The Forest That Keeps Them

CJ Morgan

The Forest That Keeps Them

This is a work of fiction. The names, characters, places, or events used in this book are the product of the author's imagination or used fictitiously. Any resemblance to actual people, alive or deceased, events or locales is completely coincidental.

Book design by Maureen Cutajar
www.gopublished.com

THE FOREST THAT KEEPS THEM

to my mom...who taught me to believe in myself

to my dad...who taught me to never give up

to june bug and little man...who taught me a love i didn't know i was capable of

to my love...who taught me that is was all worth the wait

PAST

I was snuggled in my bed sleeping when I heard the engine turn from my parent's car, the green VW van my dad calls Kermit. We were both waking up, Kermit and I, slow turning of the engine, waiting for all the right wires and moving parts to connect. When all systems trigger, it's instant and unpredictable. It is then; I awake. My heavy eyes popped open, but I laid there frozen. As my thoughts were collecting, my eyes were slowly shifting from side to side, but I kept my head completely still. I was a little four-year-old trying to wake up enough to figure out what was going on.

My room was dark except the blinding lines of morning sun that wiggled their way through the cracks of my window shade. My mom always twisted the rod that controls the direction of the blinds so they turn up. If the little slats faced down, the sun would shine directly on my bed guaranteeing that I would be the first one in the house to wake up. The rays of light that started out as small slivers expanded into rays of light against the wall where my mom painted a mural of rolling hills and a willow tree. Off in the mural's distance was a little girl holding the string of a kite. In the morning when the sun was in the perfect position, it almost brought the mural to life. In one corner of my room, I had a purple satin tee-pee set up where I could read and color. The opening of the tee-pee had colored fringe that would get tangled if I didn't constantly weave my tiny fingers through it. This little ritual became a favorite pastime when I was sent to my room for getting into trouble. My room had a sweet smell, like cotton candy and bubblegum mixed together, most likely from my strawberry shortcake doll collection. I had every one, and each one had a different scent and that was my favorite part. The dolls themselves were never something I wanted to play with. It was a bedroom every little girl wants. I loved being in my room and it was even better when my parents would come in. Maybe they liked the smell too, my mom would comb the hair of my dolls and my dad would come in after lunch in the summer and almost always fall asleep on the floor. My room felt safe, it was comforting and to a four-year-old, is never appreciated until one day, it's gone.

I laid there for only a few seconds but soon realized that when a car starts, people are going somewhere. My mom and dad were always together, they never went to town without each other, and they never left me. My mom had a love/hate relationship with the locals but seemed to enjoy the small talk. My dad enjoyed going to the seed store and fortunately, everything was located on one street. They would park Kermit and scatter in different directions but I always went with my dad. It didn't take long for the morning brain fuzz to shift into sharp reckoning that my parents and I were the only ones home, and if they were leaving, then they were leaving without me.

I shot out of bed when the thought caught up to my body. I ran out of my room and raced to the window that overlooked the front yard. Throwing the curtain to the side, I saw their car driving off the property leaving only dust from the long, dirt driveway between them and me. I called out into thin air through a weak exhale but heard nothing except the unforgiving moans and snaps of growing pains from the house.

The rise and fall of my little chest acted like a power source. I bolted out the front door only wearing my pink Cinderella nightgown with no shoes. The house faced east and the sun was bright. The cracks of sunlight through my window blinds didn't prepare my eyes for the blinding, eye-watering effect that the sun had after a good night's rest. The air felt warm and somewhere in the back of my mind, where thoughts aren't recognized right away, I knew the potential for a hot day was high.

I darted out the door letting the screen slam behind me, something my mom hated. I paused, held my breath, halfway hoping that I would hear my mom's voice raise, scolding me that I let the screen door slam shut. I was pleading with them but without a voice. *Stop!* I've been left. My heart, my paper-thin mind could not process this. *Can't they hear me?* I started to run; pebbles from the dirt road made each step feel unstable. My ankle would turn and catching my fall was impossible. I would crawl like an injured tiger for just a moment until the pain from the arrow-sharp rocks would disappear. Jagged edges of little stones would sink into the soft pads of my bare feet and after the pain; it was as if a spear would singe my skin. The fine dust from the dirt road accumulated together creating a concrete wall that wanted to swallow or crush me. I couldn't see but I kept running anyway. My arms hung low to my side, ungraceful and completely at a loss of function. I would grit my teeth, I could feel the sand between them, rough, and the sound of exploding sand would pierce my ears from the inside out. I was running, falling, crawling and crying at the same time, not understanding why they were leaving without me.

My legs moved as hard and as quick as they could with my emotions trailing behind me, screaming to be felt. Eventually, the dust from the dirt road that only moments earlier had tried to swallow me whole, had begun to settle. The fine, straw-colored sand thinned away into nowhere. The sand took me to the land of nowhere and just like that, my mom and dad were gone. I was left standing in the middle of the road completely lost and abandoned. I didn't know what direction I ran or if I turned down another dirt road. Until this point in my life, I had never experienced fear greater than the fear I felt then. I didn't know what to do or where to go. I forced my eyelids shut, then opened them hoping to find myself at the breakfast table eating oatmeal with small chunks of apples mixed in. Every time my eyes opened, I found myself still there, and the silence grew. The sand between my teeth made its way into my throat and down to my stomach. It was replaced with an echo from heart pounding inside my chest. The rhythm was more like the beat from a herd of wild mustangs sprinting effortlessly before a thunderstorm. I grew dizzy and more confused as the screams of silence multiplied.

I stood still, my breath, in-out-in-out. I looked down, my feet ached… breathing in-out-in-out… my feet are bleeding… in… out… in… out, my legs are weak… The sharp and unforgiving pebbles that were embedded in the unworn soles of my feet were expanding the same way a sponge expands when soaked with water. My mind was floating as if it were a kite in a hurricane that escaped the clutches of a child. The part of my carcass that was still alive grew numb and created a mind of its own that wandered in different directions. I took a few steps forward then back; I turned around. *Where do I go?* This thought only brought more fear. I curled my toes, gathering fine dust in between them. I took a deep breath and held it in for as long as I could, again hoping that I would hear the voice of my mom or dad, calling to me.

Both sides of the road were lined with wild, dancing sunflowers. Most of them were as tall as me. I used to pick them and bring them inside the house for my mom. My mom did her best to act appreciative, but she would hurry me back outside with them. "Oh Rainy, they have ants and spiders crawling through them. Take them back outside, and we can look at them from here." *Mommy, come get me.*

Right behind the happy, dancing sunflowers was the money. This is what the farmers would call their corn crop. Most of them made their living off the corn produced every year. This was all I could see. The world as I knew it had disappeared and all that was left were sunflowers the same height as me, the money for as long as the eyes can see and this dirt road that leads to the end of the earth.

The corn stalks swayed with a surprise gust of wind and the sunflowers that were once happy, danced a wicked dance. A black raven flew up and out of the deep corn and cawed at me, the poor, lost little girl that was left behind. He was taken up and away with the wind and I continued to follow him with my little blue eyes until he was gone. The sky was streaked with lines of white. At Christmas, my parents would tell me that these lines were from Santa's sleigh but the truth of that story vanished when the raven disappeared into them. The raven took all the people left in the world to the white lines in the sky and even those would eventually disappear. No one could see me except the dancing sunflowers crawling with ants and the hungry money that snickered behind them.

The wild mustangs started to sprint, I couldn't see them but I heard them coming. *Run little girl.* I ran toward the evil corn stocks hoping they would spit me out to the wind as they did with the raven who disappeared in the streaks in the sky. This is where my parents went, I grew sure of it.

I hurried off to the side of the road, slipping down the sandy embankment and into the dark depths of the field. The wind would blow the corn stalks over the top of me, calling upon all the other stalks to follow. I was their next offering, a sacrifice to the crop in hopes of taking over the world. The corn stalks would sway back and forth, causing the day to turn to night like a light switch being flicked on and off. I tried to stay in between the rows of corn, but the master of stocks would push me over. If I didn't fall, they would slice into my arms or punch me, tease me, and toss me around like a kid on the playground being bullied. The more I tried to run the more fear I felt. The pain grew in every step I took. The ground below me produced flowering vines with thorns that held my feet hostage, only letting go just enough, so I could plant myself into more thorns. The delicate nature of the leaves fooled me when they took their turn, cutting into my skin leaving slashes of their names behind, so I will never forget them.

I could no longer see the road. I didn't know if I was going forward, back to the road or across the field. As I ran, I would look behind me, but all I could see were the blind corn stalks looking for me, reaching out to take me in and cheered an evil laugh upon capture. They taunted me with whispers no child should ever hear. "Run... little girl run." I was encased with the rawest form of panic.

My heart was beating outside my little chest. My skin was stinging from the poison injected as they tore into my skin. I wasn't strong enough to stand my ground and when I tried to scream, the madman that lives amongst the wind would capture it. He would take my sounds and disguise it as the whoosh you hear right before the bells of a wind chime would sing. I would stumble, get up and stumble again, sprinting as fast as I could. In-out-in-out went my chest and somewhere behind me, the herd of wild mustangs. *Run.*

Just as I thought I would be tortured to death, I shot out of the end of the cornfield like a cannonball. The sun was blinding but I kept running, covering my face with my arm until I realized I was free. I eventually came to a complete stop and spun around to look at the cornfield. It was still moving, swirling around looking for me. I could hear them whispering, *come back little girl.*

I wasn't going to turn myself away from the cornfield even though I couldn't see where I was going. I waited until I was far enough away and no longer hear their laughter. I walked backward until I felt I had a safe distance and it wasn't long until I spotted a big red barn. I staggered over, leaned up against it, and slid down the wood siding to the ground. The barn was warm from the sun, and I was hidden by the tall grass that has now surrounded me. I could hear myself crying and was comforted by it. My hair was stuck to my face and the corners of my mouth. My tears ran down my cheeks meeting up with the blood that was dripping from my nose. I tried to wipe it away but the tears made my open cuts sting. I reached at my nightgown and noticed it was torn and shredded with parts of it missing. The cornfield has it; it took a part of my pink Cinderella nightgown as a reminder of the girl who got away.

I had so much pain come at me all at once. My feet were covered in thorns, and I was too exhausted to pull them out. My legs had deep cuts, bleeding from each one. My eyes were swollen and heavy and I couldn't keep them open. The sun was hot against my burning skin but I couldn't move. I sat paralyzed and my mind slowly shut down. I could no longer function.

"Well hey there, you're just a little bit," a man said softly.

Looking up, I saw a man standing in front of me blocking the sun from my eyes. He held his hand forward as if I were a dog and going to smell him. I didn't take his hand and it was then I realized my little fist was clenching a long black feather. The raven left behind a piece of himself and somehow, I picked it up. I didn't remember picking it up and wondered if I tried to catch it as he flew from the corn. A feather is all I had as proof I was running for my life, the edge of death and for whatever reason, I wasn't about to let it go. I needed this feather like I needed to find my parents.

I was confused and wasn't sure who to trust. The man knelt down on one knee and smiled, a warm and trusting smile that did very little to combat the confusion and loneliness I felt.

"Where are your mommy and daddy?"

"They forgot me," I said quietly.

"Awe, I bet they didn't forget you. Come here."

He didn't wait for me to respond, reached underneath my arms and picked me up. He was a gentle man with a soft voice and I felt safe even though I was taught not go with strangers. He never asked me questions like how old I was or what my favorite color was. I liked that about him because I didn't want to talk either. As he rested me over his hip, I could tell I had gone to the bathroom on myself. He didn't seem to mind, or he didn't care because he didn't say anything. I didn't want to look at him, I kept my head turned over his shoulder keeping a watchful eye on the cornfield as it got further and further away. I clenched the single black feather in my hand and my mind was somewhere between trying to remember the raven and what the man was saying as he carried me. I couldn't tell if he was talking to me or to himself but it was clear that he was going to call the sheriff. He also mentioned chocolate chip cookies.

He opened the screen door with one hand and propped it open with his foot while a woman removed me off his hip. She carried me into the kitchen but unlike the man, she held me away from her body. She sat me down on a chair that was cold against my skin. She knelt down on her knees and said, "You must be a little lost," her voice shaken.

I whispered. "My mommy and daddy forgot to take me with them."

She stared at me for a moment as I looked down at the floor. I wanted to look up at her to see what she looked like but I didn't have the capacity both emotionally or physically. My head was heavy and the muscles in my neck could barely hold it up. I rested my hand on my cheek, knowing I was squishing my face. Suddenly, she jumped up to her feet and her quick movement startled me. I wanted to cry, I felt like I was on the verge of breaking down but I got the feeling that the woman in the kitchen wouldn't be able to handle it. She hustled through, going from one section to another, clanking dishes, running water, and pacing back and forth as if she didn't have a clue to the fact she was standing in her own kitchen.

Through the door from the kitchen, I could see the nice man in the hall, holding the phone to his ear. "Hello, this is the Conley Place; seem to have found a little girl out here by the barn." He smiled at me, which was reassuring. "I reckon, thought she was a sick calf. Went over to see the fuss and there she was all wadded up into a little ball… that'll do then."

He hung up and paused briefly, still looking at the phone attached to the wall. It was yellow like the one we have at home. Before walking back, he looked at me first, the same look he gave to the yellow phone, and then he smiled. He put his big hand on my head and messed up my hair and the force practically knocked me off my chair.

"Sheriff O'Malley is on his way, got people looking for you, I reckon." He glanced out of the corner of his eye toward the woman, but she didn't look back.

"So little bit, next time you feel like going on a cross-country sprint, bring along some shoes."

I liked the nickname he gave me because I was just a little bit. I missed my parents, I wanted to go home, but I didn't know where I was or how I got here. One thing I didn't forget was the angry cornfield that tried to kidnap me or worse, kill me. The thought made me shudder.

"Here is a cookie and milk," she said.

I looked up to her but didn't lift my head all the way. She had black smears from her eye makeup going down her cheek and her hair was pulled tight into a bun on the top of her head. Not one strand of hair was out-of-place, and the bun was so tight it caused her eyes to slant.

A cookie and milk weren't what I wanted, but I reached out for it anyway. I saw where my arms were cut and bleeding down my arm and into the palm of my hands. It scared me, but I was also in awe of the way it looked. It reminded me of the scattered crayons I left in Kermit one afternoon. They melted all over my Wizard of Oz coloring book, mainly the color red because I was coloring the brick path. Some patches of blood were dark and cracked while other areas looked shiny and bright.

"Thank you."

I picked up the cookie and tried to take a bite from it, but it was too hard. If the cookie hadn't looked so good, I would have thought it was a rock. I tried again, using my teeth to shred some crumbs into my mouth, but I was just making a mess. It reminded me of a Christmas ornament I made for my mom and dad. It looked like a little gingerbread man but trying to eat it would break my teeth. Maybe she accidentally used that recipe instead of the one my mom uses for chocolate chip cookies. She watched the whole thing, hoping I would award her baking skills by a positive reaction but I couldn't give that to her. Instead, she reached over, grabbed it from my hands and threw it away. Then she walked over to the other cookies sitting on the counter and tossed the rest of them away too. To my surprise, she took the bowl with cookie dough and threw it all away but this time she pitched the spoon in the trash as well. All that made her appear happy. She walked back over to me and handed me my glass of milk. "Drink this instead." I did. She wasn't anyone I wanted to mess with I guessed. I drank the whole thing and slowly held it out staring at her. She took it from my hand and set it back down on the kitchen table as if she was reading my mind. She placed both hands over the top of her head trying to find a wandering or out-of-place strand of hair. I couldn't imagine that being a possibility with how tight her hair was pulled into her bun. That fascinated me once again.

She redirected her focus out the window and within seconds, she melted into herself. "Thank God. Sheriff O'Malley is here," sounding relieved. She turned toward me with her stained face and smiled. It wasn't a kind smile; it was forced which made me uneasy nonetheless.

She picked me up from the chair but instead of under my arms as the nice man did by the barn, she placed her hands over my arms making my neck disappear into my head and my arms straight to my sides. It didn't hurt when she picked me up that way but I couldn't remember ever being carried like that. My skin was stinging from her hands and I couldn't wait to be set down. She held me away from her again, but I could tell I was a little too heavy for her. By the time we made it to the porch, I was almost to my feet.

As soon as I had both feet planted on the ground, I felt instant pain. I couldn't take one single step. I didn't want to look down at them, I knew they were bleeding and I could feel the thorns piercing deeper into my skin. If I looked down, I knew I would start to cry. There was no way I was going to take one single step. The pain was too intense just standing, let alone trying to walk. I wanted to sit down right where I was on the porch but I wanted to go home even more.

The sadness I felt that my parents might not be there overwhelmed me. I wanted to be a good girl and not cry. I hoped that if I didn't cry, they would know and maybe they would come back.

"Come on little bit, Sherriff O'Malley is here to take you home." He motioned for me to walk over but I didn't move.

"Come on, it will be OK." His voice raised a little more but I stood perfectly still. I didn't want to talk; I was speechless at this point anyway.

Sheriff O'Malley walked toward me, and the closer he got, the better I could see his facial expressions. He winced and wrinkled his face but I didn't know what it meant.

"Oh God," he said as he got closer.

"No, oh no, does it hurt to walk sweetie?"

He knelt down on the porch step, looked me in the eyes and I nodded my head. As he stood up, he grabbed hold of both legs like he was going to hug them and stood up, taking me with him. It was much better than the way the woman carried me. I didn't get propped on his hip like the nice man did either. He carried me using one arm, completely wrapped around my legs and if I bent at the waist, I would fall over. I knew I needed to keep my body straight as he walked toward the police car.

I looked over my shoulder and saw the woman gazing out but I couldn't tell if she was looking at me. The nice man was standing at the back door of the police car and open it when we got closer. Sheriff O'Malley sat me slowly in the back seat and it instantly stung me. I lifted myself off the seat as soon as he sat me down.

"Whoa, I bet that seat is a little hot huh?" I nodded, and the sheriff placed his jacket under me.

Police cars are strange and definitely not like Kermit. The back seat was hard, and hollow with a wire wall that divided the front from the back, which I didn't really understand. I sneezed a few times from the dust that built up in his car. The inside was covered with a thin layer of fine sand that settled there permanently. I didn't know if I needed to buckle my seat belt and felt a little insecure in the back of the car. My mom and dad always buckled me in and told me it was safer. So I grabbed hold of the strap and placed it across my legs.

As we drove away, I glanced back at the house, and the woman was still standing behind the screen door looking more like a silhouette with a rock on top of her head. I decided that I really didn't like the bun she wore. I saw the nice man over my shoulder and I slowly lifted my hand up but not as a wave goodbye, more like an acknowledgment. I wiped my face with my arm and I closed my teeth together still feeling the grit between them. The milk didn't make it go away. I remember thinking very clearly that I was thankful that woman wasn't my mommy. That was the last time I ever saw her.

I didn't know where I was or how I got there and the thought raced into my head that I might not be going home. Nothing looked familiar when I peered out the side window and I felt lost all over again. On the tip of my vocal cord were so many questions I wanted to ask but I couldn't force the sound. *Can I go home? Where's my mommy and daddy? Where am I? Why is your car so dusty?*

We drove for miles and as soon as we turned a corner, everything became familiar. Excitement grew, but I also dreaded the idea that my mom and dad left me. I didn't know if I was being dropped off in a house where I would be all alone. I sat as straight as possible, so I could see out the front of the window. Tears fell out of my eyes and burned my cheeks as they rolled down.

My mom ran toward the police car that was also bringing along a trail of dust. We didn't even come to a complete stop when my mom ran over to the car and placed her hands on my window. Sheriff O'Malley stopped the car and popped out to open my door, but before it was even open all the way, my mom grabbed hold of my body and picked me up, holding me tight. I was relieved in an instant. All the fear, pain, hurt and terror vanished as soon as she picked me up.

"Oh Rainy, why did you leave, what happened?"

She was crying. That was the first time I ever saw my mom cry before and it made me cry even more, but with a voice I didn't have a few minutes ago.

"I saw you and daddy leaving in the car." That's all I could manage to get out between my sobs.

"Rainy, we would never leave you. Your daddy stayed home sick today. I ran to town for a few things."

My dad slowly emerged from the house, and he clearly didn't look good. I never knew my dad to wear his pajamas in the middle of the day. His blonde hair was tossed in every direction and his white shirt was wrinkled. My mom walked with the Sheriff towards my dad then handed me to him. My dad could barely hold me, but he did anyway. I hugged him around the neck and his face was prickly against mine, it stung my skin but it was also proof that I was home.

"I must have been out like a light to not hear you run out." He tossed my hair around and I imagined he made my hair look like his.

My dad carried me in the house, not letting the screen slam shut while my mom walked Sheriff O'Malley back to his car. My mom bent over to his car window, thanked him for all his help, and apologized to him for all the trouble we caused. Normally I would be afraid I was in trouble but this time, I knew I wouldn't be.

My dad handed me off to my mom once she got in the house, went straight to their bedroom and crawled back into bed. He moaned a little and covered himself up with blankets while my mom carried me to the bathroom.

The last thing I remember about that day was my mom giving me a bath. I was old enough to know that the warm water would burn the cuts I had all over my body and feet but I also trusted her.

She sat on the end of the bathtub pulling out stickers and thorns from the bottom of my feet for what seemed like hours. Now and then, a tear from her eyes would roll down her cheek and fall gracefully into my bath water. It was so quiet in the house, and all you could hear was the gentle ruffle of water and her tears falling in. She would stop occasionally and stare off at something for a brief moment and then gathering herself enough to give me a small smile. I remember how pretty she looked that day. Her long blond hair was falling out of her clip that held her hair from her face. Her eyes were glossy and full of tears but it only made her look more beautiful. She moved slowly and gently and I remember feeling so much love for her.

In the tree just outside the bathroom window perched another raven making me wonder if it was the same raven who flew from the cornfield. I wanted to believe he was the same one letting all the other ravens know with his deep and gravelly voice that the girl from the corn was safe. Maybe he was looking for the feather he dropped. My mom didn't make me leave it outside like the sunflowers I picked.

When she got me out of the bathtub, she wrapped me up in a towel that was warm, just out from the dryer. The heat felt like warm sunshine giving me a hug, I was shivering because the water was beginning to cool. She handed me the raven feather, held me tight in her lap and put cream on my legs and feet with bandages. She felt warm to cuddle up with her and I fit perfectly across her lap.

My memory fades in and out after that but before I went to bed that night I remember telling her, "Mommy, I like your hair and your cookies." She laughed a little, gave me a hug and told me she loved me.

This day was the first memory of my life.

Chapter 1

There comes a moment in every child's life that turns them into an adult and the world as we know it changes instantly. It's a world where parents can no longer make everything better. I was only four years old when the cornfield tried to swallow me whole, and they fixed it for me. When I was seventeen, I caused total devastation that my parents couldn't fix. The veil of childhood was lifted and I entered adulthood within seconds. I've been running from it ever since and with every giant step I take, I become more and more lost. I have been in full sprint away from the things I don't want to remember; the same things my parents haven't been able to repair.

I ran out of this small town when I was twenty and got married to the first person who fell in love with me. I was in love with the idea of marriage but I didn't marry for the right reasons. My mom and dad understood my desperation and probably knew that I would someday move home, but they supported me anyway. They celebrated the moment, knowing that was all it would be.

I remember being at home on the morning of my wedding day, my mom and dad took me on a long walk. Ever since that day I got lost in the cornfield, I never went in that direction. I didn't need to either. It only leads to Conley's Place, essentially a dead end. I realized at that moment just how impressive it was to live there all that time and not go down those roads. I took notice that I wasn't scared or felt any kind of fear. I told my parents how silly it was that I never went in that direction.

"What a weird feeling, all these years of living here and riding my bike or hanging out with friends, I never wanted to go down this road," I shook my head.

"Well, it just goes to show that sometimes, the fear of fear is worse than the actual fear itself," my dad said slowly.

"I guess so," I replied. "But dad, the fact that I never went down this way wasn't because I was scared. This road doesn't go anywhere."

"Maybe so," he said with doubt. "But you're the only person to really know."

There wasn't much conversation after that. I think I was supposed to learn something but I didn't. I assumed the walk was meant to be a coming-of-age kind of moment but I purposely glided over it as if it didn't exist. I am very good at doing that. I can avoid any kind of emotion or deep moment by playing dumb and pretend the moment doesn't exist. If that walk had happened a few years prior, I would have been open to emotions but it didn't and since then, everything changed.

We passed the same sunflowers on the side of the road as I did when I was four, but they weren't dancing. We passed the section of the cornfield that belonged to Mr. Conley and everything looked so small compared to how I remembered it. The corn looked like corn, the raven that flew from the depths of the field was just a raven and the breeze that blew through my hair was just a breeze. There weren't any monsters in the corn, the raven wasn't carrying messages from the dead and the wind wasn't telling secrets of horror.

The power of imagination has the ability to entertain us as children for hours on end. As adults, we are taught to use rationale and logic but what we don't realize is rationale and logic can be the very poison that kills imagination. In a desperate attempt to save it, we rename imagination and call it creativity. Creative minds are considered normal when we enter the life sentence of adulthood. If an adult is labeled as having a wild imagination, they can risk the potential of being diagnosed with a personality disorder.

I just want to be normal, unaffected by any kind of feelings. I do this by hiding under layers of chaos that I create or gravitate towards. I suppose this is why marriage seemed like a good idea. As my parents and I walked together, I focused on the crunching sounds under our feet. Three people and six feet walking along a gravel road can create a distraction for anyone listening hard enough. I focused on the beat of the step, the grind below the soles of the shoes and the lift-off of the toes. Again, again, again, the same pattern of six feet inside six shoes walking along a normal road where emotions are non-existent and silence can't be heard.

Once we got to the entrance of Mr. Conley's property, we all stopped for a moment. My brain was vacant for a brief second but slowly caught up to the fact that I couldn't hear the gravel crunching below our feet.

"Whelp," I said, "not really a dead end when you consider old Mr. Conley over there tinkering in the barn."

I didn't wait for a response before I added, "I wonder what happened with the lady he married."

"She couldn't handle the farm life I guess. She just up and left one day." My dad said. I couldn't help thinking to myself that maybe she and I had more in common than I thought.

"The only thing I remember about her was that she made terrible chocolate chip cookies and her hair, it was always in a tight bun and it made her eyes squint."

My mom laughed a little, and before any further conversation could continue, I started walking back. I could tell they wanted to say something and even though I didn't want to talk, I managed to thank them for taking me on a stroll down memory lane. I talked about how our imagination as a child can really leave a lasting impression, but I was glad to have finally walked down the dead-end road.

"Funny," I said, "even though a road might not take you anywhere you want to go, it's still a road home to someone."

I was fully aware this was not the point of our walk. I have a way of steering conversations away from the topic intended but still, appear to be thinking deeply or passionately.

"Your mom and I wanted to tell you a few things. You're leaving this tribe today, but it's important that you create a new one. You need positive and supportive people. You will always have us, we won't be going anywhere, but we also want to see you happy. Create a tribe that will see you for who you are and what you offer."

What the hell? He didn't just say that. "Wow dad, those are some great words you put together." I couldn't help but laugh, "Did you get that off a greeting card?" I patted him on the back and kept walking.

"Well, getting married is a big deal and no, I didn't get it from a greeting card."

After a long pause and silent walking, my mom said, "He read it on a bumper sticker." We laughed; my dad could find humor in just about anything, even if it was about himself.

"Well OK, I saw a bumper sticker that read, 'your vibe creates your tribe' and I thought it was good advice. Plus I added in a few parts."

I understood my dad's point of it all. It was kind of him to send me off with sound advice. All I had up to that point were my parents whereas most of the people I knew already had a tribe they belonged to. I've been on the outside looking in for years, and whether I wanted to admit it back then, I saw how important it was to attain.

Getting married seemed like it would offer much more than just something to belong to. It created chaos in my life that kept me from recognizing feelings or memories that I feared would destroy me.

I hate silence, I fear silence as if it were a monster; the same monster that consumed me in the cornfield and the same monster who shattered my life before I ever had a chance to start it. Chaos is much simpler. Inside chaos, I can't hear the pounding of memories inside my head or feel the pain, the guilt. I suppose in creating this kind of distraction also distracted me from the writing on the wall with my marriage. There are so many things I missed, all the signs that were clear to most people were simply ignored because I was, and still am, incapable of letting any kind of emotion surface.

Now here I am, years later and divorced, back to the very town I ran away from.

Being back home with my parents feels like failure and comfort at the same time. I want so desperately to have them dust off my britches but of course, they can't. Even though their love runs thick through my veins, they can't mend what it is that brings me home. I am completely shattered from the inside out and lost beyond measure. This isn't the kind of lost I felt in the cornfield when I was a little girl. In reality, being lost is to know where you need to be and where you have come from. I don't have any direction; I have no clue where it is that I need to go, only where I have been. This adds a feeling of despair and hopelessness to the fear of being lost. I don't belong anywhere; I don't have a place in this world like I did as a little girl.

Now I question if this is what rock bottom feels like. Having to move back home to my parent's house at the age of thirty-seven to a town that still loathes me isn't my idea of success. I don't know the answers and until now, I stopped asking altogether. My first memory in life was controlled by an overactive imagination and all the years leading up to this point, I have been completely checked out. I turned my active imagination into the adult version and thought I could just creatively get through life.

My whole life has brought me here; at a crossroad, literally. Remembering my dad's words when I left the first time to get married put a lump in my throat. I swallow hard, hoping some of the past will go down too. It's all so thick and heavy but I need to go. I don't know where but I know I need to go. I also don't trust myself. The thought comes into my mind briefly that I am just running away again.

I shift my jeep into drive, turn my lights on and I slowly inch forward. I look into my rear view mirror, and I'm not surprised to see my mom standing on the front porch. I watch her in the mirror getting smaller and smaller as I come to the end of their driveway. I turn onto Western Drive and I do my mental checklist. *I have my clothes, food, money, my lucky raven feather…* that's about as far as I get when I approach the intersection of Western Drive and County Road 8. I come to a complete stop, something I rarely do at this particular Intersection. The dust from the dirt road is trailing behind, never giving us distance. It feels like an unwanted hug.

The early morning darkness is everywhere. I didn't realize the world is capable of this much darkness and silence. As I sit idle, the dust settles and I immediately take note of the paired companions that are hitching a ride. Darkness is a distant friend of mine that I have been ignoring for years, silence is another distant friend but much more obnoxious. I have been running from both, but they finally caught up to me. I'm too exhausted to run, too broken to fight and I surrender to their self-invite in hopes of actually enjoying the company.

East or west, right or left. I know I need to decide on my direction but doubt my ability. Thoughts keep bouncing back and forth between the distraction of my companions and what direction I should go. I look at the seat next to me and see a road map. *Dad must've put it there.* The thought makes me smile. He didn't like the idea of me traveling by myself, let alone without a map. I tried to explain to him last night that I didn't need one.

"Dad, I'm on a self-discovery mission and I want to follow the map of my intuition. You know, just like you and mom did."

"That is different," he replied, "You weren't my daughter."

Dad always had a wild way with his words.

I take in a deep breath and close my eyes. I want my car to move in the direction I was supposed to go. Now at this moment, when I am faced with a simple decision of going east or west, I wish for something to take over, perhaps by the forces of some other free will besides my own. I open my eyes and with no thought at all, I turn my signal up and west I go.

My decision brings relief, giving time to collect myself. County Road 8 is extremely long. It is one of the longest stretches of county roads I have ever traveled, boring as well. The speed limit is 45 miles an hour. It is impossible to do unless you're riding on a horse or in a tractor. I guess the county keeps the speed limit low so a person can have time to react if a cow or two wander into the road, which is not unheard of. Out in these parts, it's not uncommon to receive a phone call from a neighbor to say, "Hey Shaffer, your cows are out, and down but the gulch up by the north pasture." I also believe that when these old farmers do decide to go to town they need a long straight road with very slow speeds to collect their thoughts. The transition from farm life to town life can be quite a jolt to an old farmer. So I find myself thankful for that dreadfully long, boring road. This way, even though I am obviously going west, I need to figure out which exact road to take. I have lived in Colorado all my life, so I am familiar with Interstate 70 and it doesn't take long to decide to take the road well-traveled.

As time passes, I settle into my seat. My nerves, while still noticeable, are decreasing in intensity. Once again, I look back into the rear view, like my mom on the front porch, my town is growing smaller and smaller behind me. I keep both hands on the wheel and simply drive. Miles pass miles and not much is thought of, something I'm good at.

Looking at all the travelers heading east confirms that my decision to travel west is a good one. The sun has made its entrance full force, and I am relieved not to be facing it. I am a grumpy traveler and I have been since I was a child. Forget the sing-along songs and the car travel games that most families do on a vacation, I would sleep. It wouldn't be ten minutes into the trip and I would be out like a light. I was this way on simple outings to the store too. My whole outlook on traveling was, "wake me up when we get there." However, I love to drive.

Eisenhower Tunnel is fast approaching and there is something about this tunnel that makes me feel like a child and an adult at the same time. The memories of going through it bring comfort. My dad would honk our horn several times and said it would bring us good luck on our trip, which was is a better story than the one he originally told me. I questioned why he honked his horn when we drove through a tunnel, and he told me that he didn't honk it; the car automatically does it when driving through it. I knew the probability of that happening was slim, even as a kid. So, the story of it being good luck was the story we stuck with. It probably did bring good luck because I can't remember having a bad trip when we would honk through the tunnels.

As I enter, I want to honk my horn with a childlike craze. I want to roll down my windows and yell like an idiot with no cares in the world. Sadly, something inside me can't. This is the first time I have driven through the tunnel on my own and used this as an excuse to reserve my inner child. I drive the speed limit and I don't follow anyone to close. My dad would be proud.

I glance up long enough to read Continental Divide on a computer operated sign. All of a sudden, I feel very far from home. The Continental Divide is quite a milestone in my journey even though it is only a six or so hours away. In some strange way, it symbolizes change. Maybe it is the way the water flows. Water is a powerful force that can be so destructive and beautiful at the same time. At the top of the Continental Divide, water goes east or west. The water doesn't care which direction it travels once it falls from the sky. It simply flows east or west, never giving its purpose a second thought.

I would like to compare myself to the water but I can't. I am awkward and clumsy. I need to have control and controlling water is like controlling a wild animal in the circus. At some point, it will explode.

While I descend the pass and still in the tunnel, my Jeep picks up speed. I notice my steering wheel wanting to pull to the right and it's rapidly getting worse. I come out of the tunnel along with all the other westbound drivers and it isn't long until I hear a loud pop! Trying to maintain control, I pull off to the side of the highway and stop as fast as I can. I turn off my car in record time and jump out. *Fire! Run! Oh, wait. My tire blew up. Perfect!*

I feel defeated. I feel like that little girl, left alone in the middle of the road. I curl my toes, a habit I have grown into when I am in a situation that needs a little extra grounding. This time, I don't feel fine sand between my toes, just my socks, bunched up inside my shoes.

Not only do I feel defeated, I feel a bit silly for exaggerating the situation. I stand for a moment, taking in where I am, where I am going and where I have been. I really don't want to admit this, but maybe my road trip is a bad idea. Maybe this flat tire is a sign that I should turn around and go back home. I stare at the road and to the tunnel where all the cars are coming through it. All these people are going somewhere with focus and luck. *Just go home…you don't belong here either.*

I walk back to the Jeep, sat down and wilt behind the steering wheel. I run my hands through the raven feather, which after years of touching has become thin and stringy. It is a far cry from the strength and courage it once had. This feather would no longer carry a raven in flight and for the first time, I see the comparison between the feather and myself.

PAST

When I was a kid, I was lucky enough to always have a bike to ride. It was my ticket to freedom and imagination and my dad knew that. My mom would worry about me as every good mom does and my dad would tell her that it was an opportunity to see the world at my own eye level. My first bike was a tricycle. It was a Radio Flyer, cherry red, and white. He always made sure all my bikes were in working order, and he took my bike repairs very seriously. Even my tricycle underwent tune-ups from time to time. He oiled my bike chain, checked that my wheels had the perfect tire pressure and made sure my handlebars were nice and straight. I never had a chance to complain of a flat tire or broken chain because he was always one step ahead.

One summer afternoon my friends were all gathered around the front of my house playing and showing off their latest and greatest toys. I was particularly impressed with my friend Anna's new roller skates. She could skate well, but what was even more impressive was the fact that they lit up. She would ride her bike over to my house and hung her skates perfectly from the handlebars. In the country, dirt roads and fields were the only things that separated me from my friends. It wasn't the miles of distance between houses. We just saw that as a chance to become who every child wants to be when they grow up; fast, free and no fear of failure. Once Anna would get to my house, she would put on her skates and roll around on my parent's concrete driveway, spinning and skating backward even though there wasn't much space. This was the same place we would all play 4 square too. No one ever used a kickstand to prop up their bike; instead, we all laid them on its side. A mound of bikes would collect at the front of my house like a bunch of biker members who are planning their next big ride. A huge weeping willow covered the driveway shading it so my dad could work and making it possible for all of us to hang out. Leaning against the trunk of the tree was an old broom. It was just part of the tree, part of the ritual. We would sweep the driveway of fallen branches and leaves creating a clean slate for the next big event our imaginations would conceive; always taking the broom back to the tree. Nothing is more aggravating than going for the broom just to realize someone didn't put it back.

In the midst of the action of roller skating and the imaginary Olympic Games between all my friends, my dad drove up, smiling inside the flat windows of Kermit. My parents were the only ones of all my friends who drove a Volkswagen van. All my friends' parents owned huge trucks with hitches; mostly Fords but some had Chevy trucks or a Dodge Ram. Not my parents, we drove Kermit everywhere and everyone knew who we were just by the vehicle we drove. Just like my bike, my dad kept Kermit in beautiful shape. It was spotless and it looked brand-new.

I could tell that he had something in the back because of his facial expression when he pulled up. He was excited but I didn't pay that close attention to it.

"Neha," he said, "Come help me unload this." My dad is the only one who calls me Neha.

We all ran toward the van and someone yelled, "Hey! Rainy, you're getting a new bike."

I could see the handlebars through the windows and tried to be the first one to look. I couldn't quite understand what I was seeing and why everyone was laughing. So, I did what every other kid would've done. I laughed too.

"Well sweetie," my dad said, "I found this bike in the ditch up by Swanson's place. He said it's been there for years. Oh, it's a little dinged up, but underneath it all, I bet we could make it a real beauty."

There it was, the ugliest bike I had ever seen, but the worst part was the pride my dad displayed. He was smiling ear to ear assuming that everyone's laughter was of joy for me, and not to the hideous mangled pile of metal my dad called a bike. It didn't have any tires on it and the seat was torn and hardened from the years of sun, and weather. The only color I could see was from the inside of the seat cushion where the padding had popped out. It was yellow with rotting stains and dirt deep within the fibers. All I could do was stand there as my laughter turned into a forced smile and then into a blank stare.

"Holy cow, that thing stinks!" Someone said.

"It's covered with cow poop." Someone else said.

There was this unspoken moment and everyone backed away. Some covered their noses with their shirts and others just backed up slowly to their bikes but eventually, everyone just... sort of left. They all hopped on their fancy bikes and rode away, laughing and looking back over their shoulders. I could tell they were all talking about me, and I can only imagine what they said.

"So, Neha? What do you think?"

"Thanks, dad," I said. "I'm sure you'll fix it up to look great."

There was a pause and I didn't know what to do or say to get out of there fast enough.

"Rainy! Hey guys, time to come in, dinners ready." Mom was always good at her timing.

I took off to the house and went to the bathroom to wash up. My mom stood in the doorway behind me.

"Honey, dad is just trying to help, and he knows you need a new bike, we just can't afford it right now. He'll make it work, he always does."

How does she always know how I feel? She always knows how I feel.

"Yeah, but mom, did he have to show all my friends? I mean really," I started to cry; "it smelled so bad, and they are all going to tease me."

My dad walked by right when I said that and our eyes met briefly but I just looked away. I was embarrassed, I was mad, I was embarrassed for him, which was odd considering how angry I was. He didn't say anything at dinner that night and that's how I knew he heard what I said. I couldn't help the way I was feeling. My parents were so different from other kids' parents. When it was just the three of us, I didn't care about being different. However, I grew tired of recycling everything we owned and worse, everything other people owned. Looking back, I could see how much this hurt him.

I remember falling asleep on the couch that night purposely to avoid the good night rituals my family had. I would hug my mom, hug my dad, and wander tirelessly to my bathroom to brush my teeth. Most of the time both my parents would come to tuck me in and that never changed even as I grew into my teenage years. That night, my dad carried me to bed and I pretended to be asleep. I never quite understood why my parents would think I could stay asleep after being picked up, carried down the hall, through the door of my room which by the way, my head would hit almost every time, and then placed into bed. I always managed to keep my eyes closed with a soft sleeping face. I thought this little trick was pretty clever acting on my part.

That night after my dad laid me down; he kissed me on the cheek, brushed the hair from my face and whispered "Sorry Rainy," and simply walked out.

I often wondered if he knew I was awake that night when he said that but I'll never ask.

A few months later, I came home from a dentist appointment and noticed that my dad was working in the garage, which wasn't unusual. He stopped whatever it was he was doing and asked, "Well, how did it go?"

"OK, it only hurt a little, and my lip isn't as fat as it feels."

I could barely talk, but dad understood every word.

"Well- be careful, just because your lip is numb doesn't mean you still can't hurt it," he said.

"OK, dad." I took off.

There have been plenty of times in life that my dad's advice stuck, and this was one of them.

When I got to the front door, I notice something out of the corner of my eye. *A bike, a NEW bike!*

"Whoa," I whispered in disbelief.

"Mom," I yelled, "There's a bike out here!"

By the time she got there, I had already checked it out. Purple. Not just any purple, purple with silver sparkles. It had the coolest banana seat I had ever seen. It was velveted and soft and I couldn't stop touching it. Not only did it have a basket in front, but there was also a basket on the back of the bike too. The handlebars had purple streamers hanging and a little bell that dangled down. I rang the bell and the ring brought a huge crooked smile to my face. This bike was perfect, it was so pretty. It was my redemption back into the bike club that I never lost in the first place. My friends will envy me I thought to myself. They will all envy me; they will all want to ride it.

"Well, what do you think?" My dad asked.

"Dad, it looks like it's going to be fast!" I said smiling. I forgot all about my numb lip and how ridiculous I sounded.

"Hey, can I go show everyone?"

"Just be back in 20 minutes Rainy," mom said

"Thanks for my new bike dad."

When I got to the end of the road, all the gang was hanging out.

"Hey check it out! Rainy got a bike."

Everyone stood around and admired it. Their very words I can't remember, but their voices echo to this day. They played with the purple streamers and touched every inch of the bike. I can still remember the afternoon sun and the smell of Swanson's fresh-cut alfalfa in the field next to us.

It wasn't until a few months later my dad informed me my bike was due for a tune-up. I sat and watched carefully of his every move.

I knew that someday I would need to know all this stuff. I handed him all the necessary tools and I felt quite proud of the fact that I knew all of their names.

"Grab the oil can up on the shelf in the cabinet, to the left," he said.

After I opened the cabinet, I saw a can of purple sparkle spray paint. I looked at my dad who was looking back at me, and we smiled at each other. I realized that my bike wasn't brand-new, it was, in fact, the busted up stinky bike he brought home a few months earlier.

I closed the cabinet quickly and said nothing. I handed him the oil can, and we went back to work. He didn't say anything to me either. I guess there was just this unspoken *thank you* that my dad heard at that moment. We never spoke of it since but that little experience taught me a lot. I not only learned to change my tires, oil my chain, straighten my handlebars but more importantly, I learned a lot about my dad that day. In an instant, I saw a man who held onto his pride regardless of anyone else's terms or opinions. He took a broken bike and with patience and time, created something perfect. He was humble; he kept his pride to himself because it wasn't about him. He did this for me, and not for his ego. He became my hero before I knew what a hero really meant.

Chapter 2

As frustrated as I am, I find myself relieved that my dad taught me all the things he did about my bike, and later, about my car. In order to get my driver's license, I had to learn to change a flat tire first.

I open the back of the Jeep access and start preparing myself mentally for the dirty task at hand. As I take the things out of the tire access door, I notice my cooler in the back seat. *A snack seems like a better idea*. I open the cooler and pull out a peanut butter and jelly sandwich. Mom makes the perfect peanut butter and jelly, peanut butter on both sides of the bread, and jelly in the middle.

"This way, the jelly won't make the bread soggy," mom would say every time. I don't want to have kids of my own but that advice always made me want them, so I can pass on that particular lesson. I think it is simply genius.

I sit down in the back with the hatch open, my feet dangle down and I watch traffic. This way, I don't feel so stupid; most people probably think I stopped for an early lunch. I don't know why I care what people think anyway. I take a big bite out of my sandwich, tasting it completely.

"Crap!" I said, still with a mouthful of food, pushing it off to one side of my mouth.

Just then, a big semi-truck rolls down the pass slowly, turn signal on. He is pulling off right behind me. I don't really know what to think but I can remember my dad saying, "I'm not going along with this idea of you traveling across the country to find yourself or whatever it is you're looking for. As far as I'm concerned, you can find yourself in our yurt but if you do go, don't go off with anyone, especially strangers. Most truck drivers will help you, just watch out, and follow your gut."

His truck stops about 50 feet away and I just keep eating. I don't want to appear scared or worried. After taking a drink of water and I swallow the last of my sandwich, I start feeling a little perturbed that I didn't enjoy the last of it. Then the driver waves at me. *What does that mean*? So, I wave back but careful of the type of wave. I don't want to appear too childlike or too girly. *If this guy is up to something, he is going to have one heck of a fight.*

I do this weird farmers military salute wave that I swore a long time ago that I would never do. I've seen one too many farmers do it and it just seemed silly to me. Where those boys learned to wave like that is beyond my knowledge, but they all do it, and they do it well. Maybe, in order to graduate high school, they all had to learn it. It's an entire conversation all in one movement.

"Howdy fellow farmer, crops going great, the family is healthy, the old tractor is needing a fixing, tell the wife hello and holler if you're needing anything."

When you get a farmer's wave back it generally means, "Good to see you too, crops going great, the wife is having some bunions removed today, I'll be by after lunch to help with that old tractor."

And it never fails; they always came by after lunch to fix something on the old John Deere.

Now, if you happen to express a farmer's wave and you don't get a wave back it can only mean one thing, they are not a local.

I laugh to myself as I watch the guy get out of his truck. It is the kind of laugh that doesn't bring a smile to your face but instead, makes you exhale from your nose just enough to make your torso move. If he is up to no good, he'll be doing it pretty slow. He is as fast as molasses.

"Hey, kid!" He hollers.

"Hello!" I yell back.

He walks to his passenger side door, opens it and pulls a few things out. He shuts the door, takes a hammer and pounds each tire a few times, checks out a few other things I know nothing about and put it all back in his truck and doing so in one swift movement. Then, he starts walking my way. Slowly.

"Kid looks like you got you a flat one," he said.

"Yeah, I'm just eating lunch." *Dumb, it's not even lunchtime.*

"Looks like to me you need to be fixing that flat tire instead."

"My dad is on his way." *Liar.*

"That's good, your daddy taught you well." He said matter-of-factly.

"Yeah, I know how to fix it, but my dad is not far behind. Just eaten my lunch, waiting."

Liar.

"Well, that's good. If my little girl were in this situation, I tell her to say the same thing to some stranger that came along to offer help. It's a little early for lunch though." And he laughs to himself.

He was a sweet old guy but I'm not sure what to think or say for that matter.

"Well, at least this thing has a full-size spare." He glances at me as if he knows that wasn't my original quote.

"Well, let's get this tire-"

"Oh that's OK, my dad is coming," I interrupt.

I feel a little stupid saying that again, but by this time, I'm sure he knows I am lying. I think he gets the idea that I am just doing what I have been taught my whole life when it comes to strangers. I half-way trust the guy. What I become more afraid of is the poor fella having a heart attack in front of me. He is a gentle cross between Wilford Brimley and Santa Clause. His suspenders are leather, a surprise to me for some reason. His jeans look brand-new, never been washed. His gray, thinning hair is slicked back and his small wire-framed glasses make him look grand-fatherly. He is wearing cowboy boots and a nice western shirt complete with a pocket protector that houses a tire gauge. *How convenient.*

I am deep in concentration, having a mini fashion show in my head when he clears his voice softly. He smooths down his mustache as I narrow my attention to make eye contact.

"I'll help you with that tire and when your daddy gets here, you can tell him you changed it all by yourself; make him proud."

"Um, OK. I will pay you though."

His voice lowers, "Nah, you can pay me in that extra peanut butter and jelly sandwich you got sitting over there. I haven't had one in years, at least one that looks that good."

I smile at him just in case he is joking. He quickly gets to work which leads me to believe that he is completely serious. I feel bad about the kind gesture he is making. The only thing I can think of doing to ease my guilt is to start talking.

"You're getting one heck of a peanut butter and jelly sandwich. My mom made it for me, peanut butter on both sides of the bread. Yep, the bread won't get soggy that way. I tell ya what..."

I was rambling. I go on talking like I have never talked to anyone before. I am grateful and I'm trying to let the guy know just how much. Not even knowing what I'm saying, the words are echoing in my own head. He isn't listening either but I just keep on talking. Silence is deadly after all.

He works diligently and stays focused. I am impressed at the speed in which he moves. My dad would be too.

Then, what seems to be one swift movement, he is done. Just like that. He grabs a rag from his back pocket and nods at me a few times. I realize I am still chattering about something that was irrelevant to the situation, and he is trying to be polite.

"So anyway, looks like you're done..." I interrupt myself.

"Yep, and when your daddy gets here you tell him the tire pressure looks good. There should be a tire shop or a mechanic in Silverthorne or Dillon. It's just down the highway a few miles. Don't let it go either. Where there is one flat tire, there is sure to be another. You don't want to take a chance on not having a spare.

"OK, no chances," I repeat. "Fix my flat. Got it."

"Thank you so much." I add.

"I need the exercise" he smiles, "I've been on the road for days."

I know he told me where he is headed and where he has been but I can't remember. I am too busy rattling off some light conversation just to ease my own comfort. I feel guilty then. He goes for days without having a good conversation with someone and I blew it for him. I want to sit and chat with him. Let him talk for a while.

"Well," he said, "I better get back on the road; head this old lady back into the wind."

"OK, well I guess I should let you get going. Wow, thanks again for doing this."

With so much preoccupation going on my head, I don't know what to do from here. I stand and watch him walk back to his truck, this time, a little less stiff. He buckles his seat belt and looks into the side mirror, slowly moves forward away from the pull off and back on the highway.

"Hey," I yell, "your sandwich!"

He pulls down on his air-horn, which scares me to death. He smiles again and simply drives away.

"OK! I yell again," I will catch up with you on the road somewhere!"

I know he can't hear as I said it, but by yelling it out loud, it somehow convinces me to keep going.

I load up my Jeep in record time. I don't know why I am in such a hurry. I am disappointed in myself that I didn't let him know how much I appreciated his help. My heart feels empty and sad knowing deep down inside I will never see him again.

I stand for a moment longer, long enough to bring myself back to reality. The cars hurry by and the noise of the highway is almost too much. It amazes me how much noise can come from rushing cars driving by. Not knowing what else to do, I get back in my jeep and close the door. In an instant, complete silence. There it is again, sitting right next to darkness.

Chapter 3

I take the off-ramp at the Silverthorne/Dillon exit. Without having much time, I knew I need to make a choice on which direction I should go. Right or left, once again I am faced with a directional dilemma. One would think I would choose to go left, being that the last right turn landed me a flat tire.

A big part of me wants to go home. I can too. Mom and dad wouldn't think a thing about it. Dad would probably say something to the effect, "Well, didn't take you long to find what you were looking for." That would be his way of making light of the situation.

Something inside my soul won't let me do that. I have run my whole life. Something is pulling at my core. I can't turn back until I find out what it is. So, I take the old man's advice and decide that stopping to fix my flat tire is a good idea. It's something anyway.

I sit straight up in my seat as to get a bird's eye view of the town. I squeeze my eyes shut hoping that when I open them, all the answers will appear. I pay close attention to the power that drives my inner conscience. I want to go against it, but the part in me that does things that I have no control over steps in; much like the simple way we have no control over the way we breathe.

It doesn't take long to spot an auto garage. This isn't your typical car repair shop. The front has glass bay doors that open up so people can pull in. It is a deep pine green stucco building with log siding that makes it blend in with the mountains that surrounds it. It looks so much prettier than the old beat up car shops back home. There aren't any old broken down cars sitting outside with weeds growing up through the floorboards. I don't see any cars parked up on blocks or hanging from a tow truck. I also noticed that there aren't any grease spots that I need to worry about stepping in. It feels welcoming and I don't get the idea that there will a bunch of males inside wanting to feed on the first woman they come across.

As I walk up to the door, I notice the beautiful hanging baskets and planters full of flowers. I could smell them as I walked by and busy hummingbirds are everywhere. When I open the front door, a little bell rang and I could see a man behind a metal desk reading the newspaper. The place has such a familiar smell that reminds me of my dad's garage, the only difference is the smell of coffee that is neatly placed in the corner.

I pull down my shirt and straighten my sleeves knowing I must look like an orphan. I smooth out all the creases and clear my throat. The man slowly folds down one corner of the paper and looks at me, and then goes back to his reading. He looks to be about my age but I can't tell with the newspaper covering half of his face. His hands are clean and the closer I get to the desk, the more I can smell him. Between him and the flowers outside, I instantly like the place.

I was about to say hello when he mumbles, "I'll get your tire fixed in a minute."

"Oh. OK." I said. "Yeah, I can just wait."

I turn around to go wait outside when I hear his newspaper wrestle. Several little odd noises came from somewhere inside but I can't tell where. It sounds like car repair noises but more random and from what I can tell, no one else is here.

"Well, nothing in here worth reading." He grumbles partly to me, and partly to himself.

I decide to head out the door to watch the hummingbirds, but he must have thought I was going to leave. He scoots his chair back to get up and it screeches along the concrete floor. I can see him now in full view away from the headlines in the newspaper. He's wearing tight navy blue pants and a light blue shirt with his name printed on a patch. Patrick. The name fits too. He stretches around a little as if he is just getting out of bed. Part of his shirt comes out of his pants, but he doesn't notice, or doesn't care, I can't tell which. He slowly brings his foot up on the desk and tightens his boot strings.

"Zeus, mind your manners." He said.

"I'll help you get that tire out, and I'll see if I can fix it." He adds.

"That sounds great," giving him a smile. *Who is Zeus?*

I begin to open the door, but he reaches over me and holds it just like my dad does for my mom.

"Mind your manners." Words barely audible.

I peer behind me hoping I am not the only one who heard that. That's when I see Zeus for the first time.

"That little dude over there is Zeus. Long story but he is part of the shop."

"Oh my goodness, an Umbrella Cockatoo. He is beautiful!" I said.

"You know your birds," he said. "Yep, Zeus there is full of himself. He will talk your ear off if you let him. And don't tell him anything you don't want everyone else to know, he can't keep a secret."

I want to stay and look at him for a while. Hell, I want to hold him. I have always loved parrots and often thought of getting one of my own someday. Patrick is holding the door open, so I know I will need to wait to meet Zeus formally.

We walk through the parking lot to my car without saying a word. He opens up the back door to the Jeep and moves around a few things, so he can get to my tire. He rolls it to the big doors and, I just sort of follow him, not knowing what else to do.

"So how did you know I need my tire fixed?" I ask.

"The spare, it's clean," he said.

He is gorgeous; the type of man that you will find in a calendar or holding the hand of a beautiful woman and this makes me nervous. I don't want to say anything or start a conversation with him for fear that I will say something ridiculous.

When we get back inside, I go to the bird and glance at Patrick to make sure it is OK. He has a beautiful smile painted on one-half of his face and I notice the length of his hair. I'm sizing myself to him, comparing my own outward appearance to his and I find myself relieved that my hair is longer than his. The length of a guy's hair is as important as his height. Personally, I never want to be taller than a man is and I want my hair longer than his. His teeth are as white and as straight as the lines on the highway and my mind is shifting around topics for a general conversation that I can have with him, but instead, I bite down slightly on the corner of my lip and smile.

"Well hello, Zeus," I say in the calmest voice I can come up with.

"Hello, Zeus." *I'm talking to a bird.*

"I think I have a spare tire that will work. Same size anyway. It won't be the same brand though. To order this exact tire you're looking at a day or so." He said.

"OK," I said. "That will be fine."

"What will be fine?" He asks.

"Um, just the tire you have will be fine," I repeat.

"And Zeus doesn't like very many people, he tolerates me, but I think I even drive him crazy after a while."

I am hoping I don't sound as silly as I feel. I can literally feel my face turn red and I can't put two words together. I am talking to a bird and trying to carry a conversation with Mr. Handsome pants who's fixing my tire.

Patrick walks to the back of the shop and my focus turns back to Zeus. He crawls through his cage and lifts his leg up like he wants me to pick him up. What a beautiful bird, he is all white with the friendliest face. Under the crown on his head, the feathers are sunshine yellow. He stretches a wing out, and I can see the yellow under his wing. He is healthy, unlike a lot of birds I've seen. His feathers are perfect, and he hasn't picked at himself. A sign of a happy bird.

"Good Boy," Zeus said in a weird monotone voice.

"You ever handled a parrot? Zeus seems to like you. You can take him out if you want." Patrick said.

I glance over at Patrick and smile. I am so excited to pick him up that I feel almost childlike.

"Hey little man, you want to come and see me?" I ask Zeus.

I open the cage and Zeus comes right over. He bobs his head up and down and whistles at me. I can't help to laugh, and then he laughs back at me. This carries on for a while but when he places his head down in my chest, it makes my heart melt. I scratch his head, and I can tell Zeus likes it just as much as I do.

"Zeus, you never cease to amaze me. He likes you. A lot. In fact, I don't think he has ever done that with any other person before." Patrick said.

"Do you like me, Zeus? Well at least someone likes me. You are a good bird, yes, you are a good bird." Zeus kisses me.

I glance over and watch Patrick. He shakes his head and continues working. He moves with purpose and he is extremely confident. Now and then, he will whistle but I can't make out the tune. It sounds good regardless.

His unbelievably good looks make me curious about my own appearance. It occurs to me that I have not looked in the mirror since leaving home.

I clear my throat and ask, "Can I use your girls' room?"

His eyes are incredibly blue and I can feel my face turn red again. He brushes back the hair from his forehead and looks me dead in the eyes. I take Zeus to his cage and close the door.

"I don't have a girls' room per se, but the bathroom is through the office, down the hallway." He said.

Stupid. I have never called the restroom a girl's room. I sound like a prissy woman that wears makeup to bed.

"Thanks," I smile again and walk away. I wonder if he is watching me, but I'm not about to turn around and look.

As I walk down the hallway, I notice a little chalkboard on the door that has BATHROOM neatly written. I am sure it is female handwriting and I can't help but wonder if this is his girlfriend's writing. On the other side directly across from the bathroom is a break room. It has a small kitchen table and chairs and a mini refrigerator with a microwave on top. There is also a sleeping cot that looks like it has just been slept on. Everything is clean, the walls have ski photos hanging and vintage snowshoes neatly placed.

As I open the bathroom door, I can smell his cologne again. There's a small stand up shower in the corner that is still dripping water and a towel hanging over a curtain rod. The bathroom is just as clean as the break room. In the other corner across from the shower is an area set aside for all his ski equipment and a coat that has RESCUE written on the back.

I catch myself in the mirror, and I'm horrified. I have a big glob of jelly on the side of my face, my hair is ridiculous, and a black streak that looks like grease under my nose and chin. I immediately start washing my face and try desperately to salvage my hair. *Maybe he hasn't noticed.* I smile in the mirror to make sure I don't have anything in my teeth. That would be just my luck.

When I go to leave, I can't resist looking in the medicine cabinet. As I open it, the thought crosses my mind that this would be a great set up for the old stick-marbles-inside-so-some-snoopy-person-like-me-would-get-caught prank, but I open it anyway. I am somewhat surprised by its contents, Band-Aids, a brush, toothpaste, toothbrush, and lotion. I am hoping to find something that will make me less attracted to him. I don't know what in particular but I find nothing. As I close the cabinet door, I notice a box of dental floss next to his hairbrush. My stomach flips. *A man after my own heart.*

I shuffle out of the bathroom feeling a little guilty of intruding on his privacy. I get the feeling he must live here but I also don't want to think much about it.

I go back to the garage and Patrick has taken his work shirt off and is wearing a short-sleeved T-shirt. He put a blue bandanna over his head that made his blue eyes stand out even more. I can see where he has strong arms but not the type of muscles you grow in a gym. His chest is as cut as a fine line on thin paper. His hands are strong and a complete mess at this point but I don't mind. He works diligently with focus and strength.

This is the type of guy that a lot of girls would take notice in. However, not too many of them would win him over. I soon begin to realize that unfortunately, I am probably one of them.

I walk toward Patrick from the other side of the shop but keep a safe distance from him hoping he won't notice my nervousness.

"How is the tire repair going?" I ask, wringing my hands together.

He looks up and stares into my face, "almost done." Then starts to whistle again and Zeus chimes in.

He makes me feel comfortable in the most nervous sort of way. Maybe it's because my mind is occupied somewhere between the bird, my journey, and him.

"All done," he straightens up.

"Wow, that didn't take long at all. Thanks." I look down to the ground, unable to look at him.

"Grape jelly or strawberry?" He asks.

"Excuse me?"

"It was on your face, grape jelly or strawberry?" He asks again.

I can't remember any other time in my life that I was this embarrassed but much to my surprise I reply, "Oh- grape. I keep a little extra around in case I get a craving."

I think my response surprises him too. I'm not sure, but I can almost bet he makes a lot of girls nervous and my answer to a rather embarrassing moment probably isn't the answer most girls would have said.

"Trick!" A man's voice hollers from the parking lot. "Your mother sent me with some muffins this morning. She said you need to give me a haircut too."

An older man strolls into the office area carrying a plate of muffins. Patrick looks just like him and it doesn't take long to figure out that he is his dad.

"Hi, dad."

"Hi, dad," Zeus repeats.

His dad goes to the coffee pot and pours a cup. He looks up and sees me standing, and he is a little stunned.

"Oh, hello, sorry if I interrupted something." He shoots Patrick a look that carries a half smile just like the one his son has shown me a few minutes ago.

His dad is wearing the same uniform that Patrick is wearing but the patch on his shirt reads DAD. I feel more at ease knowing that someone else is here to distract me from the butterflies that are flying in my stomach.

"That's OK, I am just getting ready to leave," I said.

"Son, you need to tell us when you bring a pretty girl home, so we don't come over interrupting something."

"Dad, this little lady pulled in a few minutes ago with a flat."

"Good Boy" Zeus interrupts, and then makes the sound of an air hose.

I can tell they are both rather embarrassed but I think it is cute. I watch the two of them have a conversation back and forth talking about my tire, the muffins that were sent by mom and the hair cut that dad needs before he is let back in the house. I'm starting to feel as if I'm eavesdropping.

"Your mom also said that you need to give me a good clean shave. I'll get the stuff." His dad's voice trailing off in the distance.

As he walks away, he starts whistling the same tune Patrick did and it is unbelievably sweet.

"Sorry," Patrick said. "That, if you haven't guessed, is my dad. He's a good old guy, keeps me in line."

"Yep, looks like you have a close family," I said.

"What makes you say that?

"I don't know really. I just think-"

Patrick interrupts me, and I can't be more relieved. I know myself; I have the potential of rambling on about nothing.

"Well, yes, as a matter of fact, we are close."

We smile at each other but I look away quickly.

"So, where are you headed?" He asks.

"I don't know to be honest. I'm going along with whichever the way the wind blows."

He has no response and I can't help but wonder if he thinks I'm crazy.

"Here's the total. I'm only going to charge you for the tire." He hands me an invoice.

"Thank you. But you don't need to do that."

"You're right, I don't need to do it, but I want to." He responds with the corner smile I have come to appreciate.

"Besides, Zeus likes you. He might not forgive me if I didn't." He said.

I head out to the Jeep and his dad was waiting for me, leaning up against the side of it looking off into space, rubbing his hand over his chin.

"I'm going to hang this spare back up for you, get it out of the way. Where are you headed?" Patrick's dad asks in the same voice Patrick has.

"I don't really know."

"Oh yeah? One of those deals' huh? Trick just got back six or seven months ago from some backpacking trip, said he found his soul out there. I'm just glad I've never lost my soul. Sounds like a lot of work to me." He said.

I found it endearing that his dad called him Trick. It is a cute nickname, but I question if it is just short for Patrick or if he has tricks up his sleeve that I should be aware of.

I laugh. "Well I'm not sure what it is I'm looking for but, I'm sure I'll know what it is when I find it."

"All set." He said as he dusts his hands off on his pants.

"Here's my money," I said.

"Oh-no… you better just give that to Trick. I do my best to stay out of his business."

"OK, thank you for putting this back." I give him a heartfelt smile but in truth, I want to give him a hug. I miss my own dad already.

Patrick meets me halfway in the parking lot, I give him my money and thank him one last time for his help. He wishes me luck and I ask him to say goodbye to Zeus for me. He and his dad stand in the parking lot and watch me settled in. I roll down my window and I wave goodbye. They both give me a wave back and I grin. It is adorable how alike they are, both standing the same way and have the exact same wave.

"Thanks," he said "If you swing by on your way back through, Zeus would love to see you again and maybe he'll drop a feather for ya, looks like you could use a new one. Besides, I can give you a tune-up."

His dad quickly looks at Patrick as if he were shocked at what his son just said. I think Patrick embarrassed himself but covered it up well when he winks at me.

I realize my old and thin feather was visible and why Patrick suggested a new one. I pick it up to confirm that I knew what he was talking about, and wink back. "Definitely," I said.

Chapter 4

The only way I can get out of the parking lot from the auto garage is to make a right-hand turn and go north which isn't the way towards the highway. I'm not completely sure of the direction I want to go but the fact that I have no choice in the decision makes it easy. Besides, I know that if I can turn the other way, I will end up driving back home. I wait for a few cars to pass before placing myself amongst them. It feels good to be among others going in this direction but the only difference is, they know where they are going, where they have come from and where they belong. I don't have anything like that to hold onto other than where I have been and I would like to forget it.

I notice again the map my dad put on the seat next to me, and the thought crosses my mind to open it up to find out exactly where I am and where this road leads. As I reach for it, it suddenly falls between the car door and the seat making it impossible to recover while driving. In some strange way, this grabs my attention back to my driving as if I am being scolded for taking my eyes off the road. I grab the steering wheel with both hands and look ahead. I can't shake the feeling that this is all just some stupid mistake, and I need to go call a good therapist.

The way the mind works has always amazed me. We can have conversations with ourselves and offer a variety of advice all from one mind. We use our heart-mind, our logical mind, and our intuitive mind to give advice to our present mind based on situations from the past regarding our future that may not be relevant to each other. It's no surprise to me that people's minds snap or break down. I think it's a protective mechanism in order to keep people from complete system failure. Sadly, it doesn't always work and our brain will create irrational people and events that serve as protection. I am overly aware and slightly paranoid of delusional thoughts and constantly question whether I am thinking and seeing rational or if I have fallen into a world that I can barely understand. Sometimes, I just can't tell.

The day is far from over; early afternoon, but I want it to be over and I don't see why I can't let it be. As soon as I make this revelation, I barely read a sign as I drive past that read, CAMPING 2 MILES with an arrow once again, directing to the right. I might be the only one in the world that notices stuff like this and the ball inside my brain is bouncing off coincidences and free will. Two miles pass slowly when there's excitement to get there. When there's dread or doubt toward the destination, it appears too soon. In my case, I couldn't think fast enough. I need to make a decision on whether I am going to keep driving or pull off for the day. The logical, intuitive and heart part of my brain is racking up points as the ball bounces off them and all I want to do is keep it from dropping. GAME OVER.

I ease up on the gas, looking behind me to see if I am slowing down any kind of traffic with my inability to make a decision. No one. I slow down even more. The turnoff is approaching, so I shrug off the thought of failure and pull into the camping area. At first glance, I don't see any kind of designated camping areas but soon realized that the campsites are further down the dirt road. I drive as slow as I can, not wanting to stir up dust as I inch along each campsite. I roll my window down and was immediately greeted by the smell of someone's campfire. A rumble in my stomach reminded me that it was lunch-time, and I still have a peanut butter and jelly sandwich waiting. The idea is both comforting and unsettling because I feel like I'm about to eat someone else's sandwich from the break room at work. My thought is interrupted by another thought that I might not find an open campsite. As soon as it enters my mind, I find an area that is open.

Children are busy playing, running around looking for the perfect marshmallow roasting stick or fishing pole. Moms are content with dusting off britches, mending hurt feelings and kissing little boo-boos while the dads are concentrating on their efforts in collecting kindling, wood, logs, paper, and whatever else it takes to create the best campfire in the whole campground. It is an unspoken competition between males that only men understand.

Being here feels good. The pine in the air fills the inside of my lungs and in some strange way, I can taste it. The slow lazy breeze carries a low hush through the trees causing the aspens to rattle joyfully. Once the breeze reaches my face, I close my eyes and take a long deep breath. There's a small place in my heart that is calm and I decide that this is right where I need to be. I don't want to move, so I lean back in my seat, noticing that this is the first time all day that I actually feel relaxed.

I have a perfect view of the lake, so blue; I can't tell where the sky stops and the lake begins. I don't know where I'm going from here or what tomorrow brings but one thing is for certain, I belong amongst these trees.

I sit up straight from my sleep, chilled from the night air and sweating from the fear of my nightmare. My chest is heavy and I can barely breathe. I try to focus on something but it's too dark and I can't tell if my eyes are open or closed. I reach out to my side and find the door handle and pull frantically. It's locked, I can't get out, and I can't find the button. I cry out something unrecognizable from somewhere deep within me but get interrupted when I hear a snap of the door locks. I can't open the door fast enough and my legs can't keep up. I fall out head first catching my fall with my hands as the rest of my body slides to the ground. I'm dizzy and every time I move my head, the images from my nightmare drag behind in slow motion. My mind is racing and I just want to distract myself with something but there isn't anything. I can't help but hunch over as I try to stand up in a desperate attempt to change the struggle in my mind. My legs don't feel like my own, and I am slammed back down to the ground. My muscles can barely support me, and my body no longer feels like my own. Pandora's Box has been opened again and I can't find the rationale needed to close it. In the lowest part of my abdomen, I have a burn, a physical pain that feels oddly familiar but haunting. I cradle my head between my arms and squeeze them together in hopes of forcing this memory out of my brain. The fear and confusion are enough to make me run home, but I can't move my feet. Instead, I start throwing up and I can't stop. I can't even catch my breath long enough to prepare for it. I roll into the fetal position still bracing my head between my arms, noticing the saliva dripping from the corner of my mouth. I can't tell if I'm fading in and out of sleep or something more delusional but whatever it is, I want it to stop. Somewhere in the back of my mind, in the area that is still rational, needs water or food.

I prop myself on one elbow and put my legs underneath my body and roll onto my feet. I stagger over to the back of the jeep and manage to open it and find some water and out of the same desperation, I grab some food and shove it in my mouth with tears pouring from my eyes. The food swallows hard. It doesn't want to go down and it just gets stuck mid-way. My stomach hurts but I eat anyway. I keep stuffing it in, following it with water to help force it down hoping the emotions will go down with it. I am fighting myself in a pathetic attempt to keep my sanity but I'm exhausted.

Leaning against the side, I slowly inch back to the front but unable to dodge my own vomit. I pull myself in and sit back in the reclined seat. I grab a blanket from the back seat and bury myself, hoping I can bury myself alive. I curl up in my best fetal position once again, noticing my ears are plugged and I can't hear anything but my heart pounding. This is the darkest place I have been in a long time. I am completely at the mercy of my own mind. I start rocking myself back and forth, holding my head within my arms. My heart hurts, my soul hurts, the inner depths of my core hurt.

"Please stop... Please, I can't do this," I cry out loud, feeling my saliva make a web and building upon itself in the corners of my mouth. Defeat surrounds my world and I tumble back to sleep out of pure desperation.

PAST

I moved back home with a broken life as well as a shattered soul. My parents knew that I would someday return home with a failed marriage and an even more shattered life, but they welcomed me home with open arms. After 5 days of not eating and sleeping all day, my dad came into my room, pulled me up and took me to the shower.

"You smell Neha. You need to shower, you need to eat and you need to get on with your life," my dad said as he helped me walk to the bathroom.

Of all the showers in my life, I remember just a few and this was one. I sat on the bottom of the bathtub with the water running over my head. I cried just as many tears as water was coming from the shower head. It was more than a cry, it was a mournful explosion of my soul. This cry was from the heart, not the ego. There is such a huge difference in the sound the soul makes versus the ego. When the soul cries, it comes from such a deep place. It hurts, the heart literally hurts. It is a physical pain that can't be described, only felt. Having a broken heart is a loss to the soul. I never cried so hard in all my life. Even on the worst night of my life, I didn't cry like this. So many times when people cry, it is a way of expression. They are expressing to others to hear them, to listen to them. This kind of mourning wasn't the kind I needed others to hear. This was a cry between me and the part of me that was dying.

I could have stayed in the shower for the rest of my life, but the water heater wouldn't let me. The water started to get cold and the rest of my shower was what childbirth must feel like. It was cold and unwanted but it was my time to re-enter the world and make some kind of sense of it all.

My mom brought me one of her summer dresses. It was hot that morning and a summer dress seemed logical. She sat me down at the table and brushed my hair as I picked at the fresh fruit waiting for me. I looked out the front windows of my childhood home and wished I was that same little girl whose only worry in life was fear that her mom and dad left her. I wanted to wear the same pink little nightgown and go back to bed in my room where it smelled like strawberry and cotton candy lip gloss. *I wish I was still a little girl…*

My mom kept brushing my hair even though it didn't need it. I think this was her way of letting me know that she was willing to listen to me if I wanted to talk. I didn't want to talk.

Life stood still; no friends, and no hometown that welcomed me back. All I had, were my parents.

"I love you, mom."

"I love you too Rainy."

"What do I do from here?" I asked.

"Nothing, you stand still and let the dust settle. You need to simply feel."

"I don't want to feel," I whispered.

"At this point, you have no choice."

I didn't think I had any more tears left in me, but I did. They fell from my eyes like a fast water leak and I cried like that for days on and off. It was not the same cry as in the shower. This was just random, almost uncontrollable but silent and short-lived. The tears would leak out of me without notice and leave just as quick.

My nightmares were getting worse shortly after I moved back home. Or maybe it was the voices, I couldn't tell what it was exactly. It seemed real, and it was enough to make me not want to go to sleep at night. I would wake up soaking wet, vomiting and scared to death. My mom woke up several times with me to hold my hair back as I threw up. Finally, she told me I had to go to therapy.

"No way mom. I am not going to therapy. Everybody knows everyone in this town, so there is no way in hell I am going to therapy."

"There's a new therapist, she isn't from around here and I think you will like her."

"You already met her?" I felt betrayed.

"Rainy, you are not handling life. You need help. We need you to do this." She said.

I didn't want to go to therapy. I know all too well what happens when I start talking about my past so instead, I decided to do what many native women did before me. Doing an earth walk was often done when a woman lost a child or husband from the death of a battle or sickness. They would leave their tribe to grieve and seek clarity and wisdom. Returning from an earth walk was a gift to members of the tribe and the elders would seek messages from the Great Spirit. That called to me more than going to therapy. I needed more than just an understanding, I needed answers.

Chapter 5

My eyes are glued shut from dried tears. When I manage to get one eye open, the sun beating down on me was enough to not want to open them at all. As my eyes peel apart, my brain wakes up too. I throw off the blanket, kicking it to my feet and swing open the door to stir the air. The pine smell and crisp morning air surrounded me like an emergency paramedic surrounds the dying.

I amount to nothing at this point in my life, but I had hopes that my nightmares would stop. I feel like a failure. I was so confident that I could fight this inner battle and take a win but instead, it happened again.

I force myself to get out of the Jeep and walk around. I can hear the morning chatter from other campers, and the innocent morning voices of the kids already planning their imaginary lives. The smell of coffee and pancakes randomly slid under my nose and I crave the entire situation. I want to be them, any one of them. After watching them for a little while, their laughter managed to gently blow a tiny smile over to me, and I take it in.

The subtle breeze washes through my hair but it isn't at all pleasant. I can smell the vomit that was entangled in it from last night. I stare down at my clothes and see the disgusting mess and horror still lingering on them, reminding me that, yes last night was real, my past is real and extremely alive; more so now than ever before.

I gaze up to the sky and hope the morning sun will come down and clean my very soul through its ray's or perhaps take me away from all the pain. I want to be that little girl again, the one that was so innocent and simple.

"Rainy…" A voice whispers.

I look all around to see who is calling my name. It is a whisper that I can barely hear, and I'm beginning to wonder if I hear it at all. But then, I hear it again in the same slight whisper.

"Rainy…"

I spin in a circle but I still don't see anyone. I look over my shoulder and the thought occurs to me that I am behaving as if I were a crazy woman filled with paranoia. I try to open the door to the Jeep but I can't, it's locked. My feet are losing traction from the gravel beneath me, and I am unable to run. I try to hold on to the vehicle as I slip my way around to the passenger door. It was locked too. I pull on to the handle and shake it with furry.

"Rainy…jump." Another whisper.

"No, please," I mumble through my lips. "Emma?"

Her name. I haven't said her name in so long. The voice is familiar, just not a voice I have heard in such a long time. *It's her…*

I shake the handle once again and the door flies open, so I don't hesitate a moment to leap inside and slam it shut behind me. I crawl over to the driver's side, and the moment when my keys slid into the ignition, I felt a twisted sense of freedom.

I take off but my tires take a few seconds to catch on that I am getting the hell out of here. I stir up a bunch of dirt into the clean air but it isn't my intention; I just want to leave. This time, I don't look in the rearview mirror to see what I am leaving behind. I get to the entrance of the campground where the dirt road meets the pavement and I don't second guess on which direction to go, I make a hard right turn and accelerate up the road. My heart is pounding inside my chest. I have no control. I feel like someone has control over me instead. My instinct to run away flies through my head, so I try opening the door to bail out but I'm not surprised it won't open. *I am going crazy. I just tried to jump from a moving vehicle.* This seems like enough evidence to indicate someone has gone mad.

I work diligently on my composure, to gain control over my thoughts. I think back to what I learned in therapy years ago. *I don't hear voices.* I sit stagnate behind the wheel, driving unconsciously. My heart settles inside my chest automatically but my mind is still grinding and piecing together what happened, that voice. I wish I had brought my cell phone with me, but I purposely left it behind because I need to disconnect from the world but I don't think I was prepared for this. Besides, I can't call my parents. Not like this, telling them about the voices I hear in my head would go over about as well as the time I told my math teacher to solve his own damn problems.

This is the morning of day two and it feels like I have been paddling upstream the whole time. I tell myself to ease up on the idea that I am going to have some major ah-ha moment of self-discovery, at least not yet and at the rate I am going, it might not happen at all. A few tears run down my cheek as I realize I might not have the capacity to do this, to do any of this life in general. Everything hurts and I just can't keep hurting. I feel like I've tried to heal, I tried different paths but the only thing I learned for certain is the fact that I can't turn back time. I can't take back all that I have done or the people's lives I ruined. This life, these nightmares and the constant battle I face is my punishment and life sentence and only in death can I truly feel the freedom I'm searching for. This knowledge makes it so difficult in carrying on from day to day. I wake up every morning feeling dread because I am awake and I fall asleep every night in fear of a nightmare or simply the agony of knowing I will wake up in the morning. One foot goes in front of the other and the saying I've heard too much of, that time heals all wounds, is enough to make me want to scream. The only wounds they are healing from is the Lego they stepped on in the middle of the night. Time hasn't healed this, it can't. What I carry with me will never go away.

I use my shirt to dry my face and blow my nose. I don't care, I don't care if snot dries into a hard glob on my shirt. I have puke in my hair, dirt all over my pants and now, snot drying on my shirt and I can care less at this point. But I do need to pee and that is not something I am willing to wear.

RESTAURANT/STORE. I'm pretty sure this is about the most random place to have a restaurant or convenience store. The only thing I have seen over the past few miles is the lake and the people fishing it. I haven't even seen that many houses to warrant a restaurant or store but who am I to judge.

I second guess my decision to blow my nose on my shirt. Perhaps I didn't think that through. Now I need to go into a public place and I decide quickly that I would rather people see that instead of the vomit I have caked in my hair.

"Where are your bathrooms?" I ask as soon as I get inside.

A young man points to the corner of the restaurant and I move quickly. I walk through a small general store that sold fishing tackle and bare food necessities. The entire place is filled with the smell of bacon and toast and the sounds of silverware clanking on the plates.

I fling the door open, relieved that it's a single bathroom and not multiple stalls. I lock the door behind me and drop my bag. I need to hurry, people get kicked out of places if they think bums are bathing in their restrooms. Right now, that's exactly what I have become. I quickly strip my clothes and toss them in a plastic bag. At some point, I will need to wash them. That is one thing I never thought about when I was preparing. *Why didn't I think that through?* I put my head in the sink and run cold water over my hair using the hand soap on the counter and I wash it several times to make sure it is clean. I use the same soap to scrub my skin from my face to my feet, creating a pile of water on the floor. I don't wait for the water to warm up, I don't want to waste time. It is painfully cold but I don't care. Cold water drips from my hair and down my back sending chills straight into my bones where it settles. My skin rises to attention, goosebumps. *Why do they call it goosebumps?* I grab paper towels off the wall and wipe up my mess. I searched through my bag with fierceness until I find some clean clothes to put back on. I force them over my wet skin and shake into myself, forcing my clothes to hang off me instead of sticking. It feels good to be clean but even better, I didn't get caught. There is something about cold water that can make a person feel cleaner than warm water but only on hot days. This was going to be another warm day but not like home. In the mountains, it doesn't get as hot. I lean into the mirror, and I am white as a ghost and my lips are purple. My eyes are outlined by red tracks creating a haunting image, too familiar.

I jump at myself when I hear a sudden knock at the door. I gather my things as fast as I can, force them in my bag, and open the door. I slide around a lady careful to avoid eye contact and kept my head down trying to hide my insanity.

Chapter 6

"Good morning." A waitress yells from the back of the restaurant.

"Hello," I answer quietly, trying to muster a smile and leave without being spoken too again.

"Sit down wherever," she said.

Her comment stops me dead in my tracks. Everyone looks up from their plates of waffles as I try to keep my head down without running into the wall or a person but it's too late, I already drew attention to myself. The restaurant grows a little softer, conversations slow for just a brief moment and the only thing I can think about is my wet hair. Someone is going to find out I took a mini bath in their sink and I'm focused on what to tell them if they ask.

"You can sit over here," said a soft, trembling voice.

My attention is pulled to an elderly woman sitting next to the only window in the place. The restaurant got deathly quiet after she spoke and if I had a knife, I could cut the tension in the room with it. This suddenly went from being about me to being about her.

I look over my shoulder because I feel like someone is behind me, pushing me to move. I walk through the restaurant like a bull in a china shop as my dad always said. My bag is hitting the heads of every other person sitting down, trying to enjoy their breakfast. I apologize to one, excuse myself to another, and this continues until I finally reach the table. I can't remember any other time in my life where it felt like it took years to sit down in a restaurant. I casually gaze the entire place one last time in hopes of finding an empty table and chair, so I can excuse myself from having to sit across someone I don't know. All I can hope for is that she will leave soon. Perhaps she was waiting for her check and once she leaves, I can eat my meal in peace, or whatever you call it.

She is sitting in the sun ray from the window, casting a beam of light that is ever so graceful, just enough to show her years. She is beautiful in her own way, almost angelic but not quite. Her eyes are incredibly light, gray and colorless, something I have never seen before. She appears to have so much peace about her and it places me on the verge of feeling just how much turmoil I have. She isn't your typical looking elderly woman. She has white hair that is unusually long and it's loosely braided, sweeping towards the front. She has strands of runaway hair falling out of the braid and gracefully framing her hallow face. She is very thin but doesn't appear weak or sick. She wears Birkenstock sandals with wool socks and if solace were served in units of measurements, I would receive a tablespoon because now I see where we have something in common. Her sandals are worn, the cork is almost gone, and the soles are showing holes. Her skin is paper thin but at the same time, it glows. She looks almost homeless, or poor and I instantly feel sorry for her.

I'm in the process of saying hello when the waitress comes over to take my order, not even allowing me to greet the woman who has surrendered her table to me. She pulls a pencil out of her hair which I am a bit impressed with, but not fully ready to give her my order. I don't see a menu, and she doesn't offer one. I don't even know what I want to drink. I quickly jump from thinking of Birkenstocks and my wet hair to thinking about what I want to eat. She looks as if she is going to write down my order, so I am totally thrown off when she tells me, "I'm going to bring out some pancakes and orange juice. That's all we have. The bacon is gone."

She is just about the most unfriendly person I have come across and my mom would tell me to be kind regardless, a person never knows what someone might be going through. Still, some people have a way of making you feel wanted and instantly welcomed and then there's my waitress who needs a vacation or therapy.

She leaves me sitting across from a stranger and I'm left with no other option than to focus my attention towards her. I can tell I'm the only person in here that is not a local. Everyone one else blends together. The men are wearing some kind of fishing attire, vests with lures dangling off netting and rubber boots. They slowly refocus themselves away from me, picking up where they left off in their newspaper or eating, mainly pancakes. The noise from the kitchen is loud enough that trying to have a conversation is almost useless without raising your voice which I am not willing to do at this point. I take notice of the entrance that uses a screen door to separate the outdoors from the indoors. It creeks and slams shut almost every 30 seconds from people coming and going, my mom would cringe.

I make eye contact with the old lady who is now smiling at me.

"Thanks for letting me use your table," I said.

"You're welcome."

She sounds so sweet. Her voice is soft and shaken, much like the rest of her. She looks as if she is waiting for someone and glances out the window. Her legs are directly planted flat on the floor with no obstacles in her way making me wonder if she will be leaving any second now. Her hands lay in her lap, and she subtly fiddles with the seam in her pant leg and her fingers are crooked from arthritis. She has four plastic bags filled with groceries placed on both sides of her feet with the handles still sticking straight up as if she just let go of them. I think it is interesting that she has enough groceries to fill her bags because the grocery store attached to the restaurant is little to be desired. I have seen gas stations with more selection of food than this place. But what do I know, I ran through it so fast that I might have missed the aisle where all the good stuff is.

"Do you come here often?" I ask.

I realize from the grin on her face that I just used a tacky pick-up line that is favored by desperate bar leeches at 2 am. I smile back as if I read her mind.

"I suppose when all else fails, using a classic one-liner to start a conversation takes the win," I don't wait for her to respond.

"One order of pancakes," interrupts my waitress who needs a vacation.

"Thanks," I said.

That is fast. I'm surprised at how little time it took to whip up such beautiful round little bites of heaven. I spot the butter on the table and it's not little individually wrapped butter pats but rather a whole stick like we have at home. I can tell its real butter which is my favorite and take note of the genius idea. It makes me question why someone would ruin such a great thing like butter by placing it into small foil packets that are barely enough to cover an inch of food.

I look around and back down at my food, eating, but once again, not tasting. So many things are running through my mind, like small little movie clips reminding me that nothing has changed.

She shifts her body slightly to a more comfortable position and winced to herself in pain which get my attention. I want to say something to her, but she beat me to it.

"My name is Ellie." She said.

"It's nice to meet you, Ellie. I'm Rainy, this is a beautiful part of the country. Are you lucky enough to live up here?"

"Oh yes," she said sweetly, "I've lived up here for over 50 years."

"Wow, I can't imagine living in one place that long," I said.

"Well, you're still young."

She nods her head and gives a warm smile. She is being polite in letting me finish my breakfast. The aftermath of last night and this morning left me hungry and I just now realize it. I can tell Ellie notices how hungry I am, but she doesn't seem to mind and frankly, neither do I. In some strange way, sitting across from this sweet old lady, makes me feel like I am home. Our eyes will meet up occasionally and each time, I just look back down at my pancakes and the community butter I have been blessed with. I give it some thought on how weird this situation is, especially for me. I have been blocking people out of my tribe ever since the dreadful night that changed my life. Not only that, no one wants to have anything to do with me anyway. This is my way of protecting myself from the harshness that humans can infringe onto one another. But Ellie is different. First of all, she doesn't know me from Adam. That's the great thing about strangers. They don't know anything about my past and I don't have to tell them either. The fear and anxiety that I went through last night and this morning are slowly diminishing by simply sitting across from her. There's a definite, undeniable connection but I don't want to destroy the simplicity of it by over-analyzing the dynamics.

I finish the last bite of food about the same time my plate is whisked away by the waitress without hesitation. My fork isn't even out of my mouth, and I'm suddenly left without a plate to set it on. I grow a little annoyed with that lady and if I had a little more pep to my step, I would say something to her. I set my fork down on the table and I'll be darned if the waitress didn't pick that up too, along with the orange juice that I haven't even finished yet.

"How were the pancakes?" Ellie asks.

You're good Ellie, you are good. Ellie knows I am about to say something to the waitress.

"Filling, I had a long night, so they hit the spot."

"Are you feeling better?"

"Yes, actually. I am now," I said, surprised by how much better I feel.

"So what brings you up this way? I know you're not from around here. I've never seen you before." She asks.

"I'm passing through, I stayed the night at the campground down the road, such a beautiful lake."

I know I didn't answer her question, I don't know what brings me up here or where I am going, but I am not about to tell her that.

"Very beautiful indeed," she said.

"The fishing is good I hear."

"I haven't gone fishing in years." She gazes out the window.

I was ready to leave, I want to get back to not knowing what the hell I'm doing but I can't find a way to finalize my conversation.

"Do they bring me the bill or do I go pay someone?" I ask.

"You will go to the counter," she points with her crooked finger.

Ellie's focus shifts from me over to the young man clearing off tables. She nods her head toward his direction and said, "My ride is running behind schedule and I could sure use a ride home."

Oh God, no. No No No. I swallow hard and wish I had some water. I want to jump out of my seat as if I didn't hear her, but I feel like I am glued to the chair. My ears start ringing and Ellie is staring at me waiting for a response. I can easily say no without giving an explanation but I can't seem to get the words out of my mouth.

"It's just about 5 miles up the road." She adds.

I stare at her, trying to find a lie floating around that I can use. I never like to admit this but lying comes easy for me. Perhaps I just got used to telling them. Either way, I can't figure out why something isn't popping into my head. I was able to lie to the truck driver, even though he didn't buy it, *why can't I come up with something now?*

Ellie stands up and I can't believe what is happening. *I won't take her home. I can't. I won't.* The screaming in my head is so loud that I didn't hear the silence that took root from every single person inside. I could feel the tension though and it was stronger than any of the screaming in my head. Everyone froze except Ellie who gathered her bags and took a few steps.

"Well...see, I don't have room." I said.

I look up to her with relief that I am able to find the lie file in my brain but it doesn't last.

"I saw you get out of your Jeep, you have room." She didn't look at me.

She rests her hand on my shoulder as she slowly walks by but it might as well been a touch from the dead. It gives me the heebie-jeebies but I manage to grab my bag and walk behind her.

As I approach the counter, I feel week in the knees. I look at the cashier completely expressionless until our eyes lock.

"I hope you know what you're getting into," his young voice mumbles.

I hold my breath for a second after he said this and look over my shoulder to make sure he is talking to me. I want to respond or better yet, ask a million questions when suddenly, without notice, the screen door slams shut, cracking like thunder, and I jump. I glance through the screen and see Ellie standing at the foot of the steps waiting patiently. The air is heavy and quite, sending chills through each vertebra in my back. Nobody is moving, everyone is watching and I know I need to leave. There is nothing friendly about this place.

I keep my mouth closed and put one foot in front of the other until I finally make it out the door and down the stairs. I wish I knew what he meant. I also wonder if I'm the only person who heard it. I want to turn around and ask him but my legs won't hear of it and at this point, I feel like I just escaped the twilight zone so going back is not in my best interest.

Once Ellie starts walking a little, I notice how quickly she can move. I suppose I'm expecting her to walk slow, hunched over and cautious of her steps but instead, she moves with ease. When we get to the Jeep, the thought crosses my mind to tell her I lost my keys, but they are in my hands so that is a short-lived idea. Then again, where would we go if I could tell her that? Certainly not back inside. By now the waitress has probably made a voodoo doll of me.

I open her door with resistance and slowly walk to the driver's side. I stand in place for a moment secretly hoping the jeep won't start. I realize I didn't help Ellie and I didn't even think to help her with her groceries. Not something my parents would be proud of. It's too late now, she is already in the Jeep. I am more nervous than I have been in a long time. My hands are cold and sweaty, my heart is racing and I can't figure out how on earth I got to this point.

"Come on Rainy," she said with her shaken voice, "jump in."

All of a sudden I hear the same voice from this morning. "Jump Rainy. Go to the edge and jump..."

PAST

I was ten-years-old to the day and my parents had a swimming party at the recreation center in town. All my friends were there and having a blast playing water games and jumping off the diving board. Their screams of joy and laughter echoed throughout the pool with random whistleblowing of the lifeguard followed by warnings to walk, no running. I, on the other hand, sat on the edge and watched. Having a birthday party with all my friends seemed like the best idea in the world. I could picture myself being lifted into the air while everyone celebrated the triumph of turning ten. It was, after all, a milestone into the double-digit club. I had visions of being surrounded by friends wanting my attention; pulling at me to follow them or even better, following me. But that was not the case, I was ignored. Not that this was unusual for me, but this was the first time I noticed.

I've always known there was something different that separated me from my friends and my parents from other parents. Being just a kid, it's hard to know the action that sets off judgment from other people. I couldn't put my finger on what it was that separated us from the rest but as I got older, I started to see the differences.

My mom was sitting in a chair across the pool, and we would periodically make eye contact, giving me a sweet, assuring smile every time. She was aware of the growing division between my friends and me. I think she understood the feelings because it also affected her, but I never wanted to question it. Even if I wanted to ask why I was treated differently, I wouldn't because I didn't have the words to form the question. It was easier to just feel it rather than question it. That simple.

I sat as my friends would call out to each other to have them watch a trick or an impressive flip from the side of the pool. I was never called to watch anything and I wondered if they remembered it was my birthday. The party was in full swing, going on two hours, but I was ready for it to be over. I didn't feel like opening presents or eating cake, I just wanted to go home and ride my bike, or play with clay at the dining room table while my mom made dinner. Whatever I wanted to do, I just wanted it to be the three of us.

Now and then, my mom would talk to one of my friends or go into the lobby of the rec center. I didn't pay attention to what she was doing until one by one, my friends decreased in numbers. Before I knew it, everyone was gone.

A person would think this would be a great disappointment to a ten-year-old kid, but I was relieved. My mom knew me better than I knew myself, and she could tell that the party diverted from my birthday celebration to a get together for everyone else.

My mom ended my party early by telling all my friends that I had an upset tummy. When we went to the locker room, she gathered all the cards and gifts and asked me to carry them to the car as she carried the cake. I couldn't wait to get home, maybe my party was better than I thought it would be. Being a ten-year-old girl with presents to open was something to look forward too even if they were sympathy gifts.

We loaded up Kermit and I climbed to the front seat, a place I didn't get to sit in very often. I was usually stuck in the back.

"Well kiddo, I'm sorry the party was a flop. Did you have any fun?" She asked.

"Yea, it was OK, I mean I didn't hate it or anything, it just wasn't like I thought it would be."

"The good news is you don't need to have friends to be important." My mom said.

"The good news is that I get to go home, eat cake, and open presents!" I grin.

"That's my girl," she tossed my hair, "that's a positive way of looking at it."

I studied her just a little longer than usual. She always had a way of making me feel better by confusing the day right out of me. I laid my head back and rested it on the seat while watching the fluffy clouds move quickly through the sky. My eyes were tired and I wanted to doze off but mom suddenly spoke up.

"Rainy, do you know how long it's been since I jumped off a diving board?" She asked.

I didn't answer, partly because I didn't know she could jump off anything, let alone a diving board.

"Well, a long time, and I really want to again, so I was thinking that maybe tomorrow we could go back to the pool and do it together, I mean, if it's OK with you."

"Sure Mom," I said as enthusiastically as I could.

She smiled, not for me to see but to herself. I could tell she genuinely wanted to do this and I realized that she was doing it more for her rather than me. My mom always knew when I needed a pick-me-up but this wasn't for me, and I was OK with that.

When we got to the house, mom parked the van and pulled the keys from the ignition but instead of getting out, we both sat there in silence for a minute. I lifted my head off the seat and sat up straight as we both looked out the front windshield. Kermit made weird clicking noises and subtle swishing sounds from the windshield washer fluid much like the sounds our house makes when it's deathly quiet.

"Thanks, mom."

She knew the reasons why I needed to thank her and I didn't need to wait for her to say anything else. That gave me the perfect opportunity to jump from the van and run to the house. I had a feeling she would tell my dad about how my day went and I didn't want to be a part of the conversation. I flew through the front door and straight to my room, so I could avoid the questions.

The next morning, I woke up to my mom bellowing out the song Surfing USA at the top of her lungs. She would sing some and laugh some and I could also hear my dad chuckle from time to time. These were not the usual sounds at my house this early in the morning. Most mornings I woke up to the sounds of clattering dishes, soft voices and the smell of breakfast in the crisp morning air.

I rolled out of bed, curious about what was going on. I was surprised to hear my mom and dad were in their room.

"Mom?"

"Hi Rainy, come in."

I absolutely could not believe what I was seeing. My mom and dad were standing on their bed in their swimsuits, pretending to be surfing.

"Dad is coming to the recreation center this morning." My mom said smiling.

My dad had never been swimming as far as I knew. Even worse I had never seen him in a swimsuit. I wasn't sure to laugh or cry. My parents are both attractive people, but stylish- not so much. They seemed to think they were pretty hip back in the day. Hippie maybe, but all I knew them to be are my parents and nothing else. From time to time I would hear them giggle and mess around but it was far and few between. They were usually pretty serious and talked about boring stuff that people are doing on the T.V. I couldn't understand why people like to watch the news when so many other shows were on. Mr. Rogers's Neighborhood was on T.V at the same time as the news, so I never got the chance to watch it. Now, that was a good show, Mr. Rogers always seemed like a nice guy but I couldn't be for certain, they changed the channel as soon as things got good. I was lucky to watch Bob Ross though. He was fascinating, not to mention extremely talented.

On a typical day, they had more serious moments than silly. So seeing them like that was downright weird to the point that I wasn't sure I liked it. I stood in front of my parent's door to their room half paralyzed, hoping it was a joke.

My dad's legs hadn't seen the sun in years. I couldn't remember seeing anything as bizarre as his legs. His upper body was just as white. His head, neck, and arms had a beautiful tan, but unfortunately, it didn't go with the rest of his body. In those parts, you would call it a farmer's tan. Mom, on the other hand, looked good. She didn't have any sun at all and was completely white, but she wore it well. She had on a green one-piece swimsuit with little yellow daisies all over. It was fitting for her. I was unaware that my dad owned a pair of swim trunks but at least they weren't cut off jean shorts. Nonetheless, he still looked like a freak show.

I suppose my parents had a style all their own, and it certainly wasn't the typical farmer attire. Dad was handsome and mom was just as pretty. Most of the time dad wore jeans and t-shirts and my mom wore pretty little sundresses. There were times he wore a hat but that was mainly in the winter and was one my mom crocheted for him. She took pride in placing his hat on and would adjust it carefully. Most times, he would readjust the hat to go crooked which gave him even more attention from mom. She loved it though, it always ended in a hug or a kiss, but she always straightened it again. When he came to kiss me good-bye, I would move his hat back to the crooked position. This became another unspoken ritual for the three of us.

"So uh, are you guys going to wear that?" I asked.

They jumped off the bed, both at the same time making the light on their nightstand rattle.

"This is the style kiddo." My dad answered.

"Yeah, but not for you guys"

"What do you want us to wear then?" He asked.

Good question I thought. I didn't have an answer for that.

"Dad, are you coming with us?" I asked?

"Your mom is diving today and I want to be there to see it. I haven't seen her dive in years. Get on your suit and shoes, were burning daylight. Mom packed peanut butter and jelly sandwiches to eat for breakfast. We will eat on the road."

What is my dad going to wear for shoes? I can't remember my dad wearing any shoes other than hiking boots with red shoelaces. In the summer when he changed clothes at the end of the day, he would slip on Birkenstocks if he needed to run down to the mailbox or grab something from outside. *Why in the world are we eating peanut butter and jelly sandwiches for breakfast?* These thoughts were racing through my mind.

Sure enough, dad left the house wearing his is hiking boots, red shoelaces not tied and flopping all over the place.

When we got to the recreation center there weren't a lot of cars in the parking lot and I couldn't have been more relieved. My dad went to the front to pay and nobody gave their attention to his unbelievably dorky ensemble. In fact, they acted like they see swimsuits and hiking boots every day.

"I will meet you girls at the pool."

When my mom and I went onto the locker room, she placed all our stuff inside a locker and grabbed some goggles out of her bag. She shut the door to the locker, took the key and pinned it to the inside of her swimsuit. I was impressed with her. She acted as if she did that all the time.

"Mom, how come you have goggles?"

"Oh, I like to have them when I dive."

"When did you get them?"

"I've had them for a really long time. Come on dad's waiting."

She smiled again, a certain smile that lit up her whole face.

"I haven't seen those eyes sparkle like this in years." My dad said as he kissed her.

Now that's about enough. I thought to myself.

The pool was empty, at least of anyone I knew and my stomach could relax. There were old people in the water doing laps and other things that looked like a cross between dancing and drowning.

"Rainy, come and sit on the edge and watch mom jump with me." My dad said.

I went to the edge and plopped down next to my dad. We dangled our feet onto the water and I found my focus narrowing in on the nonexistence color of my dad's legs once again.

"Pay attention Neha. Here she goes." My dad nudged me with excitement.

I watched my mom climb the ladder to the diving platform. It was so high up in the air, almost to the ceiling. I noticed that everyone who was minding their own business minutes earlier, stopped what they were doing to watch and I wanted them to quit looking at her. I felt the need to protect her from the embarrassment she was about to embark on but the fact that my dad was at ease, made me less worried.

She stood at the top of the platform and put her goggles on. She waved at us and smiled and my dad gave her a thumbs up while I waved back. She walked to the edge and jumped up and down on the board and stopped. I was already impressed that she could stop jumping on the board so easily. She walked back to the end of the platform and made some adjustments, turning a big round wheel with her foot. She wasn't smiling anymore and I went from caring what everyone thought to fear that my mom might be scared. I never wanted to jump off the high board, although I admired the kids that did. They had guts that I wasn't born with. I looked at my dad's face for reassurance and found a grin from ear to ear and I knew he wasn't scared for her at all.

"Just do a cannonball mom!" I yelled at her.

I didn't really know what a cannonball was but I used to hear other people say it as someone was about to jump.

Then it happened. She jumped a few times on the board and every time her feet left the board, she was as straight as an arrow. Her arms would rise above her head effortlessly and her legs looked like they were glued together. Her feet were pointed straight below her like a ballerina leaping through the air. Her last jump was high above the board and while in the air she curled her body into a ball and did several forward flips. As she fell closer to the water she opened up her body as if she were a flying angel. Logic knows she was going fast but for me, time slowed down. She was beautiful. She went into the water head first without a splash and I had never seen anything more impressive in all my life.

She swam to the edge of the pool and quickly got out. She was very excited and you could see it by the smile on her face. Everyone in the pool area was clapping and my mom took a bow with a shy childlike grin.

"Good job!" My dad said laughing. "Did you see that Rainy?" he added as he quickly jumped to his feet, pulling me up with him. He gave my mom a hug and spun her around like you see in the movies. They both were laughing and my dad's voice cracked.

"Oh man!" She said with more enthusiasm than I have ever seen.

"It felt great. Better than great." She added.

She took her goggles off and rang out her wet hair. My dad handed her a towel and said: "you looked great, better than great." He hugged her again.

My mom looked at me, but I didn't know what to think or say for that matter. I was thankful that she didn't make a fool out or herself, and I was shocked that she was capable of something like that. My parents were talking amongst themselves but I felt invisible. The eye contact that was exchanged between them made me uncomfortable. For reason's I couldn't explain, I felt sad. Up to that point, I always felt like my mom and I were always feeling the same things. She always seemed to know exactly what to say because she understood me because she felt the same way. But at that moment, she didn't and it made me feel like we were worlds apart. She didn't seem to have any fear, and she had such bravery. I didn't have any of that and I questioned how she could understand me when she wasn't the same as me at all. I knew I needed to say something. Anything.

My dad walked away and hollered back over his shoulder to us that he was going to sit in the hot tub. Then he winked at me.

"Rainy," she said, 'just between you and me, I was scared to death to make that jump. It's been such a long time. So? Did I seem nervous? How did I do?'

I felt so many emotions all at once and hearing her say that brought tears to my eyes. I desperately needed to hear those words but I didn't know it until she spoke them. I felt reconnected to her again, but not because I learned she was nervous or scared but because she shared those feelings with me.

"Mom, it was so great! Just like the Olympics, when did you learn to do all that?"

"I did a little diving back in high school and college. I loved it." She said.

"You know what else Rainy? I was just about your age when I jumped off the diving board for the first time. I was so scared."

"Do you get scared every time you jump off?" I asked.

"No, only if I hadn't done it in a long time, like today. After a while, your fear goes away, or maybe it simply changes into excitement and anticipation. It's easy to get them confused. Do you understand that sweetie?"

"Yea I do mom, but can you be excited and scared at the same time?" I asked.

"Of course, but trust me the fear will go away. Do you want to try it? Not dive like I did, just jump. We don't have to but if you decide you want to try, I can help."

"I want to but I don't know what to do. It's so scary and I don't know if I can do it."

"Just hold on to my hand, that's all you need to do. Gravity will do the rest. Being scared is part of life, it's a good thing. Fear is meant to keep you safe, not keep you from growing."

I didn't really hear what she was saying or maybe I didn't want a life lesson. The only thing that registered is that she would jump with me, but I know for a fact that you can't jump off the diving board with anyone.

"I can't hold your hand mom. It's the pool rules."

She took my hand as we walked over to the diving area. She waved at the lifeguard and she waved back.

"I already took care of that," she said proudly.

"What if I get up there and I change my mind?"

"OK, so what? You change your mind, we are all allowed to change our minds."

"So I would just climb the ladder back down? Will I get in trouble?"

"Nope, no trouble. There is no rule that says you can't climb back down the ladder." She said.

"OK, I will just go up to the top and see if I want to jump," I said nervously.

"Good, that's a great place to start."

I went ahead of her and when I got to the fifth step, I peered down to make sure she was still behind me.

"You need to keep climbing if I'm going to follow you up." She said.

I held onto the sides of the ladder and looked up toward the top. I had a lot of steps to go and I could hear my mom below me telling me to take one step at a time.

"When you get to the top, you can hold on to the rail of the platform. It goes half-way out so you can still hold on and make room for me to get up."

"Oh, OK," my voice was shaking.

I decided to look down and surprised myself that it didn't freak me out. My mom looked at me, and we both stopped for a second.

"Probably not a good idea to look down eh?" She asked.

"Um, it's OK actually, if I fall, I will land on you."

"Really?" She smiled.

When I got to the top I held on the rail and inched my way over, so she had room to stand. I was in awe of how high I was which meant the water was far below. My mouth was dry and I the thought of letting go of the railing and walking out to the end of the board made it impossible to swallow.

"OK Rain, how are you doing? Still want to jump?"

"Yea, so wait. No. Not yet. How do we get to the end, there's nothing to hold onto. I don't want to fall off the side." I said,

"The railing goes as far as the side of the pool, as soon as the railing ends, the pool begins. If you fall off the side, you will land in the water, not on the ground. So are we going?" She said slowly.

"Yea, grab my hand," I said.

As we inched ourselves toward the edge, the board bounced a little which wasn't something I expected and I yanked my hand from hers and held onto the rail. One more step closer and the railing would be gone and would be left to walk the rest of the way hand in hand with my mom.

"Want to keep going?" She asked.

"MOM!" I raise my voice, "yes just wait!"

"Take your time. The board will bounce a little but you won't bounce with it like I did. That takes a whole set of separate effort." She said calmly.

I reached out to her hand, and she took hold as we both walked to the edge. I didn't want to look anywhere other than my own feet, but I wanted to know if my dad was watching.

"Is dad watching mom?"

"He sure is." She answered.

She takes her other hand, and waves at him and I can't believe she is so calm. I am to the point where I can't turn around even if I wanted to. The thought crossed my mind that I might end up staying up here for the rest of my life. I'm too far down the board to turn around. I wouldn't have anything to hold on to and the railing was no longer within reach.

"We're here, are you ready to jump?" She asked.

"No, not yet, just a sec."

I needed to breathe. I had barely taken a breath since I climbed the ladder which seemed like ten days ago.

"Yep, I'm ready, just don't let go of my hand," I told her.

"On the count of three," she said.

Together we counted, "One… two… Three…"

And we jumped.

Chapter 7

I can't get a grip and I find myself in another world and I know Ellie has no clue of the emotional state I am in. If she knew, she wouldn't want me to take her home. I keep going back in my memory of the diving board and my mom. She would hold my hand right now but I don't have her here. *1...2...3... I'm jumping.* The only difference is, this time I'm jumping alone.

I clear my throat knowing the jibber jabber coming from Ellie might require a response. I keep thinking of the truck driver that helped me yesterday and how terrible I feel that he had to listen to my nonsense when it was clear he probably hasn't talked to anyone in days. I just let her talk, admittedly, I don't want to talk anyway. I want my mind to go blank, just like a blank piece of paper. I need to concentrate on my driving and nothing more.

The nerves under my skin are pounding, compiling sweat into the palms of my hands. Every ounce of water I have inside my body is coming out through my hands and all I can do is hold onto the steering wheel.

Ellie makes a motion with her hand toward the direction I need to turn. All I can see is a dirt path lined with tall pine trees. The path has been driven on but not very often. Two grooves in the dirt are separated by a small mound with low-lying flowers and other green plants that are probably weeds. The path disappears up the hill into the trees.

A part of me feels angry that I am in this situation in the first place. I don't want to feel this way but it's not like she bullied me into this situation, if she only knew what I did to the last person sitting in the passenger seat.

I follow the dirt road staying in between the grooves, hearing the flowers and weeds dragging under the Jeep. An old worn hand-made sign is not far from the entrance labeled Private Drive No Trespassing. The road is long and winding and barely drivable. I drive slowly in order to keep my wheels out of the deep ruts. Something to concentrate on other than the moment.

As I pull up to her house my first thought is that she can't live here and the real house is somewhere behind this neglected pile of boards.

"Well, it's still here." She sighs.

"I didn't know that was a concern." I blurt out.

"It's pretty run down, I always wonder if I will come back and find it laying in a pile."

"That wouldn't be good, I suppose it would ruin a perfectly good day," I said.

I am shocked that anyone can live here, especially her. I take in the condition of her house with a growing concern over her safety. Even though it looked dead, it was very much alive. A deep breath leaves my body and the house seemed to do the same as if this old run down shack and I are holding our breath at the same time.

"Ellie, do you live here alone?" I ask.

"Mmm umm," she mumbled. "Honey, can you grab these bags?"

I walk to her side and open her door, grab her bags and hope she has herself under control. I don't think I can handle a trip to the ER because she trips and falls.

The covered front porch has collapsed on one end and the paint is peeling off like a snake shedding skin. The ground is covered with pine needles and pine cones and the tips of the trees blanket the sky. The trees form a canopy which makes this closing morning feel more like dusk. Every so often the sun peeks through the trees that are swaying by the breeze.

I can hear a wind chime in the distance long before I actually see it. I follow behind Ellie as she takes the lead, stepping carefully onto the porch stairs. She isn't a slow elderly woman and I find myself wanting to call her Miss Ellie instead of just Ellie; makes me think of the old movie, 'Driving Miss Daisy.' I, on the other hand, feel awkward and clumsy and my mind is still getting over the fact that I just had someone in my Jeep. The steps let out a scream as soon as my feet land and all I can hope for is that I don't fall through.

As she opens the screen door, I drop the bags from my right-hand and grab it thinking it was going to fall from the hinges. It is only connected by the bottom hinge and even that doesn't look like it is going to hold much longer. She walks through the unlocked door, something I could relate to from back home and I walk in behind her. Ellie sits down on the first chair directly off the entryway from the door. I'm still holding on to the grocery sacks wondering what to do with them as she motions toward the kitchen.

"Some of those things need to go into the refrigerator, would you mind?" She asks.

"Sure."

I walk through her small living room and into the kitchen which is equally small. There's a square table against the wall with two yellow matching chairs. Her sink is clean and has no dishes in it except a teacup on the corner. I place the groceries on the table and was a bit confused on what I should do next. I unpack what few groceries she had but I feel like I am invading her privacy. I put the cheese and other things that go into the refrigerator and feel saddened by what little food she has in there. I take out a few cans of soup from another bag and organized them on the counter. I feel a little uncomfortable sifting through her cabinets to put it all away. I fold the plastic bags as neatly and methodically as I can just to take up time, so I can take a glance around at the rest of her house, from what I could see anyway.

When I glance over to her, she has her head back on the chair with her eyes closed. As run down as this place is, I can tell she is relieved to be home. It is so quiet up here and I take note that I am still being chased by my companion, silence.

There's a faint smell of lavender that brought life to the air, and she has plants throughout the kitchen. I check the soil in automatic response to something I've watched my mom do my whole life. I'm not surprised to find them recently watered. The floor is wood through-out but worn down and dull. The walls are fragile with not one picture hanging, but I can still sense a story between each board. There seems to be something much bigger than me in this house but I don't fear it. In fact, I feel calm.

Her ancient, rounded refrigerator rattles and hums quietly only to stop seconds later making the house even more still. That's when the clock on the wall takes over. I imagine its ticking is the heartbeat of the house. It is steady and strong and reminds me that time isn't standing still; not in the least.

I know I can't keep standing in the kitchen, so I make my way back to the living room. I watch her breathing for a few moments, wondering if she is asleep but also questioning whether she is still alive. She looks relatively comfortable in her own way which leads me to believe she sits here often. Surely she isn't asleep knowing a stranger is in her house. I conclude that the odds of her sleeping outweigh the alternative.

I need to leave, driving her home wasn't part of my plan and I want to get back on track. I shift my weight from one leg to the other, so I can lean over the couch and grab a blanket to cover her with. Summer up here doesn't warrant the same temperatures as it does back home and I find myself with the chills. She will surely get cold after a while. I walk toward her and lay the blanket on her.

As I turn to walk towards the door, the floor creaks sounding like a slap of thunder compared to the stillness of everything else. She opens her eyes and catches me looking at her. I feel a wave of sorrow for her, but I don't know why.

Her eyes refocused, still gray and colorless.

"Oh, my. I started to doze off a little, those trips to the store always wear me out." She said.

"That's OK. I put a few things away. I don't know where all of it goes."

"Thank you so much. And for the blanket too."

She sits up in her chair and asks if I have it in me to stay for a visit. *Have it in me… if she only knew.*

"Sure," I drag out the word. "I've got a little time, then I need to get going."

"Where are you going?" She asks.

"See, that I can't answer. I don't really know where I am, I mean… as far as… it's not like I'm lost really, I just got off track and ended up here." I stutter.

"Oh? Are you going somewhere important?" She asks.

"No, I don't think so? I had a flat tire off the highway yesterday and I stopped to have it fixed. I don't know how I ended up this way… just driving along."

Ellie nods her head but I can tell she is confused and I know I am not making any sense. I wring my hands together and curl my toes up trying to find my words or find my old friend; distraction. I can still hear the clock on the wall in the kitchen, ticking away. Her furniture is so out of date that it is now back in style. I am surprised by how clean everything is considering how old and run down things are. She has a few windows cracked open and I can smell the forest that surrounds the old house. Her white sheer curtains blow loosely as if they are dancing with each other. Without thinking, I sit on my hands, a terrible habit I picked up as a toddler and I still do it when I find myself in an awkward situation. I watch the white curtains rise and fall, then twist and twirl only to fall still for a brief moment until the breeze blows just right. People need music to dance just like the curtains need the wind.

"I see you have a few lavender plants throughout the place. I love the smell of lavender. The real stuff, not the stuff they make in a factory and sell in stores." I said.

I reach over to the plant and pinch a tiny piece off and roll it between my fingers. Something my Mom did, but this gives me a chance to take my hands from underneath me.

"Well that doesn't make sense, why would someone make a scent in a factory when they can just get it from a plant?" She asks.

"Wow, this lavender smells so good, so much sweeter than the lavender my mom has planted."

"That plant is about as old as you are." She said.

"That's probably why it smells so good. I was born on a good year." I smile.

Ellie was amused by my quick comeback. "Not too many people visit me anymore. The company has been nice."

She slowly stands up and folds the blanket to put back on the corner of her couch. I stand up with her thinking this was the extent of our visit.

"I get too comfortable under that heavy old thing and I may never get up," she giggles and sighs at the same time. "I'll make us some tea," she adds.

"Oh, actually, I think I should be headed back down the road."

"Where are you headed?" she asks again.

"I don't have a specific place, I just decided to go for a drive."

"Where do you live?" She asks.

"Way out in Eastern Colorado, small little town, my parents still live there."

She disappears into the kitchen leaving me standing in the entryway. It's not like I can't just walk out the door and take off but I don't have the heart to leave like that. It's the same soft spot that got me up here in the first place, but I realize I like her company. The best part of this situation is the fact that she doesn't know who I am or what I have done.

"I'm making some tea, I have a few different types." She said from the kitchen.

"You know what, I think I will stay for tea," I said, as I walk into the kitchen.

"You mentioned that you don't know where you're going? Are you lost?"

"In the sense of the word, I guess I am. Maybe not lost-lost, but lost in a way that needs a little quiet time and reflection." My voice trails off.

Water flows from the sink to the tea kettle, and she sets it down on the stove. Meanwhile, I wonder why all of a sudden I turned into a chatty Kathy. I pull up a chair to the table and sit down while Ellie takes two small teacups and places them on the table. She brings over a few different boxes of tea to choose from and I decide on the peppermint and raspberry.

"This is a great place you have up here. It smells so clean." I said quickly.

"Yes, I suppose it does. I've been up here so long I don't smell it much anymore." She responds.

"How long have you been up here? You mentioned over 50 years?"

"About that long. Long enough to know that the winters are brutal, the days are long and the nights are so quiet you almost feel guilty of eavesdropping on conversations between the owls."

She pauses for a moment and gazes out the kitchen window.

"I think that sounds nice in a scary kind of way. At least for me. I tend to migrate toward people. Funny thing is, I don't really like people. I mean, I like some people, family and such. Do you have family that visits?"

"No," she responds with little excitement.

"I would love to hear a good conversation between owls," I said.

"Well, if you're not going anywhere, in particular, you can. I have an extra room here."

"I didn't mean to insinuate that-"

"Oh, but wouldn't that be fun?" Ellie interrupted, "Sure!" She answers her own question. "I think it sounds like a lovely idea!"

She has the sweetest grin and her gray eyes open up wide, and she reminds me of a child who has just come up with a great plan. I laugh out at her enthusiasm and find it contagious.

The day goes on as I sit across from Ellie, dabbling in general small talk. We drink our tea slowly, with purpose and I mention that this must have been what it was like when Native Americans roamed the land hundreds of years ago. We imagine the conversations between tribes who visit other villages, passing the pipe around inside their tee-pee or huts where it was warm in the winter and open to the sky in the summer.

The tea kettle whistles from time to time, and we take turns grabbing it from the stove, neither in a hurry to take it off. We laugh as we mock the strange whistle the kettle would make, filling the voids and quiet moments with noise. When it's Ellie's turn to catch the kettle, she pretends to be a conductor of a famous symphony, waving her hands while holding her spoon.

She pours honey in my cup followed by more hot water and a new tea bag while I sit and let it seep. The tea goes down my throat and I can feel it warming every inch from the inside out until it settles into my core. We talk slowly, laugh often and find ourselves connected by the years that make us so different.

"Tell me how you got your name. It's so unusual."

I smile. "I get that all the time. My whole name is Rainy Sky O'Neal. I was born on a rainy, Wednesday night. My dad calls me Neha but that's a long story. I also think the seventies had a lot to do with my name too. "

We both laugh. "Well, I just love it." She said.

"It says a lot about you and your parents." She adds.

"And you?" I ask.

"Eloise Doris Baxter. Named after my parents' parents. Not as great as yours that's for sure."

We are feeling more comfortable with one another, oddly like old lost friends. Our conversations get deeper as the day gets shorter but I still find myself still wanting to be the perfect stranger.

"Tell me a good story that will last all night." She said.

"Oh, well I don't have many," I said with embarrassment.

"Sure you do, like what exactly are you are searching for?"

She has the same tone of voice she used at the restaurant and it immediately brings me back to reality. She looks at me with her piercing hollow gray eyes and it makes me feel uneasy.

I clear my throat and began to speak. "I... uh, I will know what it is when I find it."

"Or when it finds you..." her voice trails off.

I force a smile and wiggle around in my chair. I wish she didn't say that. "Well I can say this, I just left my folks house yesterday and it's already been a good adventure."

The life from our conversation is gone, and I'm probably the only one to know it. That one question, that one remark and gone, just like that. I have become an expert at reading people or reading a room and this went south in a hurry. The trick is to not let on that I am aware of it. The second part of this talent is the ability to create the illusion of being clueless while being fully aware. I must continue with the same enthusiasm in my voice, grandeur of my actions and unresponsive expressions in order to give life back into those who may or may not be affected. The complicated part is when other people besides myself feel the life leave. Then I must make them feel singled out from having those emotions in the first place. After all, nobody wants people to feel sorry for them, so acting as shallow as possible is vital. This works with awkward conversations, hurt feelings, and topics that need to be avoided. The bonus part of the whole thing is that sometimes, I too forget and I can feel the freedom of the void return to its natural form.

I begin talking to her about my flat tire and the truck driver and how he fixed it for me for payment of a peanut butter and jelly sandwich which I never gave him. I told her about the cute guy at the repair shop. I told her how good he smells and I even told her about the embarrassing glob of jelly he spotted out on my cheek. We talked about the empowering movement of being free and alive. With every word I speak, Ellie's uncomfortable questions got further and further away and if she had any guilt for asking them; that too is gone. She hangs on to every sentence like a lifeline pumping her full of life.

When a train pulls into the station, it starts to slow down miles ahead and if a person is paying close enough attention, you can feel the drag of power gearing down. It is so subtle and almost impossible to notice until suddenly, the train is at a complete stop. Most of the time, people don't pay attention to the slowdown, they are in tune to the very beginning, and the very end. Sometimes, they don't care about what happens in the middle. This is another talent I have mastered. I have the ability to know when the train is getting close to the end much like this experience is coming to an end.

My words become few, my enthusiasm grows sleepy and eventually, I come to the end. I have nothing else to say, and neither does Ellie. She fiddles with her napkin and goes into a trance. I'm not prepared to say anything more, especially about myself and Ellie isn't going to either. Perhaps she too has these talents.

"Well, I can't believe we have been sitting here all day." She said after a long pause.

I glance at the clock, horrified at the time.

"Six?" I jump to my feet and the chair tips over backward. "Oh my God, I have to go!"

"Goodness Rainy, you startled me, and I thought you didn't have anywhere in particular to go."

"I don't," I said.

"Then why are you so worried?" She asks.

"I don't know!" I say with frustration.

I just stand dumbfounded, staring in her eyes looking for some kind of answer that will give me a little direction. She stands up slowly and I'm still clueless.

"You look so confused, you need to eat." She said.

For the normal person, I suppose that makes sense but for me, I feel like a burden.

"To be honest Miss Ellie, I can't stay. I don't want to be a burden. Besides, don't you think it's a little weird to have a stranger you just met sitting down at your table to eat your food?"

"At this point in my life, I would invite a serial killer into my house. Besides, we aren't strangers anymore. Just sit back down and let me do this."

"Can I help at least?" I ask.

"No, I have all the help I need right here."

She opens some soup and places bread in the oven and I gather from the evidence that this was going to be my dinner. A part of me wants to go get my cooler and bring it in with the intention of sharing food but I don't want to risk appearing ungrateful. Not only that, but I fear if I step outside, I will try to make a run for it or worse, Ellie will catch me. Not likely, but she did just say that she has all the help she needs; perhaps to chase me down. My thoughts are mangled, my emotions are charged and I just want to remain unknown.

She continues to make dinner while I just stand here not knowing how to help. She walks over to the sink with her back facing me, and I can see her reflection in the window just as clear as if I were watching her in a mirror. Then, she does something I'm not expecting; she slowly moves her hand to her aging face and wipes a tear that is rolling down her cheek. As I sink down into my chair at the table, my heart breaks into a thousand little pieces.

I'm so concerned about becoming a burden to her that I can't see how lonely she is. Maybe I'm not so great at reading people or reading a room. This whole time, she just needed someone to talk to, to listen to or to simply be around. A few hours ago Ellie crashed into my life by having the only chair to sit at and this whole time, it wasn't about me. It has been about her. The tear that fell from her gray eyes shed so much light on a piece of the puzzle that I need to see. She doesn't have any answers, I have hers. Just maybe, we hold answers for each other. Just maybe, she is as scared as I am. Can it be possible that this is exactly where I am meant to be? She has emotions bigger than herself just like I do. It doesn't feel so random anymore and even though I have no control over what happens next, I think I understand why.

She serves my soup and toast much like the way she served my tea and as she sits across from me, I can tell she is embarrassed and humbled with the meal she is serving.

"Ellie," I said looking directly into her eyes, "Thank you for making me dinner, I love soup," I said.

Our spoons clanked on the bowls from time to time, and that was the only sound in the house. Of course, the ticking clock on the wall is doing its thing in a perfect tick, tick, tick tempo that I have already grown accustomed to. I eat slowly and so did she. Neither of us looks up from our food. I'm sure we are both deep in thought, probably thinking of the same thing.

When we finish eating, I get up to do the dishes while Ellie watches. It feels good to be here and the feeling takes over so quickly. I dry the last of the silverware and decide to sit back down at the table. She places her thin curled hand on top of mine; a gesture that didn't bother me this time.

"Start over again, with your stories. Go back to the beginning, where you left your parent's house. From the beginning."

I smile at her and I watch her expression settle deep down into that part of us that can only feel content and love. I take a slow deep breath and she follows. She closes her eyes and listens only with her ears. It seems like my voice travels through her ears and turns into music because of the simple way she would tilt her head to the side, then to the other. Dancing. Just like the curtains need the wind, the body needs music and the soul needs words in order to dance. For just a brief moment, I belong somewhere other than with my parents. I like belonging here; sitting across from Eloise Doris Baxter. My friend.

Chapter 8

Waking up from deep sleep can be done a number of ways. We can wake up startled from an alarm clock or sudden noises and it usually takes us from a deep sleep to wide awake within seconds. I often wonder why more people don't die of a heart attack when they wake up this way. The other kind of waking up is slow and natural. It is often a long process because we float between sleep and consciousness, effortlessly drifting in and out of logic and dreams until we fully wake up. Somewhere in between logic and dreaming is a part of the mind that even to the most reasonable of people, can turn unreasonable without warning. This is the closest a sane person can get to insane and it all happens somewhere between our sleep state of mind and our awake state of mind. This is the place where our logical brain chases our dreaming brain and now and then, they collide with one another causing complete confusion.

I wake up slowly to the natural sound of nothing but find myself completely confused for the first 4 seconds. Memory, logic and reason gear up for full functioning, all wires connect, all systems go. *Ellie's house.*

Her guest bedroom provides a perfect view to the living room and part of the kitchen depending on where I lay in the bed, which happens to be dead center. There's a perfect amount of sunlight coming through the window but it isn't casting directly on me which I appreciate. The spare room looks so much different in the morning than it did last night when I went to bed. Across the hall is the bathroom where a line divides the old tile from the old hardwood floors creating segregation from the rest of the house. I fold my blankets back a little and prop myself up on my elbows looking for Ellie. I can't see her anywhere and I certainly don't hear anything other than the hoo hoo purrs of mourning doves, not to be confused with the hoo hoo of the owls. A part of me wants to plop back down and tumble off to sleep but the much more curious side decides to get up.

It suddenly occurs to me that I never talked to Ellie about the kid back at the restaurant. I wanted to ask her what he might have meant but I never did. I make a mental note that I need to do that at some point. Whether she answers me, is a different topic. The thought also runs through my mind on making the bed or leaving it the way it is. Making the bed might suggest I am not planning on staying another night but then again, shouldn't I offer to strip the bedding and wash everything? Which leads to my next thought; if I keep the bed unmade, it suggests that I plan on staying. Or, it can mean I am a slob with little regard to manners. I can't decide on the right thing to do and wonder why on earth I think of these things in the first place.

I don't have a clue what time it is, I don't wear a watch. For all I know, it is 6 am and Ellie is still in bed. I peer through my door keeping my entire body inside the room only popping my head out just enough to look down towards Ellie's room. Nothing, but I discovered an answer to my prior conundrum, if her bed is made, I will make mine. As I glide quietly a few steps, I see that her bed is half made. I quickly retreat to mine, straighten the blankets and fluff my pillow. I feel pride in declaring victory over topic one.

I make my way into the kitchen, the only place I am aware of that keeps time. It's still early, only a few minutes past seven which for some people is late. The early risers of the world would suggest that I am burning daylight by sleeping in. Seven in the morning is considered sleeping in back home and most kids who are raised in the fields don't get the opportunity to know what sleeping in feels like. My parents understood the value of sleep and didn't wake me up at the break of dawn. Then again, they don't have the typical farming mentality either.

Ellie is nowhere to be found but I know she hasn't gone far. I shuffle throughout her house, looking at different odds and ends, still not finding any photos on the wall. I make my way through the screen door that is holding on for dear life by one nail, barely squeezing through to make sure that I don't completely rip it from the door jamb. I don't want to spend too much time lingering on the porch in fear that it might completely collapse. I recognize that I should have shoes on as soon as I step onto the ground that is lined with pine needles and dirt. Some areas have patches of green low laying vines and moss-like plants. The edge of the forest creates a barrier around her rundown shack but trying to conceive what is beyond the trees intimidates me. It's thick with pine trees touching the clouds and the ground is covered with dead, fallen leaves from the aspens that have randomly taken root. Vines are crawling up and over tree branches and it softens the sharp reputation of the ponderosa pine. It gets darker the further in I try to look. The cornfield and the forest have nothing in common with each other, the cornfield looks like a playground compared to the magnitude of the vast and mysterious forest.

I tiptoe my way around the edge of the trees, walking from the front of the house to the side where the spare room window is. I eventually wander to the back of the house, finding a rundown shed made from thin planks of gray and aging pieces of wood. I'm uninterested in what could be inside but keep walking around and eventually to the front of the house.

"Good-morning." I watch Ellie walking toward the porch, not having a clue where she just came from. I said.

"Good morning, you're awake." She said.

"I have an internal clock that keeps me from sleeping too late," I respond.

"Did you sleep well?" She asked?

"I did, thanks for extending your hospitality. I've been wandering the outside of your house a little."

"Have you found anything worth bragging about?" She asked.

"Uh, no. I'm impressed with the trees- how in the world did you get so much mud on your shoes, Ellie? How can you walk with all that built up on your shoes?" I ask in surprise.

She looks down to her feet and mumbles, "just a little walk."

"Why don't you slip those off and let me clean them. Maybe make us some tea?" I ask.

"Oh, yes I suppose that's a good idea."

Her shoes have layers and layers of mud built up making them look more like round rocks than shoes, weighing about the same too. I stood at the corner of the house, and knock the shoes into each other causing dirt clumps to fly off. Little by little, pieces of where ever she has been crumble off. These shoes have been worn just as hard as the Birkenstocks she wore yesterday, making me curious if she owns a pair of shoes that still have tread on them. *Where in the world has she been?*

"I'm an old woman," Ellie shifted her body to a different position.

"Age is all in the eye of the beholder," I respond as I take a sip of tea.

"That's easy for you to say, you don't have one foot in the grave." She said lightly.

"Oh jeez, you don't have a foot in the grave."

"I know my time is coming. Count on that."

"Let's not count on anything that we don't know," I said as I take another sip of tea. "Besides, you seem pretty darn healthy, especially considering the extra thirty pounds of mud you had on your shoes." I hint.

"I suppose I could live until I'm a hundred. Oh dear, I hope I don't live that long." She said, avoiding my comment.

"Well, I don't really feel like talking about it, death? Ugh, that's just depressing." I said.

She has no idea how uncomfortable this topic makes me. Feeling depressed about it is the last emotion I have regarding death. While I have certainly felt my share of depression, the topic of death or the memories of death doesn't compare to the insanity that often comes with it.

I find it interesting that old people can talk so freely about dying. Even healthy people can have very little emotion. It's easy to share how they want to die or how they feel about it, but if you ask the person who is dying; all they want to do is talk about living.

We stop talking for a minute and stare out her living room window trying to watch the hummingbirds with no luck. We can both hear them but to actually see them isn't easy.

"You need a hummingbird feeder to hang outside the windows. I bet you could watch them from every window in the house." I said.

"That would be nice, although the food they make for those feeders is not good for the birds. At least that's what they say back at the store. They use sugar water."

"The kid at the store asked me if I knew what I was getting myself into yesterday. Why would he say that?" I said, completely changing the subject.

I know she heard me, she looked straight at me with her gray colorless eyes but didn't answer.

"Do you know why he would say that?" I ask again.

"He's just a boy who comes to pick me up for grocery shopping, he means well."

Maybe it meant nothing. I don't feel like pushing the topic, I don't feel like knowing the answer.

I rest my chin in my hands and wonder if asking another question would upset her. I know I don't like to be questioned or pushed into talking about things that I don't want to talk about. She takes a long breath in and slowly exhales and without hesitation, I do the same. I feel like my mind is slowly decluttering and my lungs have been purified. I watch as the wind travels through the trees, making its way through the leaves and pine needles until eventually makes its way through the window. The air feels warm and brings a sweet, earthy smell of wildflowers and pine.

"Ellie, why are your shoes so muddy?"

"I walk... I smell rain coming soon." She added.

"Doesn't look like there's a cloud in the sky," I said looking out the window.

"No, maybe not but the rain is coming."

Chapter 9

Ellie convinces me to stay but in all honesty, I don't want to leave. Moments have turned into hours that have turned into days. I have small simple conversations with her that bring huge amounts of joy and laughter. Other times, I find content in just watching her. She has a familiarity about her that is amusing and a complexity that brings out my curiosity.

We talk for hours, and the tension between us as strangers is now just a fine line. I believe she and I both have jagged scraps of our lives we aren't sharing with each other but I don't mind. She has a way about her that makes me feel completely at home and I have a hole in my heart that grants her freedom. I won't talk much about my past with her and I get the feeling she is hiding something from me as well. It is especially prevalent in the quiet moments when we watch each other.

In the past three days, little pieces of ourselves are exposed in our stories and actions, but we don't acknowledge it. Every time I bring up the topic of going on a walk, she insists on going alone and I drop it. She ate some food I brought, most of it was food she has never had before but I don't question how that's even possible. I recognize how she avoids certain topics but I respect her privacy.

She asks me to drive her to Silverthorne but when I refuse, she doesn't insist. She notices my fear of going for walks alone, but she pretends she doesn't. Ellie sees the walls surrounding me, but she isn't trying to knock them down.

We have fragments of our lives that control us in one way or another, we often choose it without knowing it. What's ironic about those who need to control their surroundings are often times the most out of control. I am no more found than I am lost and being up here has yanked me from constant chaos and thrown me into the unknown. I don't have more answers than I did three days ago but I haven't had the nightmares that tend to control what I believe. It's considered inhumane to control people by forces that are guided by destructive or sick intentions but when we use it on ourselves, it's considered as acts of self-discipline. I have used my own sick and destructive feelings about myself to create a world that is superficial and comfortable. So I question whether I have done it again because being up here makes me comfortable. The fact that I don't want anyone to know who I am makes me remain superficial, yet I have abandoned chaos.

From the outside looking in, Ellie appears to be the loneliest person I have ever known. But after being here for a few days, she shows content in her life. Her TV is broken and has been for years, but she doesn't seem to care. She will simply sit for hours staring out her window into the woods as if she is waiting for someone. She can't remember the last time she's been out of these mountains, but she doesn't seem to mind. Ellie has a routine from the moment she wakes up in the morning to the time she goes to bed at night. Today, she abandons her routine and sleeps on and off.

It's in the moments when she sleeps that I go outside, and skirt the edges of the trees to peer in. I circle her house taking note of all the neglect and damage from years of harsh winters and fiery summers.

"Ellie? Are you OK?"

"Yes," she whispers.

"I thought I would go out to the shed and see what tools you have, so I can fix a few things around here," I tell her.

"OK, just be careful, I haven't looked in the shed for years," she said and continues looking out the window.

I walk to the back of the house where the shed is trapped by tall grass blocking the door. As I turn the handle on the door, I hear a sound from behind the shed. I hold my breath to be completely still but after a few seconds, I turn the handle again. The door is unlocked but the tall grass is blocking it from opening. I trample on the area to push the grass into the ground so the door can open and I hear the same rustling, this time it was clear that someone or something was walking toward me.

I don't feel scared but I also know that whatever is behind the shed is well aware that I am here too. The sound of leaves crunching starts and stops, pause for a moment then start again. It is subtle and not at all like a large animal or person walking, so I peek my head around the shed. While I still can't see anything, the sound is clear, it has to be a rabbit or squirrel.

As I get to the back of the shed, I notice leaves and pine needles moving but absolutely nothing is there. Then the sound stops, so I hold my breath until it happens again. I slowly walk towards the moving leaves and stop walking once it stops moving. Logic tells me that a squirrel or rabbit is busy burrowing a hole and a small piece of me just wants to walk away but the inner child in me wants to explore.

"Please don't be a snake," I whisper to myself which becomes a small chant every time I stop moving. "Please don't be a snake." Pause...take a few steps...pause..." please don't be a snake," then I see it.

I kneel down and brush the leaves and pine needles aside and find a baby bird.

"Oh no, well hi there little bird...awe, you're a cute little fella." I said quietly. "Are you hurt? You must have fallen out of your nest huh?"

The little bird instantly becomes a male whether he was male or not. I liked calling him little fella because little lady or little girl felt weird. I look up into the trees hoping to find a nest low enough but don't see anything. I know that even if I did find a nest, the likelihood of him surviving is small.

I scoop him into the palm of my hand, and cover him with the other, and hold him close to my chest. As I walk to the front of the shed, I can feel his spiky feathers that have yet to unfold. Now that I am out of the shade, I can see him a little better, so I slowly peel my hand up and his mouth is open like they do when their moms bring food back to the nest. I don't know when birds can start to see but, I know it isn't this soon. I also know that this little guy is hungry.

He barely has any feathers and a bald bird to some people might be about the ugliest thing they ever saw but to me, he is adorable. He is large for a baby, it can't be more than a few weeks old and I immediately want to show Ellie. I don't know her well enough to be certain she won't throw me or the baby bird out the window but I can't resist sharing this with her. I feel the intense urge to mother this little fella back to the wild, and as I walk back to the house, I wonder if this is a small resemblance of what women describe as motherly instincts.

Ellie is thrilled to see my little bundle of bird and immediately wants to hold him.

"He needs food. Run into the kitchen and get some soup, mix it with a little water, so we can spoon-feed him. Just a little broth might fix him up until we can figure out what to do next." Ellie said.

I find a little can of vegetable soup, warm up a small cup and smash it together so it would easy for him to take in the same way a mom bird would feed. Ellie is still holding onto him and I dread the idea of having to set him free or take him somewhere else, in my mind, I already have plans on raising him.

He takes the vegetable concoction like a champ and his little squeals are a good sign that he might be OK.

"We need to name him," Ellie said. "Right? I think we need to keep him and care for him until he can handle being in the wild." She adds.

"Really Ellie? I mean, yes!" I smile. "We might be able to find what we need to keep him healthy."

"I think we should recreate a nest for him. There should be some boxes in the shed, you go find one and I will hold him until you get back. Then we need some nesting twigs, I will round up a few things." Ellie said with excitement.

I finally pry the shed door open after stomping the tall grass down, and I am amazed at how much stuff is piled in here. Boxes line one half of shed, neatly placed and a car on the other half. It is covered with a tarp that has at least an inch of dust resting on top. My curiosity is getting the best of me, and I quickly decide that finding a box or a good set of tools can wait for a moment longer.

The lighting inside is dim, so I push open the large door causing dust to fly. I fold the tarp slowly not wanting to scatter even more dust. Each inch I fold back feels like opening the last present on Christmas morning.

"1957 Chevy," I said out loud, shaking my head.

"Ellie, Ellie what else are you hiding?"

What a charming vehicle, old and with so much character. I only know the year of this little darling because my dad had one just like it that his grandpa gave to him. My dad sold it when I was 11 to a guy from Oklahoma. I never did understand why someone would buy a car that had to be towed but what did I know.

This car looks like it is in much better condition than the one dad had. The paint isn't rusted and the inside still has upholstery attached. Questions build and I'm unsure if these are the kind of questions I can ask Ellie or if I need to keep the pace of our unspoken language.

I refocus on why I came out here but also, the tools I originally set out to find. I empty the first box I find onto a little workbench but don't really see any of the tools I need. Gardening tools clutter the corners and what I manage to find isn't enough to do even small repairs. For now, all I care about is the box I found and getting the bird comfortable.

"Ellie? I found this, a little box. How's the nest coming?" I ask.

"I found enough to get him comfortable, we can take a rag from the kitchen until we figure something more permanent." She said.

More permanent. I repeat this in my head as we go back to the house. Any plans of me leaving has been completely cleared off the table all because of Ellie's excitement to keep the little bird and my need to make him survive.

That's what this is; a need. I haven't needed anything in so long. This isn't the need for food or air to breathe, this is a need that would make my heart heal. I hope it can anyway. I wonder if Ellie knows this about me, and maybe this is why she wants to keep the little bird. *Does she think that as long as the bird is here, I will stay? Would I stay even if I didn't find him? How long do I stay? What the actual hell am I doing?*

"Tomorrow, I need to go into town. I need to find baby bird stuff and also a hardware store, so I can fix a few things. Unless you have other tools somewhere else? I don't see anything that I can really use." I said as I wring my hands together.

She sits straight up in her chair and excitement sprung in her eyes.

"Oh Rainy, you have to take me with you. The baby will need to come with us too. He will need food every few hours. Oh my, I haven't been down this mountain in years." She smiles.

I can't help to smile back, I haven't seen a person this excited in a long time. I'm sure my smile hides the pain that settled into my chest. It's the kind of pain a person feels right after receiving bad news, not to be mistaken by feelings of butterflies or general nervousness before a person takes the stage. I feel nauseous followed by a taste of metal in my mouth that can only be understood by someone who has sucked on a penny or aluminum foil. Sweat builds up again in the palms of my hands and no amount of deodorant can handle what is building up under my arms. I can feel my heart and hear it pounding as my breathing becomes short. I feel like I am breathing inside a plastic bag and the air has turned into carbon dioxide. I know I am not thinking clearly, the room is spinning and my legs are numb and heavy.

"Ellie? I need to tell you something… something I have done. I have to tell you this before we spend one more day together. Especially before I put you back into the passenger seat of my car."

Now what have I done?

PAST

Winning the basketball state championship was a huge deal, especially in our small town. This was the girls' basketball team and the first championship win in the history of our school. The whole town participated in every sport and from every aspect. Fundraising activities were not only fundamental for every student but every business took part in contributing. This bought new uniforms, updated the football field or gym floor and even a state-of-the-art scoreboard that replaced the last state-of-the-art scoreboard four years prior. The local hardware store stocked school t-shirts or hoodies with team colors and our mascot, the Bison was a logo used by just about every business owner. There isn't anything else this small town has to offer when it comes to entertainment. There isn't a movie theater or shopping mall and all the restaurants are owned by locals, most likely passed down from generation to generation. The local newspaper is usually filled with news from the school, the latest games, the highest scoring students and stories of academic achievements. Now and then, short articles about local farmers who helped birth a breeched calf would make the second page.

It's not very often that students leave town after they graduate. Some kids will go to college but most of them stay back on the family farm. For those who do go to college, they usually return at some point with their new family. Steve Drunnen went to college and returned years later with his family to open his own private practice. Dr. Steve Drunnen is just about the only Doctor in town and while his parents are proud of his accomplishments, it's no secret that his brother who stayed after graduation to help his dad on the farm has more respect. Depending on your personality, this can be considered a great town. Everyone knows everyone which has its advantages and disadvantages. News travels fast, good or bad even if it's true or not. The people all have the same philosophy for life and can be judgmental of city people. Most Sunday's are set aside for church unless it's harvest season. When harvest season hits, everyone becomes part of the success of the other and will do anything to help a fellow farmer. It's not uncommon to see Benton's combine harvester in another farmer's field. Farms around here are divided by miles of crops but the close-knit community of like-minded people bridges that gap.

If you're popular, you're not just popular in school but with the whole town. Every generation of the town's school hero's birth the next generation of the town's heroes and on and on it goes. This narrows the gap for an outsider to hail the crown, it doesn't matter how talented at sports they might be. Our school was small and most of the time, it was predictable in who was going to marry who. A year or so after graduation, you can almost guarantee two or three wedding celebrations to follow. The birth of the next generation would soon follow and the whole process starts again.

My parents, who were high school sweethearts, didn't follow in footsteps of those before them which was a total embarrassment to my grandparents. They left this town to protest the Vietnam War and travel the United States which was considered insensitive and disrespectful. They lost many of their friends when they left but eventually, my grandparents forgave them and welcomed them home after my mom got pregnant with me. My parents got married on a Cheyenne Indian Reservation by Chief Standing Bull who is a descendant of Chief Tall Bull. My parents were passionate about Native American culture and resented holidays like Columbus Day, Thanksgiving and the Fourth of July. I was quick to learn that the school in our town was named after Lieutenant Beecher who killed hundreds of Native Americans in the Battle of Beecher Island which is also a point of interest in town. With my parents being disappointed by their ancestors and their white man ways, they were able to befriend the people from the reservation. After I was born, they took me back to Montana and had me blessed by the same Chief who married them. I wasn't given a name shortly after I was born, this was the responsibility of the elders. First, I had to grow into it and most of the time, names were not issued until much older. My grandparents didn't understand my mom and dad's ways and all they asked was that I return with a name.

Upon arriving at the reservation, it started to rain, pouring rain that drenched the underdeveloped ground. It had been months since the reservation saw any rain whatsoever and the natives were well aware of my arrival and what I brought. During my naming ceremony, I was also given to Mother Earth which is much like a Christian baptism. I was given my name, Neha. Neha, Sky Water. The girl who brings rain. My dad is the only one who calls me that and no one ever asked what it meant but Neha means rain in the Cheyenne language. I quickly became known as Rainy. Every year on my birthday, my parents talk about the night I was born, the naming ceremony and why I received my name. They retell the ceremony every thirteen moons which are also considered the cycle of moons that pass in a year. I went through a phase where the story was so repetitive and I dreaded listening to it. Eventually, I told the story which reduced the misery. Year after year, I found myself understanding more and more of how important it was to remember the honor of the ceremony and the meaning of Neha.

When my parents came back from traveling and learning the native ways, they were very well-educated and worldly. They had passion in that they wanted to change the direction the farming industry was going. My dad already started organic farming but gained full control of the farm when grand-pop died. He started raising bees which became a huge source of income for them. He only grew vegetables from seeds that weren't genetically modified and never used chemicals or pesticides. At the time, this was considered nonsense but my parents saw the movement coming and the need to educate other farmers. Unfortunately, this thought process wasn't perceived with high regard. Most times, they would blame it on the mentality of the town, other times they blamed it on the government having too much control over the farming and ranching industry. My dad was considered a hero in other towns like Boulder, which was over four hours away, but this helped our little farm grow into a year-round source of income. They were able to build greenhouses completely self-sufficient other than planting and harvesting. This success angered some traditional farmers in the area but most of them brushed it off and grew to respect my mom and dad. They were always available to help others to show new ways of doing things and even taught some old traditions they learned back on the reservation. I grew up with recycled and reinvented things but my parents were sensitive to my self-esteem. This was their way of saving the world but it wasn't always easy. I am a product of their love and differences therefor understanding and adopting the same beliefs. Being a version of my parents didn't make me eligible of the towns' hero title but it never bothered me. Instead, I was nicknamed the love child. We were different, when we went to town, we arrived in an avocado green VW van with curtains on the window and a bumper sticker that read, Give Peace a Chance. That was us, sticking out between all the Ford and Chevy trucks but with a green thumb nonetheless.

Back on the basketball court, the buzzer rang and everyone was screaming. Cheering erupted as every person in the gymnasium ran to the court. People were swarming toward their hero and my best friend, congratulating her on the winning shot. I was trying to get to her, but I am invisible to everyone; being pushed to the side without being touched.

Finally, she reached me, and we gave each other a big hug.

"God Emma, you did it, girl!" I yelled.

"We won!" she was screaming.

She grabbed my hands and told me she needed to go with the team to the locker room. It was an honor that she came to me through all the other people who were trying to get her attention. She made eye contact with me and I could see her happiness but also her relief once she saw me. She was never a huge fan of the hero title and how this small town had nothing better to do. Emma wasn't staying in this town, she was moving onto better things, college and a new life. I was the only person who knew that. Everyone just assumed she was going to marry Carter but I knew better.

I leaned against the wall of the locker room and watched the gym slowly vacate. As I waited, I eavesdropped on conversations between the parents, teachers and other community higher-ups. It's funny what people talk about in the presence of one another, bragging about what role they played.

"I told Emma to take that shot, she looked right at me and smiled." Someone bragged.

"She came to the restaurant last night and I told her to eat spaghetti, I found that the right nutrition can make a champion." Mrs. Randall bragged.

"I worked with her the other day about how to keep her head in the game, I gave her my old techniques." Bragged another.

"She told me that she went to bed last night at seven, I told her that getting plenty of sleep would keep her focused and it did, and she played one heck of a game." Someone bragged.

"She and Carter spent time with each other after school yesterday, he really makes her happy and Carter is bringing her to dinner tomorrow, so we can celebrate. Those two are so in love. Love is a powerful thing." Carter's mom bragged.

They weren't listening to each other, instead, they were just trying to one-up the other person in hopes of winning the because-of-me award. What they didn't realize was that I knew the truth of why she played the game so well. She worked her ass off, that's why. She hated Mrs. Randall's spaghetti, she can't hear a word anyone yells at her when she is in the game, and she didn't go to bed last night until eleven because… Carter. *Wouldn't they like to know what she and Carter did the night before her game?* She always dreaded going over for dinner and made up excuses that she was coming down with the flu. She was so desperate one night that she thought about telling Carter's mom that her arm might fall off. I shared the same dislike for Carter's mom as Emma did.

Emma walked out of the locker room with the team as the local paparazzi tried to get her attention. They cheered once again for her, applauded her win, and wished she would make eye contact with them. All of that made me feel out-of-place, but she never let me feel that way for long.

"Everyone is going to The Malt Shoppe to celebrate. Let's go!" She said.

"We will meet you guys there!" she hollered to everyone else.

"Wow, girl you played the game like you owned the place!" I said proudly.

"I was pretty good wasn't I?" She laughed.

"Seriously, that was intense, way to take it to the last second." I nudged her.

"I was trying to give a few people a heart attack. It was my plan all along, obviously didn't work though." She whispered.

"Carter's mom wouldn't stop talking about it. Everyone wants to take credit."

"Don't remind me, and ugh, his mom is such a Nelly." She rolled her eyes.

"Nelly? Did you just call her a Nelly?" I laughed as I teased her. "She's more of a Wilma."

"Or Betty," Emma added. "She's such a Betty."

"You're a dork, such a dork." I laughed.

Random screams and hollers would echo through the parking lot and as we got closer to the car, Emma got serious. She often did that right after a game and I knew her well enough to let her. She would get really serious if she lost the game, so I was relieved I didn't have to go through that. She would get quiet for a little while and I knew she was replaying the whole game in her head. As we sat in the car, I gave her some flowers from the back seat.

"Flowers? You didn't even know if we would win the game." She said.

"I know, I got flowers just in case you lost." I smiled and handed them to her.

"Jerk."

We laughed a little but I knew enough to let her mind go to whatever place it went after a game. Somewhere in her mind was like a movie playing but, she was the only one allowed to watch. She would replay the game or, so she said, but it seemed to be more than that at times.

"Why do people in this town see me as the only person who played the game? I feel bad for Rachel, she was amazing. Every time she rebounded, she looked at her mom but her mom would be looking at me. It got weird." She said.

"I'm surprised you noticed, you don't normally notice that stuff," I said.

"And coach only addressed me in the locker room." Her voice trailed off.

"Emma won this game tonight blah blah," she added in a mocking voice. "I can't wait to get the hell out of this town Rainy."

"Yep, me too… Hey, I think I will take road fifteen, it's faster." I said.

"No, it's not, it's a dirt road, and you can't go that fast." She said.

"Trust me, it's still faster," I said nudging her with my elbow giving her a smile.

Emma was emerging from her predicted lull and once again, the celebration continued. We eventually went back to our talking and time stood still. We were free and we were winners. I messed with the radio trying to find the perfect song and once we did, we became our own version of rock stars, Emma danced wildly as I sang every word with a passion.

It happened so fast, the steering wheel jumped out of my hands, and I was suddenly out of control. The steering wheel and the tires felt different, I was powerless.

"Rainy!" Emma yelled.

I didn't answer. I held tight, my dad's voice in the back of mind whispering, *don't over correct Neha*, but I did. Without notice or warning, the car lifted off the ground and tumbled, slamming down and then back in the air. My head was being bashed violently and the noise was ear-piercing. I could hear Emma, making sounds the same way a person does after being punched. Glass was spraying everywhere and trying to protect myself was a lost effort.

Just as fast as it happened, it stopped. I had no clue if we were upside down, or on the side. As I opened my eyes, I couldn't focus on anything. Even bringing my hands to my face was a challenge. The inside of the car was mangled and twisted, nothing made sense.

I couldn't sit up straight and I could barely breathe. The dust was thick and heavy and the smell of burning rubber and plastic was overbearing. My mind and thoughts were scattered but I soon realized we were on all four tires. The explosion of noise moments earlier turned into eerie sounds of silence.

"Oh God Emma, are you OK?"

I could feel my own pain as I reached across her body. She was covered in glass, her seat belt was tangled, and I couldn't tell where the dash of the car ended and where Emma began. It was so dark, and my eyes could barely focus but I could tell she was bleeding. I touched her face where I could see a shadow and felt the warm ooze of blood spilling over my fingers.

"Em, we need to get out," I whispered.

My seat belt had me pinned to my seat, but I was able to unbuckle it. More glass fell as I tried to open the door, but it wasn't going to open and I didn't have the strength to force it.

"My door, it's broke, I'm going to-"

"Rain, she whispered, Rainy?" She said again.

Her head was facing the broken window and I couldn't make eye contact. The light of the moon was the only light I had and as my eyes adjusted to the dark, I could tell she was pinned by something or trapped, and she was bleeding.

"Oh my God Emma, you're hurt, I've got to get you out of here."

I squirmed out of my car window, barely feeling the glass cutting through my skin. I was in pain. I couldn't walk and in the back of my mind, I knew I broke my leg. I didn't care. My only purpose was to get Emma out. I hunched over the car using it as a crutch but burned and sliced my arms on the jagged pieces while my leg dragged behind me. I had to pivot on one leg but eventually got to Emma. I broke out the rest of the window that wasn't already broken and reached over her to unbuckle her seat belt. My eyes adjusted enough to see her looking back at me. I whispered to her that everything was OK. I knew everything would be OK and I repeated it over and over because she looked scared. I continued to repeat it because it was the only words I could say.

I could feel the warmth of her blood on my skin. She wasn't saying anything but I could tell she was trying. I reached under her arms and began to pull her out but I didn't have the strength. I tried again, but the pain from my leg was unbearable and I knew I didn't have a chance. I started to panic, fearing that she would be trapped and the car would catch fire. I didn't have any hope that the door would open but I tried it anyway and it budged. I pulled on it as much as I could until there was enough room to wedge my body in between and pushed it with all my body weight until I had enough room to slide her out. I was hurting her more but I didn't stop, she couldn't stay in the car. I dragged her until I couldn't go any further and laid her gently back on the ground.

"Emma, I need to go get help. We are in a field, you're OK."

I had to crawl on one knee and drag my leg behind, but the pain was only getting worse. My head felt heavy and blood would drip on the dirt below me. That dirt road didn't have many travelers and I knew that the odds of someone coming were not in my favor. My heart was pounding, and I was helpless, I cried for help. My cries turned into screams when all of a sudden car lights came up over the hill. As it got closer, it slowed down, eventually to a complete stop. The lights blinded me. Mr. Martin came running over to me, and I was crying and yelling at him to go get help.

"Please, get in your car, go get help. Go!" I yelled.

"Rainy? Oh God! Who is with you Rainy?" He asked.

"Emma, go! She is OK, just go get someone." I yelled again.

He ran back to his car and took off leaving me on the road. The urge to get back to where Emma was laying was overwhelming. When I got closer to her I could hear her mumbling but I could only make out a few words. I lifted her up and propped her against me hoping the gurgling sounds would stop.

"Emma, look at me, you will be OK." She didn't look at me.

"Think of the game Emma, you were great."

"Rainy," she interrupted, and I held my breath.

"Yea? Talk to me."

"Tired," she whispered with her lips half glued shut from dry blood.

"I know, we will get you home soon so you can go to bed." She started shaking.

"Shhh, your cold, hang in there." I was rocking her back and forth.

"Shhh," I just kept repeating over and over while her breath was getting shorter and shorter.

"I want," and then another quick breath, "my mom."

"Me too, I know…just breathe. I know you're cold."

I continued to rock her, she felt heavy in my lap, and my tears started falling. I was terrified, confused and I didn't know what else to do. I felt an overwhelming amount of guilt. *Why did I go this way, she told me to go another way?*

"Emma, look, I can see them coming... It's OK… we are safe now… we can go home… OK? Just try to sleep."

I didn't get up when everyone rushed over. I was frozen. I kept holding her, brushing the hair from her face. People kept running over towards us, talking amongst each other barking orders and assessing the situation.

"Back up, you need to back up. We will take over." someone said.

I laid her head down gently and watched in between the crowd of people.

"She's not breathing."

"No pulse."

Medical things were flying, people were talking and all I could hear were voices melting together.

"She's OK. She's sleeping. She is sleeping." I kept repeating.

Someone came over and laid me over on a stretcher. I could feel my pain now more than ever, it was sharp and deep that had an impact on my entire body but I didn't want to take my eyes off Emma. Everyone was in the way, passing by, hovering and talking. I tried to make eye contact with, but I couldn't see her and I just wanted to protect her. A strange feeling of anger was rising and I wanted to scream at everyone to leave her alone. *She hates being fussed over.*

"She is OK," I said out loud to no one in particular. The sky was filled with lights. Voices molding together with the slow movement of human beings and I had a hard time hearing anything through the ringing of my ears. I was being poked and squeezed as dirt was tossed from under someone's shoes and onto me. I tried several attempts to get up and go over to Emma. She needed a hand to hold on to and so did I. I tried desperately to hear what she was saying, to see if she was calling out for me.

"She needs me."

"You need to lay down, or we will anchor you."

When the paramedics lifted me into the ambulance, the pain from the movement of the stretcher made me scream. I was floating one minute and heavy with pain the next.

"Emma!" I said, reaching toward the ambulance as the door slams.

"I can't breathe. Oh, my chest, it hurts." I whispered.

Not one person was saying a word. I'm not sure how many people were in the back of the ambulance with me. Now and then someone would say a random number or words that didn't have any meaning to me. A plastic mask went over my mouth and nose which made it impossible for me to speak. I laid unbearably still on my back and could feel that my head had been strapped down. I would try to move my eyes enough to see what was going on around me, but things were a complete blur. Tears would fall, roll over my temples and puddle into my ears. I became dizzy and tired and from there I faded in and out of consciousness.

I tried to open my eyes but was blinded by the lights. Faint whispers filled my head. People saying my name. I was in pain and my mouth was terribly dry. As my eyes struggled to focus, I could hear my mom's voice become clearer.

"Rainy? We're here sweetie."

She grabbed hold of my limp hand and kissed it. I could plainly tell that she was crying.

"Mom?" I barely managed to whisper.

"Shhh, Rainy, you're OK."

I start floating again, in and out of reality trying to focus on the people or voices I heard.

"Rainy, are you OK? Are you in pain?" A woman asked.

I moved my eyes to the other side of the bed and there stood a woman that I didn't recognize. I quickly looked back at my mom and my dad who was standing behind her.

"How are you feeling sunshine?" She said.

"I'm thirsty." I tried to move then but was stopped by a strap holding my hands down.

"You can't move right now." Another voice echoes from somewhere in the room.

"It hurts," I mumbled.

"Where sweetie?"

"I don't know, everywhere-" My vision darkened and the voices echoed again.

I couldn't pinpoint one area of pain over the other, and I couldn't focus on any one thing. I would wake up and travel back to sleep just as fast. I felt trapped and oddly free at the same time. Time was irrelevant and the surrounding space didn't have boundaries. Voices would come in and out but I couldn't track the conversation or stay alert long enough to comprehend what was said.

"Dad?" I whispered.

"Right here Neha." He sounded concerned.

It was easier to think than it was to talk. *What's going on? Why... where's... the accident... Emma...* It all came flooding back, the accident and Emma and pulling her out. I started to cry but not making sounds or words, just tears pouring out my eyes as the memory floods my mind. *I want to see Emma, I need to apologize and talk to her. She went home already, her mom came and brought her home. Has she been here?*

"Can Em... ma."

"Now don't you worry," my dad interrupted. "You need to rest."

"Emmm ah... was here, is shhh still here?" I asked slowly.

"Hey kiddo, you just need to rest." He whispered back.

"Tell hhuur sssorrry."

I could hear my mom cry, but somehow, even though I didn't hear him, I could tell my dad was crying too. They said nothing to me. My dad held my hand and I felt safe feeling his strong hand over mine. I fell back to the place where I was trapped and free; where the walls went down and I couldn't move.

Emma came to see me, sometimes she stood over my bed for hours, and we talked, I told her how sorry I was and that I should have listened to her. She wasn't mad at me, she looked good. Not a scratch on her.

"How...sooo muh blood off," I mumbled.

"They came this morning to clean your hair, I bet you feel better." My mom said.

"Emmaa looks bet... hur."

A new voice enters the room and demanded that I work hard at staying awake and try to eat. He had an unusual accent which grabbed my attention long enough to focus on him. His blue scrubs came into my vision first and then his blond hair.

"You're... the dent... ist from Rud... olph... Her... mey."

"Close enough," he chuckled. "You really need to start trying to move around a little OK?"

"Oohh... kay."

I lifted my hand to show him that I was strapped down but the restraints were gone. I lifted both arms and lifted my head off the bed and focused on my mom and dad. A wave of sadness drifted through me. The heartbeat monitor increased to mirror my emotions and I began to cry. Things were becoming clear and once again, the guilt was overbearing. I was so relieved I didn't hurt Emma but my parents had to go through this and it was hard to see their expressions.

"I'm sorry," I said.

"No, don't you be sorry. Right now, you just get better worry about the rest later."

"When's Emma coming back?" I said trying to swallow.

"She isn't coming back sweetie," my dad said choking back tears.

"Oh no, she's mad at me," I said slowly.

"No one is mad." He said.

"Her mom is mad." I swallowed hard, the lump in my throat wouldn't go away.

"Emma won the game," I said.

"Yes, she sure did."

"Can you call her dad?"

"I can't-"

"Use the phone." I interrupted, pointing to the phone.

"Neha," my dad pulled the chair closer to my bed and Dr. Herbie was poking my leg and making me move my toes.

"Sweetie, Emma can't come back. Emma died in the accident."

"That's not funny, and I just saw her."

"No, sweetie…what daddy is saying…um… Emma passed away, you have been in the hospital for a week now." My mom said calmly.

"I JUST SAW HER!!! DON'T LIE TO ME! NO!"

I started to scream, I was so angry. *Why would they tell me this?*

"WHY ARE YOU SAYING THIS? I FEEL BAD OK? I FEEL SO BAD!"

More people came in the room as I continued to scream. Everyone was hollering at me to quiet down but I just couldn't. They were lying to me, trying to make me feel worse. I tried to pull out my I.V.

and sit up but the pain stopped me. My leg was in a cast and I couldn't move it off the edge of the hospital bed.

"NO NO NO! DON'T TOUCH ME!!!"

"Let's sedate her." A nurse said.

"Get the restraints, give her one cc of Versed." Another nurse said.

"Rainy, you need to calm down, we are going to give you some…" A random voice echoed as I faded away.

Chapter 10

Ellie doesn't say a word or ask any questions, but she knows I am done talking. She's looking at me with a concerned expression but not the same expression all my therapists had. This is different, she has a genuine look that is friendly and accepting, which I find comfort in. What started out as being teary-eyed, has now developed into the kind of cry that takes your breath away. I wipe the tears from my face but Ellie stays silent. For the first time since the accident, I am listening to myself cry and what a strange sound sorrow can produce.

I don't want to share more than I already have, but the rest of my story is just as sad and I silently weep for the girl that once was, I weep for both Emma and myself but I don't feel like talking anymore. I believe somewhere in all the years of Ellie's life, she gathered a great deal of wisdom that is untouchable. She is able to say so much with no words at all. She is allowing me to find my own way back without making me feel alone and that is something I haven't had. My parents were the only ones who could surround me with that kind of openness and as I share a part of my life with Ellie, I am reminded why I started this journey in the first place.

I'm not sure Ellie could say anything that would have made me feel any better anyway. Over the years, I decided that I would keep my pain to myself because no one can really make me feel any better. I have heard every cliché phrase and eventually, the accident became a secret. My parents didn't agree with me and told me it was unhealthy to keep that kind of secret. It was extremely unhealthy, considering I didn't even tell the man I was married to. I kept a lot from him, he didn't know who I was and I liked it that way. My parents were always on my side, even when they didn't agree with me. They helped me keep this secret but told me they will never lie if it was brought up. I learned that what someone doesn't know about me isn't a lie, it's a secret, and I was good at keeping them.

Telling this to Ellie doesn't bother me, for the first time in my life I'm not only able to share this, but share the remorse, guilt, and regret that comes with it. I am showing everything that comes with those emotions too, the tears and the physical struggle with thoughts running havoc in my mind. My heart hurts as I sit here and cry, my throat hurts from the deep wallow of my voice and my head hurts from the thoughts that trample through it. Yet, Ellie remains quiet, nodding her head and every so often she will whisper a simple, "yea" as I catch my breath.

The accident was only the catalyst of what happened next, the other part of who I am is something I can't share. Not now, I'm too drained but I also have a place in my mind that tells me I don't need to share more than I already have. My symptoms are returning and this too weighs heavy on my mind so while I don't necessarily need to share the rest, the reality is, I might not have a choice.

I will never understand why the body responds the way it does after crying. It's a feeling that can only be explained by comparing it to something else. Its physical exhaustion but at the same time, it's cleansing. I truly believe in the body and mind connection and what our mind goes through, so does our bodies. When we have a total meltdown, the tears that follow are full of trapped emotions. In some way, after letting it all come out, we are left clean but also empty. The words that were once trapped or stuck are free but replaced with a vast amount of emptiness. Through all these years of crying and letting go of the tears, I was left empty and that is still the case now.

"This is my story I guess, it changed the direction my life was going." I sighed.

"Sure it did."

"I ruined so many lives. The guilt I live with every day is the price I pay. It's the life sentence no one knows about." I whispered.

"At some point, you will need to forgive yourself." She said.

"Ah, no Ellie. I won't forgive myself until I am forgiven by Emma's family. That will never happen. Hell, the whole town treats me like a murderer. But then again, that's what I am."

"Were you charged with murder?" She asked.

"No, but her parents wanted a vehicular homicide charged against me."

"And? Did the court press charges?" She asked.

"No, it wasn't considered neglect or careless driving so everything was dropped."

"Well, you're not a murderer then. Murder is if you intentionally kill someone. They call it an accident for a reason. It was an accident." Ellie said.

"It really doesn't matter Ellie, I was labeled a killer."

"Oh, that's just silly," Ellie said while making a hand gesture.

"Not really, and not funny either. I wasn't able to go back to school, we had death threats, my car was spray painted with words like 'killer' and people wanted me to leave town. My parents went through hell."

Ellie didn't respond and I was relieved. I know what I am, even though I didn't intend for this to ever happen, it did and I can't go back and change it. If it weren't for me driving on a dirt road, Emma would still be alive. What's worse is she told me not to go that way. It doesn't matter what people have said over the years, the accident and her death is my fault.

"I'm going to lay down for a little while Ellie. I will feed the baby bird in a few hours." I said

"OK, we will go to town tomorrow," Ellie said.

I couldn't help but feel frustrated by her response. It felt like everything I just told her went in one ear and out the other. The purpose of me telling her was that she understands why I can't drive her again. I did it once and nearly threw up my breakfast. I don't want to go through that again, but she doesn't care, or maybe she cares but trusts me regardless. The bottom line is that I don't trust myself. The distraction of this adorable little feathered friend was more than welcomed.

I fell asleep yesterday afternoon and woke up every few hours by the sound of the bird, hungry and wanting to be fed. I can tell my eyes are swollen and puffy without even looking. They feel heavy and tired but the reward outweighs it all. I shift different thoughts into my head as my body wakes up. I don't usually lay in bed like this but stretching and yawning feels particularly good while remaining horizontal. Having a moment like this is has not been on the top of my list of things to do. I recognize the oddity of the whole thing considering how much I dislike being in my head. This is new, this is the first time in a long that I don't immediately jump up and start creating distractions.

Telling Ellie about the accident feels right even if she did miss my point. I don't have any regret telling her. I am so tired of having this burden, I'm tired of carrying this weight on my shoulders and I just want it to end. I'm still irritated that Ellie doesn't mind the fact that I caused the accident and still wants to come with me today.

I can hear Ellie in the other room coughing but it sounds more like noise. It doesn't take me long to realize that she is trying to get me up with a fake cough and I can't help but to smile and shake my head. When I tumble out of bed and wander into the family room, I am surprised to see Ellie dressed and ready to go, sitting by the front door holding her purse.

"Good-morning," I said.

"Not in a hurry. Take your time getting ready. We have shopping to do." She said.

"Umm…?"

"I want to go to breakfast first," she interrupted.

"OK," I said during a yawn, "what time is it?" I ask.

"7:30" She answered.

"Nothing is going to be open this early."

"The diner is, we can have breakfast first and head into Silverthorne," Ellie said.

"I'm not sure I can handle the same waitress we had last time," I said under my breath.

"That's Debbie, she is just a grumpy lady that needs a tall glass of water and a vacation," Ellie responds.

"I'm not entirely sure what you mean by that, so I will just agree."

"She needs a good-looking man and a vacation." She said.

"What on earth does a tall glass of water have to do with her needing a man?" I ask.

"It's a figure of speech. Haven't you ever heard of that saying? Why, being from the country, I can't imagine you never heard that expression before."

"Uhh, no. I still don't get it. Plus I don't make a habit out of hanging out with the people in my town." I said.

"Well, a tall glass of water is referring to a good-looking, tall gentleman, she needs a man in her life to smooth out some of her edges," Ellie explains.

"I am not a fan of the mentality of a woman needing a man in her life," I said firmly.

"Well, a gal doesn't need to depend on a man, she can just have one handy if she wants to be entertained for an evening-"

"La la la," I placed my head in my hands, "OK, I don't need to know more than that."

Ellie laughs, "Well, now don't be a prude, its normal." She said.

"It's weird. I know it's normal but I don't want to hear about it from someone who could be my grandma." I shake my head and smile.

"I will get dressed, but I'm not going to take a shower. I'm planning on coming back to work this afternoon." I add.

As I'm getting dressed I ask Ellie if there is anywhere she would like to go or if she would like to visit anyone. I still don't feel like I know her at all and I've been up here for days now. I shared myself with her and even though I don't expect that to be a reason she should share her life with me, I think it would give her more motivation. When someone asks your name, usually they will tell you theirs in return but with Ellie, her name is all I know.

Ellie is already in the car which I assumed when she wasn't answering any of my questions. As soon as I get myself through the mangled screen door, she waves and smiles at me just like a little girl does when there's a parade float passing by tossing out candy. Now that my emotions are on my sleeve, I can take in a huge sigh knowing she is well aware of my nerves and I don't need to hide them.

"I trust you Rainy. I always will." She pats my knee.

"I know, it's just this promises I made a long time ago. I swore I would never drive another person in my car."

"You know what I think? Well, I will tell you anyway. You have been broken and putting all the pieces back together for so long that it has created your identity." She said cautiously.

I roll around different ways to respond but nothing nice is coming up. *How the hell does she know what created my identity?* However, it's the nicest way anyone has told me to stop feeling sorry for myself. I've heard different people tell me that for so long and I suppose this is one of the kindest ways so far.

"Easy for you to say," I said as I placed the box with the bird on her lap.

The first thing Ellie does is roll her window down and sticks her hand out. She looks wide-eyed and a smile from ear to ear. Her hair that was so nice and fixed up moments earlier is wind-blown, but she doesn't care. In fact, she doesn't have a care in the world. She isn't afraid of me being the driver, her hair, her goofy grin or anything else. We don't talk much, but I can feel her looking at me as if she is checking in. I don't dare take my eyes off the road but my mind is at ease just enough to wonder when the last time she has gone to Silverthorne; or anywhere for that matter.

As we sit down at a table, I take notice of a few faces, some looking familiar from the morning I first met Ellie. I want to sit by the window for nostalgia reasons but it's taken. The thought also crosses my mind that it was only a few days ago that I was here and more time needs to pass before I can label that moment as nostalgic.

There's always a second or two when I sit down in a restaurant and I glance up to see if anyone is looking back. Today, everyone is looking.

"Hi, what can I get started for you ladies-" the waitress pauses, "Ellie, it's not-"

"I would like some hot cocoa with whip cream on top," Ellie interrupts.

A few questions zip through my head but the waitress is looking at me. I am also surprised that Ellie already knows what she wants. She must have been thinking about this all night.

"I will have the same," I said.

"We will order our breakfast when you come back," Ellie adds.

Ellie opens the menu and places her head inches away. I ask her if she knows everyone here, I mention that a lot of people seem to know her as well, but she isn't paying attention to me or my questions.

"I want one of everything in here." She giggles.

"You know we can eat out for lunch too?" I said.

I want to ignore all the people staring at us but it's hard. It is so blatantly obvious that they are talking about us and I feel frustrated that I am surrounded by this kind of mentality. I hated this about the place I came from only to be surrounded by it yet again. I am about to ask Ellie why when someone comes behind me.

"Ellie? I thought that was you! How are you?" A man's voice asks.

I was about as surprised as he was.

"And look who you have here. Hi Rainy." He said.

Ellie is smiling as she looks past the top of my head. I turn around to see who she is talking to and more importantly, to see who knows me.

"Do you know Evan?" Ellie asked.

"Well, I know him as Dad, that's what his shirt said at the auto shop. His son was the one who fixed my tire." I said mustering a smile.

Ellie puts her hands together in a silent clap. "So that's the cute young man you were talking about? Patrick. Ah, yes." She grins.

I can feel my ears turning red, and I'm sure everyone can see it.

"That's OK, he thought you were cute yourself. Not too many girls get noticed by Patrick. You must have made an impression on him as well." He laughs.

"Speak of a little sunshine himself," Ellie said.

Once again, someone comes up behind me. My heart drops into the floor. It is Patrick, I can instantly smell his cologne but I can't bring myself to look. I want to melt down my chair and under the table. I know I look terrible but I also don't know what Ellie will say next.

"Ellie? Wow. It's been so long." Patrick said as he gave her a hug.

The look on his face as his brain registers who he is looking at throws me off guard. He comes across as such a confident person but the way he smiles at me adds uncertainty to his otherwise composed nature.

"Rainy? Hi, uh I thought you were long gone. I didn't know you were up here visiting Ellie." Patrick said.

"I'm not, I mean… I don't know her. Well, I know her, but… I guess I'm staying with her for a while. We just met a few days ago. Here actually, we met by that window-"

This is usually about the time when I ramble out sentences without knowing what is coming out of my mouth because I'm so far in my head to actually control what is being said.

"-Rainy and I met here the other morning," Ellie interrupts, "we started chatting and I asked her for a ride back. She took me home and hasn't left."

"I was convinced to stay. How can I say no?" I add.

I wink at Ellie, the same wink I used to give to Emma when she bailed me out of awkward situations. She doesn't do it back, smart on her part because they are both looking at her.

"What brings you girls down the hill?" Patrick turns to me.

"I am fixing, or try to fix, some things around Ellie's place," I respond.

The entire diner became quiet as soon as I said that, almost like someone has a remote control to a TV and hit the mute button. I said something that made everyone uncomfortable and I'm shuffling the conversation in my head trying to find what it is.

"Well, Ellie, Rainy, we boys better get a move on so you girls can eat your breakfast. It sounds like you have a lot to do and Trick and I, we have fish to catch." Patrick's dad said.

Patrick's dad looks around and back at me. He notices everyone looking at Ellie and me, and how quiet everyone has become. As much as I want to ask what the hell is going on, I can't. Whatever I ask will embarrass Ellie in front of them and I knew it. Even though she hasn't told me one dang thing about herself, I decide to wait until they leave to start asking questions.

We say a brief good-bye, and they walk out the diner. The conversations throughout the entire place start back up but I can tell most of them are talking about us.

"Do you want to tell me what that was all about?" I ask.

"I don't know, but Patrick is taken by you. That I do know." Ellie leans in to whisper.

Ellie is as good as I am when it comes to changing the subject. My frustration is rising as I lean in close to Ellie. I need better answers but more importantly, I need validation that what I am seeing and feeling is real.

"Do you noticed people staring at us Ellie?" I whisper.

"Oh sure, I haven't been around in a while. That's all."

But that's not all. There is something so much more to this woman than she is letting on. The last time I felt this uncomfortable was back home after the accident. I want to press this harder but this isn't the place or the time, but I won't let this go. As uncomfortable as I feel, I want to face it head-on.

Ellie and I hardly say anything to each other as we eat breakfast. She is lost in her own thoughts and so am I. I can't help to question my intentions of wanting to know what on earth is going on with this place, Ellie and everything that comes with it. Is this a genuine concern or am I creating a distraction again? I want to find a world where I can be still in a moment without over analyzing it. The fact that I am even asking these questions, or find myself this deep in thought is completely new. It's not hard to piece together why I'm tracking new territory, I just don't have the words for it. It's all parallel to this place, to Ellie and why I took off. I told Ellie a little about my life, my fears and in doing so, I have let some of my walls down. It's true that the walls we build to protect ourselves with are the same walls that won't allow healthy emotions in. I have created a cycle that feeds off of itself but now that I have recognized it for what it is, I can try to stop it. The hardest part of this whole thing is to understand the difference between situations that are benefiting me, and the ones that are used to distract me.

Patrick and his dad are out by their truck tinkering with fishing lures and fishing poles and I immediately wish I had taken a shower, or at least wore different clothes. I know I look half-way homeless which makes me want to avoid them even more. Patrick is the most handsome man I have ever laid eyes on and here I am looking like a hobo that just lost her shopping cart full of tin cans.

I don't want to make eye contact and pretend that I didn't see them but it was too late, he already saw me. He drops what he's working on and walks toward me.

"Rainy! Hey, um, how long are you staying up at Ellie's? I, well, maybe I can visit?" He looks down then back up quickly, "I mean in case you need help at Ellie's, fixing something?"

"Uhh- sure," I respond.

"How long will you be staying?"

"I don't know to be honest. This all sort of fell in my lap. Now one day leads to another and I'm still here. She needs a lot of work done and I think I will stick around and help her."

"You might want to keep that to yourself. But…I… umm, I can help or come see you or just say hello? I mean if that works, or not. I don't want to intrude or you know-"

"Sure, anytime." I smile and start walking to the jeep. Ellie is already inside.

"OK, so I will see you around sometime."

I just wave at him and don't respond. It was cute that he is nervous and stumbling all over his words. I find it somewhat empowering that a guy like him is nervous around me, but I can't put much thought into the whole thing. I can't, Patrick is the last thing I need in my life right now. I am not here to find a boyfriend or any kind of friend for that matter. *Except for Ellie.*

"I think Patrick is looking at your butt," Ellie said.

"Ellie!" I gasp.

"Oh, he didn't hear me." She whispers.

"Don't you like him?" She adds.

"No, not really. He's cute and everything but I don't need anything that Patrick has to offer." I mumble.

"Well, he is sure smitten with you."

"Guys like that don't go well with girls like me Ellie," I said.

"You sure don't think highly of yourself."

"You're probably right about that, but if I ever get into a relationship again, I don't want it to be with a fella like Patrick."

"What's wrong with him? You don't even know him." She said.

"I know his type," I said.

"Just because of the way he looks?" She asks.

"Yep, guys like Patrick know they are good-looking, they know they can have any woman they want and probably already has a girlfriend that he's tired of and sees me as his next toy," I said.

"You don't know Patrick like I do, he's a good boy who just happens to be handsome."

"Yea, well anyway. Not interested." I said.

"You should give him a chance."

"Thing is Ellie, I took a chance at a relationship once and it didn't end well. He cheated God knows how many times, he lied, he was just a terrible person. I didn't have any business being in a relationship either, I guess I just don't know how to make another person happy. So no, no way." I answer, feeling angry again.

"Like the kind of no when you said you would never drive someone in your car? That kind of no?"

I turn the radio on to avoid any further conversation. I wish I would've asked Patrick if there's a place to find supplies to care for the bird, or better yet, had advice on what to do with him next. That is about the only thing I wanted from him. He has a bird, he surely must know after taking care of Zeus. The thought makes me smile a little.

Patrick could very well be different and as much as I want to believe her, I just can't. Not only that, I don't want to believe her. That is probably the biggest admission to the topic. It's not like I don't think he's gorgeous, I am human after all but being with a guy like that is setting a girl up for heartbreak and being with a girl like me isn't any better.

PAST

Towards the end of my marriage, I decided to take up the violin instead of facing the fact that we were headed towards divorce. I needed something to fill in the holes of my heart and secretly, I thought if I impressed him enough, we could reconnect and find a way to make it work. Music was his life and just about the only avenue to his heart. He played in a local band, lead guitar and many nights, he was either at practice or performing a gig.

I would rather deny the fact that he didn't love me than face it and move back home. That was far worse than being in a loveless marriage. I started taking college classes and unable to work full time, and I knew that if we got a divorce, my life would change. This was his town, his friends and his life, there was nothing there for me. Even though I never liked that town, it was better than living in a town that wished I was the one killed in the accident.

I didn't own anything important, I owned my Jeep and the rest was disposable or replaceable. He owned his truck but his music equipment and recording studio was his lifeline. Hope was all I had that someday, I could become his muse. The issue with that mindset is, love goes both ways. I wasn't in love with him either, I was in love with the fact that I was miles away from all the other people that didn't love me. At least there, the lack of love wasn't because I caused the death of the town's hero and future queen.

The violin came naturally to me, I was good at it and I could read just about any music that was put in front of me. I loved the sound of classical music but enjoyed the grit and emotions that came with playing the fiddle. Most people don't realize the difference between the two but the sound is completely different. Once I mastered the violin, I wanted to learn the cello. The deep and mournful sound it produced called to me. I was saving every dime to purchase one and was only a few hundred bucks away.

It was snowing on the opening night of my first concert. I had a solo part so my nerves were getting the best of me. I practiced more than I needed to, the tips of my fingers were calloused and my neck muscles were tight and sore. I knew everyone was coming but the fact that my husband would be there excited me beyond my ability to control it. I had butterflies in my stomach and my heart raced faster than I could keep up. I was ready though, I knew that everyone seeing me on that stage would give them a new light to see me in.

I wore a dress that I felt beautiful in, black and flowing behind me, and when the stage lights hit it just right, I sparkled like glitter. Rehearsal brought my teacher to tears, she told me that I was meant to be on stage and it was a shame that I didn't pick up the violin sooner. She was impressed and at the end of every practice would ask me, "Why do you need me again?"

My parents were driving down, his parents and entire family were sent formal invitations to the event. I was in the local paper headlining the entertainment section for a charity event to raise money for the art complex and being a part of it was empowering. I had been practicing for 5 years, every day and some days I practiced for hours at a time. I was ready.

I reserved an entire section of seats, twenty-three to be exact. As I was warming up backstage the event coordinator asked if the reserved seating I was holding would be filled. It was getting close to the curtain call and the entire theater was filling up.

"Yes, I'm sure the snow has slowed them down a little, but they will be here."

We took our places on stage and the curtain opened. The lights were bright and it took a second to adjust. The conductor walked out from the side of the curtain and everyone applauded. My adrenalin was pumping but my hands were steady. I waited until the first song was over to look out into the audience. I glanced over to the section I reserved but the seats were empty. Not one person I invited was there, not even my parents.

Even though the audience was applauding, all I heard at that moment was silence. I knew my solo was after the next piece, so I had to compose myself but found it difficult to do so. As the rest of the section grew dim and the solo light was placed on me, I walked to center stage and the rest of the string section began to open. Once I started my solo, I closed my eyes and felt the music take over my mind and I went on auto-pilot. Ava Maria, fitting for the occasion and enough to bring me to tears, but I played through it. I cried for the fact that I was playing in what could very well be my best moment in life. I secretly cried for Emma, my loss and the pain I caused so many people. I cried for all the love lost and love never felt.

I didn't want it to be over, I loved the moment I was in. As I placed my violin at my side to take my curtsy, I took one last glance over the audience and the section I reserved was still empty. I inspired everyone in the theater to tears and for the first time in my life, they were tears of joy. I brought love and inspiration to their hearts instead of pain and suffering. Yet, through their applause and standing ovation, I was left in the dark.

When the curtain drew closed, I packed up my violin quickly, hoping that no one would mention the empty section I reserved. The greeting area was full of flowers, hugs, and photos of prideful family members wanting to capture the moment. I looked around hoping I would see my parents but not one person looked familiar and no one knew me either. I was randomly approached by different people telling me I played a lovely rendition of Ava Maria and how touching I was to watch. None of it mattered knowing I didn't have my parents, family or friends to see it.

I made dinner reservations after the show to a great little hole in the wall restaurant and before I jumped to conclusions, I wanted to see if anyone was there. I ate alone that night telling the host that my party was stuck in the snow and were unable to make it. I felt pathetic but hungry which is an odd little combination.

I had no hope that I would find them at the house that evening and it was confirmed when I parked in the driveway. The house was dark, not even the porch light was on. It was cold inside and the first thing I did was turn up the heat, I changed into my pajamas and called my mom.

"Mom? What are you doing home?"

"What do you mean?"

"Uhh, my concert? It was tonight?"

"Wha-wait, we were told it was canceled?"

"Canceled, why would it be canceled?"

"Well, I don't know sweetie, that's what Zac said. He called early this morning and said it was canceled."

"My God mom! It wasn't canceled! Why would he say that?"

"He's your husband honey, you need to ask him. He just said there was a technical issue, and they are postponing the concert and you would let us know the date it would be rescheduled."

"This is really, I can't. Mom, I don't know what to think." I said through tears.

"You need to hang up and find out from Zac about what happened. Calm down OK? Stay calm and keep it together, stop crying Rainy."

At 2:30 in the morning, Zac got home, but I was still awake. I was fuming mad but so very hurt at the same time. I had enough time waiting for him to get home that I was able to stop crying and collect my thoughts. When he walked through the door, he saw me waiting in the kitchen. He didn't bother setting down his duffel bag that was propped over his shoulder. Instead, he walked directly to me. I knew he was playing a gig, not just from his bag but the way he smelled. It was a mix of beer, hot wings and sweat.

"Where were you tonight Zac?"

"What do you mean, where was I? I had a gig at the lamplight."

"My performance was tonight."

"What performance?" He asked.

I had zero expression on my face. I also had a million questions boiling inside my brain and I wanted to scream at him but I knew if I did, I wouldn't be able to stop myself.

"You're not serious right now. My solo was tonight and you and everyone I invited didn't show up." I said clearly.

"They must have all got the date wrong." He shrugged.

"No Zac, do you think I am stupid? Do you think I wouldn't talk to my parents? You told them the concert was canceled! Why? What the hell were you thinking?"

Instead of looking guilty or like I just busted him in a lie, he threw his head back and rolled his eyes. The tossed his hands up in the air, shoved his duffel bag across the floor and took in a deep breath. As he exhaled, he moaned deeply and weaved his hair through his hands. His voice was low but grew louder as he slammed his hands on the counter. He was irritated and the way he looked at me with disgust was not at all what I was expecting.

"Yea, I did. I called everyone and told them it was canceled. I didn't want you to embarrass yourself Rainy. I was looking out for you. You're not a violinist, not to the degree they had you playing tonight. That is a big venue, so I actually rescued you from humiliation." He said.

"I can't believe you are telling me this. You have never once heard me play. In the five years I have been playing, you never once heard me play! How do you know what I am capable of?" I was sobbing. "Twenty-three people Zac, an entire section was reserved but left empty. How could you?"

"Do you really think you're that good? Come on Rainy. You have been playing for 5 years, it's taken me 15 years to get where I'm at." He said egotistically.

"You've never heard me play! Not once. You have no right to do what you did tonight. It was cruel and you have hurt me more than you could ever realize."

It was wrong that he canceled everyone from watching me perform and that hurt me more so than angered me. Even though I wasn't in love with him, he crushed me to the core but not the kind of heartache a person feels when love is lost. This was the kind of hurt that only pride is able to feel. I was so proud of myself, the music I created and the accomplishments I achieved. The one person I admired for his musical talent slammed my pride to the ground.

"Grow up and move on. Look, we can't keep doing this." He said.

"We? I haven't done anything to you!" I started to raise my voice.

"Stop being a victim all the time. I can't do this anymore OK?"

"Do what? You need to make this right Zac."

"I'm tired of making it right, I'm tired of being the one who drags emotions out of you, and I'm just so damn drained. You act like you are half dead most of the time. Can't you see it? You don't love me, you never did. I never loved you either, I rescued you from whatever the hell you were running from. You don't share anything with me, you don't open up and let anyone in. I feel like I'm married to a dead person."

"You are wrong about me, so wrong," I said through tears.

"Here's the deal." He interrupted me, "I have been feeling this way for a long time, I have tried to connect with you on a deeper level and you just can't. You are incapable of having feelings, you can't allow someone to get close to you, and I am just so sick of it! Do you hear what I'm saying?" He was yelling.

"Don't yell at me! Don't make this about-"

"I started seeing someone a while back, and she is pregnant. Rainy, you need to move out." He interrupted.

To say I was shocked would be an understatement. The air was sucked right out of me, and earth below me gave out. The entire conversation was mind-blowing and I couldn't keep track of it.

"What?" I exhaled.

"You heard me. I. Want. A. Divorce." He said slowly.

It took everything in my power to not punch him square in the nose. I was so angry but the one thing that stopped me from saying something I would've regretted was the simple fact that he was right about a lot of it. I knew I was disconnected in many ways. I had a difficult time giving all of myself to someone knowing that they are getting half a person.

I hadn't been to sleep, and I was exhausted, my emotions were extreme and cycled rapidly. After he told me he wanted a divorce, I couldn't focus on anything else other than getting the hell out of there. He went to my closet and piled my things in huge lawn trash bags while I wandered in a daze barely able to stay focused.

Later that morning he left without saying anything and I thought this would be the last of it, but he returned with a U-Haul trailer instead.

"You might as well get everything out today, I don't want you to come back. If there's anything we missed, I will mail it to you." He said.

He couldn't get me out fast enough, heaping my things into the Jeep or trailer and neither of us was speaking other than the occasional "do you want this?" The house was his before I married him, and I was never added to the loan or deed. I knew I would have rights to half of the house but the thought of going through the fight was making me sick. I hated the furniture and didn't want that either. The fact of the matter was, I didn't want to take anything other than the things that had sentimental value, which wasn't much. He packed up my bags of clothes and other things I wouldn't have thought about. He even packed my clothes from the dirty laundry. I could tell he thought about this for a long time and had a plan already in effect. Oddly, this made me feel like I was left out of the loop and that devastated me even more.

"Do you want these photo albums, if not I will just toss them in the trash."

"Just throw them away," I responded.

There were three photo albums created over the years, one was from our wedding and the other two were filled with photos of our adventures and friends we made. If they didn't mean anything to him, I didn't see the point of keeping them either.

When I had everything packed up, I walked back through the house and garage looking for anything I left behind. It was as if I was never there. I was erased from existence and became a faint memory within hours. He was starting over, he had plans and determination in his next chapter of life while I was clueless to my own.

"I think I have everything."

"Whatever you left, I will mail to you." He said quickly.

"Right, OK then. So, I guess that's it." I said.

"I have a lawyer drawing up paperwork. Is there anything you want to add?" He asked.

"The house is yours, I don't want any money from it, and I'm not going to fight you. Plus, you have debt in your name that I don't want to have anything to do with either. You take it all. If you don't, then I will see you in court." I said firmly.

"We have over 160 thousand in credit cards!"

"No Zac, YOU have over 160 thousand in credit cards. Look at the statements, it's all in your name, your purchases, and your stuff."

"That isn't fair, I-"

"Fair? Do we need to discuss the definition of fair before I leave? Because the last thing I remember is you getting a girl knocked up and asking for a divorce."

"You're the one who pushed me out." He said, sounding like a child.

"I will own my part but not today, and not with you in my life. Regardless of what I've done or didn't do, this is on you. If you can't agree, let's take it to the judge because I won't fight with you."

"Oh, and another thing," I added, "You need to pay all the legal fees. The lawyer you hired and all the fees that come with it are also on you. I won't be coming back down here so you'll need to figure out how to get my final signature and whatever else you'll need to get this done. The only time I won't mind coming back is if we need to take this to court."

I said all I needed to say, so I turned around and walked away leaving him standing on the front lawn. It felt good having the last word. Money was always an issue with him and I knew I hit below the belt with the topic. He had $18.82 in his bank account. I wouldn't be surprised if he had money hidden but I could clearly see his deposits and where he spent his money. What money he did have wasn't enough to make his next mortgage. A month prior to that, the guys were discussing their next gig and how money was not coming in. His last paycheck from the Lamplight was $438.00 and that was from 2 nights. Some guys were having to get another job to support themselves but Zac had me. I made a lot more money than he did but since I was taking college classes, that income dropped considerably. His spending habits didn't and consequently, he was in debt up to his ears.

We never joined bank accounts as normal married couples do. Partly because we never took the time to go to the bank and get it done and partly because I knew he had expensive taste in music equipment. This was the smartest thing I could do for myself and I have my parents to thank for that. They warned me to never become financially dependent on anyone or I would become trapped if the situation ever got bad. I cashed my checks through the bank in which they were issued and never used any kind of credit. Everything was cash and I stashed it until a bill was due, it was only then that I gave him money. I expected him to make the transaction to the bank and pay the bills. At times, he would try to tell me that his money was short but I always knew better. I might have appeared clueless, but I was aware of his deposits and where the money was going. I always stayed firm on what I would give monthly and didn't budge. I never told him how much I was really making an hour or how much my paychecks were. If he asked, I would lie and I also never told him about my bonus checks. He took seven lines of credit, and they all had high limits. I didn't want to have anything to do with them.

I had zipper pouches where I kept all my money. I safety-pinned them to the inside of 3 different pairs of jeans that I never wore and kept them folded in my closet. I would add my cash to the pouch without taking it off the jeans by sticking my hands through the legs. That way, if he ever walked in on me, it looked like I was fixing something instead of stashing money. He liked to snoop through my purse looking for money and the first time I caught him would be the last. I decided then that I had to take measures to protect myself.

I knew I was leaving him broke but I didn't care. I had over sixteen thousand pinned to 3 separate pairs of jeans and no way to prove I had that much cash to my name. After telling him that he needed to pay all the costs of the divorce, and knowing I had enough money to live off of, I felt like I had a soft landing. This is all I had, and I was thankful I played the game the way I did. In the end, this was the only thing I had going for me. If we went to court, I'm sure a legal accountant could have found my income was more than it was but I doubted Zac would take it that far. One thing I knew about him that worked in my favor was how private he was about his life. He didn't like anyone to know his business, something we had in common, but he didn't hide it from me as I did from him. Going to court will go against everything he tried to protect.

It wasn't until I was on the highway that I actually called my parents to inform them that I was moving home. My cell phone charged by the minute so the conversation was short. I told my mom that I was coming with a U-Haul and moving home. I was bawling when I made the call, and she could barely understand what I was saying, but she understood enough. She wanted me to tell her what happened but I couldn't. I was an emotional mess at that point and I also knew that I would regret it when the phone bill came. I knew I needed to pull myself together and make other important phone calls so this was my excuse to get off the phone with my mom. I called my cell phone company to update my new address. I called my enrollment officer at college and also advised them of my new address. The last conversation was one I dreaded the most. I had to call my boss and inform him of what happened.

When I started school, I had to rearrange my work schedule and shift into part-time. I earned my associate's degree in applied human biology and became a surgical technician. The group I worked for had several surgeons that covered all aspects of general and orthopedic surgeries. I was one of the few surgical assistants that had privileges in the main hospitals in town as well as neighboring cities. Our group was also contracted through the state, and federal prisons to be on call for the inmates of trauma or any other surgical requirements and I had access to every single facility. We had satellite offices throughout Colorado and this was my only saving grace in hopes of keeping my job. I wasn't worried about my college classes, I just finished midterms and I knew I could transfer to my nearest community college.

To my surprise, my boss understood my situation and asked to schedule a phone conference when I was settled in. Of course, I agreed, and we set a time and date but I needed to ask him if I had any job security or potential job opportunities, and he reassured me that this was actually good news for them. They needed someone for their new division in the Northeast section of Colorado that also included the prison in Sterling Colorado. It's the largest correctional facility in the state, and they needed more manpower. To hear this news was a complete relief and I knew I would be OK. At least I would be a contributing product of society even though I was a mess of a human being.

My dad came into my room one afternoon and sat on the end of my bed. I opened my eyes and saw his fresh smile.

"You're done now Neha," he said softly. "It's time to start over."

I knew what he meant. I needed to be done mourning. He gave me space and isolation to absorb all the sorrow in my life much like the way an Indian woman mourns her husband in death. The father will allow the daughter time and solitude while the rest of the tribe takes care of her children and tends to her duties. Her father will decide when the mourning is over, and she is expected to carry on. I was always thankful that he never told me this when it came to

Emma. He knew the difference between the two kinds of broken hearts.

He helped me out of bed and my mom had run a bath for me. I was weak from not eating much, and dizzy from laying down in the fetal position for days on end. My mom washed me, cleaned my hair and held my body up and out of the tub. She helped me dress as my dad waited for me at the table. He fed me, I ate and it was in complete silence. Just like my dad had said, I was done.

Chapter 11

Ellie and I spend the whole day in town. We eat little snacks found in coffee shops and wander in and out of random stores that are irrelevant to the purpose of this trip but I don't mind. I enjoy watching her and can't help to feel joy from the simple fact that she is so happy. She looks at everything there is to look at. She observes the people and the latest technology with pure amazement. By the end of the afternoon, the jeep is loaded up with things to start fixing her place. I was expecting to pay for all of this myself, with the little money I have but decided days ago that it would be worth it. I am surprised to learn how much cash she carries. She pays for everything and loves spending her money. Every time I try to buy something, she stops me from paying.

We find a pet store that is owned by a veterinarian, and we unexpectedly receive free advice. She gave us a formula and syringes to make feeding the bird easier. So far, we were doing all the right things and when she asks to see him she confirms that he was only a few weeks old. She also confirmed that the bird is most likely a Raven.

Once she told me this, my eyes welled up with tears. I'm sure they both notice but I don't offer an explanation because I just don't have the words or the time. My connection to a raven bird isn't something I can easily describe and trying will just botch the whole thing.

By the end of the afternoon, I can tell Ellie is tired. She reminds me of a toddler who is so completely exhausted but can't calm down enough to settle into sleep. She isn't delirious yet, just giggly which makes me laugh. Ellie watches the kids while they skate but can't understand why they wear their pants half-way off their asses. She is also amused that the girls wear pants so low on their hips that it exposes their underwear. She doesn't understand the type of underwear they wear either.

"It's nothing but string, what is the purpose?" She asks.

I never stopped to think about the purpose of string underwear. I laugh.

"It's sexy I guess," I add.

"Well, if a man wanted me to wear those dumb, sorry excuses for underwear, I would make him wear them first. If he liked the way they felt, we would have a deal. I have half the notion to go over and pull their pants up."

I laugh even more. It sounds fair enough, I guess it never occurred to me that thong underwear might be hard for an elderly person to find reason in. Especially if you can see them rising up from their pants. Furthermore, seeing boys wearing their pants half-way to their knees would be hard to grasp as well.

"How long has it been since you have been to town?" I ask out of the blue.

"I don't remember, years."

"Why? I mean that is a long time. Is it that you can't drive?" I ask.

"Oh sure, I can drive but I…I just don't." She answers. "Where are we going next?"

I can tell once again that she is shifting the conversation but I allow it. I know she will be disappointed knowing that we need to head back, so letting her change the subject gave me the upper hand.

I slowly inch the jeep down the long dirt road that leads to her house, and as we get closer, I can see a truck parked in front. *Patrick.* He was leaning against it with a twig in his mouth, looking up to the sky.

"Oh my God Ellie," I said calmly but wanting scream.

I wave at him as cool as I can, reverting to the trusted old farmer's wave. He recognizes it and gives me a swift wave back.

"Hi, Rainy, Miss Ellie. I hope you don't mind me stopping in." He smiles. I melt.

"Oh, Patrick, I am so thrilled you're finally up here to visit," Ellie said.

"Well, Miss Ellie, I um, really enjoyed seeing you today. It's been too long, so many things have happened." Patrick said sweetly.

There's a pause and immediate tension is forming. They both know something I don't and it makes me uncomfortable.

"I want to say hi to Rainy too." He adds.

"Of course you do," she said as she held his hand in hers.

"I am going in the house to make tea," she said proudly as if the idea was the best she ever had. "You two can unload the car, and Patrick, have Rainy show you what is in the box. She is a proud mother."

I show Patrick the raven and ask Ellie to prepare some food for him as she walks in the house. I am relieved she gave us something to do because standing here felt awkward, but standing around with nothing to talk about was worse. What I really want is the opportunity to ask questions about Ellie. I get the feeling I am the only one around here who doesn't have answers to questions that seem pretty reasonable to ask.

"Congratulations," he said, "Uhh, he looks just like you."

"Doesn't he though?" I respond proudly.

"You ladies spent the whole day in town?" Patrick asks.

"We sure did, I'm tired, and Ellie must be exhausted."

"Looks like you will be busy for a while. You must have plans on staying up here, this looks like the beginnings of a big project. With Ellie being a proud grandmother to a bird and all…a…what kind of bird is he?" He asks.

"A raven. At least the vet in Silverthorne seems to think." I pause as we both look at him.

"I think he's hungry. I also think Zeus will be jealous of Mr. Raven here." Patrick said.

"Oh Zeus, he will get lots of love if I see him again… Hey, question… I don't understand how or why this place got so run down and why Ellie is alone up here. Nothing really makes sense."

"So, you two just met a few weeks ago huh?" He asks.

"Believe it or not, yes. She was sitting alone and I don't really know what happened from there. Somehow, here I am. So, have you known Ellie long?"

"All my life. She has been up here a long time." He said as he takes a few bags from the back of the Jeep.

"I figured that. She was pretty excited to go to town today." I said.

"I bet she was, and you have some nerve taking her." His voice trails off.

"The other morning a kid at the restaurant made a remark about whether I understand what I was getting myself into. Then today you said something about keeping my plans to myself. I kind of feel like everybody knows something but me. It's making me uneasy."

"Oh, you don't know." He said quietly.

"Know what?" I asked, trying to sound nonchalant.

"Ellie, her…umm, life…what she's done."

"Done? No, she hasn't told me anything." I said.

"That's up to her then, I'm sure as hell not going to say anything."

"Well that's not very reassuring, what is she? A murderer?" I said sarcastically.

"I have said too much, and I am sorry. It's just, you're so pretty and I… um… don't think when I see you. Besides, it's not really my place to say anything."

When he said I was pretty, I about dropped everything I was carrying. I never saw myself as pretty, pretty plain maybe. But, this doesn't change the way I feel about him. He's clever and too smooth for my liking, even though he might pretend to be slightly awkward, he is too confident in his actions. I can't help to wonder if this was his way of avoiding further conversation about Ellie but I still don't have a clue as to what or how to respond.

"I'm sorry, I didn't mean-" He starts.

"No, it's OK," I interrupt, "I just don't know what to make of it all. I've been waiting for Ellie to tell me, she would rather hear about my life than share her own. I don't blame her much. I suppose I'm the same. It's not like she has come forward and said she has a secret, but I can just tell."

"It's not my story to share, it's Ellie's. I will admit when I have said too much. But, from the moment I saw you, I don't know…I just, you have…I don't have words." He stuttered.

"I will stop you right there." I smile. "You seem to be struggling a little."

We both laugh, giggle like a couple of teenagers but I don't say anything back to him. Once again, I am utilizing my skills of avoidance to steer the conversation to a topic that feels safer, controllable and less emotional.

We unload everything from the car and take it to the shed where space is limited, but I am able to move a few things around to make room on the workbench in the far corner. Patrick stands behind me peeking under the tarp at the 57 Chevy.

"My God, I forgot she had this. They don't make cars like this anymore. This one is in perfect condition. Perfect. Have you seen this yet?" He asks.

"Yep, 57 Chevy. I bet it's still in the original condition too." I reply.

"You know your cars, impressive." He smiles.

"I know a few."

"So where are you from?" He asks.

"Eastern Colorado, about 5 hours from here."

I turn around to face him, and he is dangerously close to me. I can't move back any further or I would be on top of the workbench, he is blocking the only way out unless I want to parkour over the car which feels a little extreme at this point.

"Hey Rainy, you wouldn't want to go on a date sometime would you?" He asks as he looks down.

"Nope." I was shocked and embarrassed at what just came out of my mouth. "I don't date men," I said.

"Right, got it." He turns away. "I guess that takes a little pressure off. At least I'm not being turned down because you're just not into me. So hey, we can still hang out though, I mean just as friends, some of the coolest chicks I know are gay." He begins to ramble.

"What? No, I'm sorry." I said laughing. "I'm not gay."

"But you said you don't date men? Oh jeez, I have completely made a jack-ass out of myself here." He laughs.

"No, don't say that it was funny. I didn't mean that I don't date men, I just don't date these days. Like, at all."

"Are you married? I just assumed you weren't. Not that you have to wear a ring to be married, I just-"

"I was married," I interrupt. "I'm divorced. I am not very good at marriage, or any relationship really."

"I'm sorry to hear that. Any kids?" He asks.

"No, I don't want kids. You?" I ask.

"Kids are cool, I don't think I want any either though."

We finish putting all the bags in the shed and I make room on the workbench as Patrick continues to look in under the tarp that covers Ellie's car. Neither one of us says anything for a while which is unusual for me. I smile to myself as I replay the awkward conversation we just had, and realize his question about having kids is actually brilliant. I can't help to let my mind wander in the realization that he's probably been in a few relationships where the girl wanted children, but he didn't. Usually, this leads to heartbreak and I suppose asking before any feelings develop is his way of avoiding that.

Children can bring so much love to a person's life, but they can also bring a lot of sadness. I know I have given my parents both, but it's the sadness and heartbreak I caused them and so many others that left a hole in my heart. I would never want to pass that down to my child. It's been said that children often fill those holes but I don't think it's fair to bring a child into my life where they would already have a job to do. A child is given to their parents to receive love, happiness, and support, not the other way around. I also think a child teaches parents a love they didn't know existed, or they didn't realize they were capable of. Love scares me because love hurts in so many ways. To love and be loved simultaneously is a rare and precious emotion to feel. Inside that type of love rests contentment and solace which is the strongest love there is. The only way a love like that can survive is to first love yourself. My parents have that kind of love for each other, and also with me which has been my lifeline throughout all these years. Expecting a child to be the lifeline is selfish.

Patrick stirs around the shed and eventually finds himself standing in the door looking up to the sky. His movements distracted me away from my thoughts and it is unspoken but understood that he is ready to leave.

We walk in the tall grass along the edge of the forest and talk back and forth until I stop at a little path that leads into the trees. Even with the sun, it looks like a different world. The trees are tall and close to each other but once they reach the sky, they fill out making it difficult for the sun to shine down on the ground. I suddenly realize this is where Ellie walks in the mornings when she thinks I am asleep. This is why her shoes get all muddy. I can't see how far the path goes or where it leads because it gets dark the further in it goes.

"Where does this path go?" I ask interrupting our conversation.

"Huh? Oh, I don't know." He said looking in.

He does know and I will find out for myself.

Chapter 12

"What in the hell are you doing?" I ask as I rub my eyes. I am in a dead sleep when I suddenly wake up, sensing someone is in my room. Ellie is sitting in the rocking chair in the corner of the room, and she looks ghostly and oddly iridescent, almost see-through.

"Sorry if I woke you," she answers.

"Woke me? You about gave me a damn heart attack Ellie. What on earth are you doing? What time is it?"

I sit up in bed and reach over to turn the lamp on that was next to my bed but I quickly give it a second thought. The moon is full and it brings enough light in the room. I don't want to wake up more than I already have, so I leave the light off.

"Is everything all right?" I ask.

"Yes, I just had a lot of excitement in the last couple of days and I can't sleep." She answers.

"Um, I know, but we can talk about it in the morning can't we?"

"Patrick is a good man." She said, completely skipping over my question.

"Uh, that's random. Is that what why you're here? To talk about Patrick?"

"No, not really, but I want to show you something." She whispers.

"Now? Can't it wait until morning?" I groan.

"No, follow me," Ellie said standing up, shuffling herself to the front door.

"Hang on just a second, let me get dressed or something. Where are we going?" I ask knowing she won't be telling me the answer.

Ellie scoots around the broken screen door before I have the chance to put pants or shoes on. I can't help to wonder if she is out of her mind in some way. I've only been up here for a few weeks so maybe I'm just now witnessing an episode of hers. I make the subconscious decision to follow her instead of getting dressed knowing that whatever happens from here, I will happen in my t-shirt and underwear. I don't stop to put my shoes on either which brings back memories of the cornfield. I barely catch Ellie walking around the side of the house as I wiggle myself past the screen door. I take notice of how aggravated I am and make a mental note that this stupid screen door will be the first thing I fix.

I make my way around the corner of the house just in time to see Ellie walking into the thick forest, her white nightgown and long gray hair trailing behind her. The moon casts a soft light making it possible to see the beginning of the path but it quickly disappears into the dark. She doesn't stop to wait for me, but I'm not sure I want her to. I stop when I can no longer see the path ahead of me, the moonlight is blocked from the pine trees that tower above me. I don't see Ellie ahead of me, and I don't want to call out to her either. I find myself afraid of something I know logically doesn't exist.

This isn't the cornfield, and I am not a little girl who is abandoned by her parents. I was never abandoned in the first place and as I curl my toes, the soft ground beneath my feet reminds me of that. The earth below feels comforting and as I take a few small steps, the smooth foliage against my bare ankles radiates through me, confirming that I don't need to be afraid.

A warm gust of wind pries the trees open allowing the moonlight to show the path just enough to take a few steps. I see glimpses of Ellie gliding along the delicate trail effortlessly, she knows this path extremely well.

As I walk deeper into the trees, the ground gets colder, and when I step on top of the moss that blankets the ground, water squishes over the top of my feet. Mud builds up between my toes but it calms my mind. I can hear an owl high above in the trees, keeping a steady rhythm to another owl echoing far off in the distance.

Ellie disappears down a small ravine and I can hear running water at this point. I get to the top of the hill and can clearly see her at the bottom near the water. I still don't say anything, I wouldn't know what to say anyway so it feels right just staying silent. I watch her cross over the creek and it surprises me to watch her do it so gracefully. She kneels down on her knees next to the water as I make my way down the ravine.

I pause at the edge of the creek not really wanting to cross over it. Ellie has shoes on and the thought of how uncomfortable it must be to wear wet shoes enters into my mind but leaves just as fast. I look to see if I can avoid crossing the creek but I have no choice. I can't stand across from her on this side of the creek because of a small waterfall that is carved into the side of a hill.

The hush of the forest is replaced by the ripple sounds of water as it wanders carelessly over the stones and rocks. I put one foot in and then the other feeling the cold travel up my legs and eventually taking my breath away. It is deeper than I anticipated and the stones below my feet are slimy and unsteady. I take my first step and the water goes past my knees but the further I get to the other side, it becomes shallow again. As I clumsily get to the bank of the creek and climb out of the water, the more impressed I am with Ellie and how quick she crossed. I kneel down next to her and take a moment to catch my breath and find my bearings, noticing that even in the dark, this place was beautiful.

"This is really pretty. But why couldn't we wait until morning?" I ask shivering.

"Because I don't want to. I don't like coming here in the day time. Not very often anyway."

There was not one word I could think of saying at this moment. She looks back down at the water and her head gently tilts to the side in the same way someone looks at art on the wall. The trees cast a shadow over the water but when a gust of wind would flow through, it moved the tress long enough for the moon to cast a glare over the water. I take my hand and brush it over the top of the creek, feeling it run through my fingers. I wonder how deep this little area is and I wait for the next rush of wind to move the trees aside, so I can see into the water.

My focus in is harmony with the wind and the movement of the trees and I hunch down a little closer. A huge gust blows through the ravine and forces the trees to the side long enough to see clearly. I gasp and fall back on one hand and it sinks into the moss. I can feel the cold, wet ground seep through my underwear as I dig my feet into the ground to force my body to move away from the edge of the creek. My free hand slaps over my mouth, keeping me from screaming.

"Oh my God Ellie!"

PAST

"Rainy, honey? What are you doing out of bed?" My mom asked carefully.

"Emma is coming to get me."

"Well, why don't you go lay back down and rest for a while?"

"No, I'm done resting, I want to go home, Emma said she will take me home and wants to spend the night," I said as I peered down the hospital corridor. "She won the game last night, you guys should have seen her winning shot. It was exciting."

My dad came in the room holding my clothes that were neatly folded with brand-new shoes placed on top. Once my mom got my dad's attention, she shook her head which I could see out of the corner of my eye.

My parents would leave and come back in the room on and off the whole morning and sometimes only one would come back just to have the other leave again. I knew they were talking to the doctors outside my room and, sometimes I could make out what was being said. My mom's voice would rise in disagreement to something being said and my dad would interject with a calm voice, deep and firm.

"We can't fix this. This is the best thing for her." My dad said.

"I can't let this happen, she just needs more time." My mom said through sobs.

"I know this isn't easy, but in my opinion, this will be the best thing for her. It's a lovely place. She will take this at her pace. There are long term consequences if this isn't addressed now." Dr. Stevenson said.

All three of them came back to my hospital room and the doctor explained that instead of going home, I would be going to a place to heal my brain. My mom was still crying and my dad could hardly look at me at all. He sat at the end of the bed and stared out the window, eventually placing his hand in mine.

"Can Emma come to visit? I have met so many new friends. Can they come too?" I asked.

My mom started to answer and from the tone of her voice, I could tell she was going to say no. Dr. Stevenson interrupted her and I felt a sense of relief knowing that if the doctor said they could visit then it was decided. He didn't answer my question but instead tried to explain where I would be staying for a while.

Following any kind of conversation was difficult for me, even if there was only one person talking and no one else was around. I felt like I was listening to an entire crowd of people talking at once so instead of trying to focus and follow along, I would go into a trance.

The brochure on the coffee table in the waiting room was less than impressive but I still picked it up to look at it. The Brain Integration Center, it read on the front. One would think they would find a different photo for the front cover, instead, it was a generic photo of a family appearing to be happy with a cute puppy in the background playing on the grass. The inside was worse, a lot of words describing the facility and the type of care offered. Photos of brain imaging were randomly placed with words under it in small fine print; normal brain function, abnormal brain function.

"Rainy?" A woman I never saw before was standing at the entrance of a long hallway decorated with handmade paintings and drawings on construction paper.

We all stood up at the same time, but then my parents were called by another woman behind the front desk.

"Hi Rainy, I'm Maryann. I am going to show you around while your parents take care of all the boring parent stuff. Sound good?"

"Uhh sure, will someone let me know when my friend Emma gets here?"

"If Emma comes, we will let you know." She answered.

I liked that place even though I knew I wasn't going home. It looked more like a hotel and not a hospital. She was walking a lot faster than I could, and I was trying to look at the different drawings taped to the wall that lined the hallway. As we made our way down another hall, we passed the gym where someone was in a small pool moving around and other people were using exercise equipment with blank expressions on their faces.

I had my own room but nothing over the top. I had a bed, a small chair in the corner with a light on a table and a bathroom where shampoo and all the normal bathroom items waited for me.

"This is your room for a while. Everything you need is here and if you need anything else, the nursing staff is right outside your door. You can watch T.V in the lounge area where there're snacks and different things to drink. I think we even have a spiced chai tea on tap." She smiled.

"OK, thank you. Can you tell Emma and the others where I am when they get here?"

"If they come, we will let you know." She repeated.

The next morning, I woke up and showered but the nurse needed to help me. My leg broke because of the accident and it was in a cast and brace that I couldn't get wet. I told the nurse that I was excited to have Emma visit. I explained that I talked to her, and she was excited to visit too. I didn't have the best clothes to wear, my parents weren't exactly sure what to pack for me, but I had clean socks and underwear, so I suppose that's all that mattered.

In the lounge area, a selection of fresh fruit, dry cereal, and oatmeal with all the add-ins was displayed neatly on the counter with a toaster on the end. Even though the food was what we might have at home, the way they placed everything on the counter took the ordinary out of it all.

The nurse helped me get my food to the table where another person was eating breakfast and minding their own business. The day before when Maryann was showing me around the facility, she called the other people who stayed here as "stayers" which I suppose sounded better than nut jobs.

I was watching The Price is Right, fully engulfed in the showcase showdown along with other stayers who were watching. Some would watch a little and start talking to themselves while others would spontaneously shout a random remark to no one in particular.

"Rainy?" A man's voice said from the corner of the lounge.

"Right here," I said as I stood up and grabbed my crutches. "Is Emma here?"

"No, she's not here. My name is Dr. Edwards. I will be talking with you for a little while today and then you will have some scans and tests done. Sound good?"

"Sure, my friend Emma is going to come over today, I talked to her last night," I told him.

"OK, and we are going to talk about your friend Emma a little today too."

He was an ordinary looking man, nothing that set him apart from any other person I've talked to. He had a kind voice, a sympathetic face with a smile that reassured even the toughest critic that he was easy to talk to. He pointed out his family in a picture frame on the end table across from me and smiled contently as he looked at it. In the picture, he was sitting next to his wife and two little girls with fall colored trees in the background. It was a typical pose that seemed to match his ordinary and traditional first impression.

The front wall in his office was lined with huge long windows with a view of the parking lot below and off in the distance, the Front Range. He had several bookshelves fixed with trinkets and photos along with books placed perfectly on each shelf. His chair was green and mine was orange. Other than the color, they're the same. He had a long chaise lounge chair which was bright purple sitting near the window but it didn't look like anyone sat over there. The art on his wall was abstract and brightly colored, matching the chairs in his office. The art and colors were less than typical and a little modern or edgy for what seemed like a traditional kind of person.

"So Rainy, the first thing I would like to do is make you a promise. I promise I will always tell you the truth. Is that a good promise?"

"Yea, that's great. Thanks."

"That means that I will never lie to you, do you understand what I am saying?" He said.

"Yes, I get it." I sighed.

"So, what's the one promise I will always do?"

"You will never lie to me. You will always tell me the truth." I repeated.

"Yep, do we have a deal?" He shook my hand and added, "I read that you had a car accident a few weeks ago, I am sorry you had to go through that. Do you remember anything about that night?"

"Well, Emma won the state championship, so we decided to meet the team for ice-cream. I hit a soft spot of dirt on the road and lost control of the car. It could have been worse though."

"When you say it could have been worse, what does that mean to you?" He asked.

"Someone could have died," I said as I adjusted my leg.

"So was Emma with you?" He asked.

"Yes, I helped her out of the car. She's always thanking me for saving her life." I answered.

"When is the last time you talked to her?"

"Last night, she will be coming today to visit me," I said proudly.

"Do you remember anything when you were at the hospital?" He asked.

"A little, I slept a lot. I was in a lot of pain too. I remember my parents talking to me, and maybe a few of the nurses and doctors but the details are a little fuzzy. I made new friends too. I'm sure my parents have told you about them but this one girl, her name is Three, it's a nickname I think. I mean, who would name their daughter Three? But anyway, she only came to visit once and left. She didn't talk much."

He was writing down notes on a yellow notepad, and I was curious to know what I said that was so interesting that he had to write it down.

"When is the last time you saw Emma?" He asked.

"She came to see me at the hospital. I talked to her last night too. I think. I mean, I just talked to her." I felt confused.

"Did anyone else talk to Emma?" He asked.

"No, well, maybe. I don't know." I responded.

"Is there anything you want to talk about with me?" He asked.

"Not really, I mean I don't really know why I am here or what this place is," I said.

"Well, we are taking a look at your brain, we want to see if there is any kind of damage or injury from the car accident. If so, we will try to fix it."

"OK, that's what I assumed," I responded.

"The next step will be for us to take some images of your brain and other tests that will seem pretty silly to you but they will give us a lot of information." He smiled

"OK, sounds good. So when do I get to go home?" I asked.

"I don't really know, that will be up to you." He said.

"Can I have my parents come to visit? Emma?"

"Sure, anyone you like. We have visiting hours a few times a day."

"Emma might not know when those hours are. I will call her. When are the visiting hours?" I asked.

"I will have the nurse fill you in on those details." He said.

A few days went by and most of my time was spent sitting across from someone answering questions and getting different scans of my brain. I had a blood test but the nurse told me it was the only one I needed to have. It was nice being out of the hospital but I still wanted to go home and sleep in my own bed. After a week or so, I started taking medication at night that made me very sleepy. I was having terrible dreams and waking up soaking wet from sweating. My parents would visit me every evening but their last visit they told me they needed to head home for a few days and check in. I was OK being left there and I knew Emma would be coming to visit soon.

"Hi kiddo, how have you been doing?" Dr. Edwards asked.

"Good, I think I'm good. I've been doing a lot of tests and keeping busy." I said.

"What is today? What day of the week is it?" He asked.

"I think its Thursday."

"Today is Wednesday." He stated.

"That's right, Wednesday. I get lost in time lately." I said.

"Has it been nice having your parents visit at night?" He asked.

"Yea, I mean I would rather go home, but I guess I will soon enough. They won't be visiting for a few days. They needed to take care of a few things back home."

"Has any of your friends come to visit you?"

"No, I have been expecting Emma to come, but she hasn't yet. Well wait, I talked to a friend I met at the hospital. That was nice but she said she was leaving." I answered.

"Why do you think she hasn't come to visit yet?" He asked calmly.

"I can't call her, the nurses won't let me use the phone. Can I call her from here?" I asked enthusiastically.

"So how were you able to talk to your other friend if the nurses won't let you use the phone?" He asked.

"I mean, she just came to visit I guess," I said. "So, can I call her?"

"No, you can't call her from here. Why don't you think you can call her from here Rainy?"

"You have a phone, so I don't really know. But it's stupid that I can't call her." I was agitated.

"I was talking to your mom and dad yesterday, and they said Emma wasn't at the hospital. They also never met any of your other friends. Let's talk about Emma, why do you think she wasn't there?" He asked.

"She was there, I don't know. Maybe she came when everyone was gone."

"The nurses never left, and there is a sign-in list of everyone who came to visit and I don't see Emma's name on here." He said.

He handed me a piece of paper that had my parent's name written with dates and times all the way down the page.

"She just didn't sign in. She probably didn't know she needed to sign in. We can ask her when she comes to visit." I said.

"What if she doesn't visit? How would that make you feel?"

"Sad, really sad. She's my best friend. If she doesn't come to see me it would mean that she's mad at me, probably because of the accident. But, I've already apologized to her."

"Why would she be mad about the accident?" He asked.

As he was writing down my answers, I didn't have an answer to his last question.

"Why would she be mad about the accident Rainy?" He asked again.

"Maybe because she didn't get to celebrate her win. She won the state championship. Or maybe because the accident scared her. We can ask her once she gets here. I just need to call her."

"How would Emma describe the accident if we were to ask her?" He asked.

"Her mom was mad. I remember calling her mom one night from the hospital. My mom and dad left for the night. Yes, I remember now. Her mom was yelling at me and told me to never call again. Why would she do that? Maybe that's why Emma isn't here yet."

The memory became very clear at that moment and I started to cry. I remember calling Emma's mom in the hospital, and she was angry. She screamed at me, but I couldn't make out what she was screaming about. I couldn't understand her. All I wanted to do was talk to Emma, but she wouldn't let me.

Dr. Edwards handed me a box of Kleenex.

"Sometimes people have emotions that we don't understand right away but you will. We will keep talking about it. Why don't we call it a day and talk more tomorrow? Until then, you have a journal so you can use that to write down your thoughts, maybe ask yourself why her mom is so angry with you. How does that sound?" Dr. Edwards asked kindly.

A few days passed and I didn't use my journal but I thought a lot about why her mom would be so mad. All it did was make me angry and I really didn't want to think about it. I knew I was to blame for the accident but, I was OK. Emma was OK too and, I didn't really understand why she was so mad.

The medications they gave me didn't help with the nightmares but I didn't tell anyone. I didn't want to take more medicine because I was already too groggy in the mornings and more medication would only make that worse. I would wake up and sit straight up in bed but I could never really remember what they were about, a song was playing though. I could remember that and it would get stuck in my head. I grew to hate that song.

Dr. Edwards wasn't in his office the next day when it was time for me to meet with him. I could hear him outside the door talking to one of the staff members but I couldn't make out what they were saying. I decided to sit on the long chaise near the window and wait for him. It was soft velvet material with deep rivets that made it look expensive. Perhaps it was expensive but I wanted to sit on it anyway. It was comfortable, especially with my cast. I didn't think it was a good idea to prop my feet up because of my shoes but it was so much more comfortable than the other chairs in his office. The cast was becoming more aggravating as the days passed.

A single raven perched himself on a tall light post in the parking lot below and even though I couldn't hear him, I could tell by the way his body moved he was calling the way only a raven can. Ravens have such a deep and meaningless call, not even close to the pretty chirping sounds that songbirds make. Their gravelly caw never bothered me, even in the early mornings when they gathered in the trees outside my window.

"Hi, Rainy. How are you this morning?" He asked as he finally came back into the office.

"Pretty good, a little tired. I want to take a nap."

"Why don't you sit in the chair across from me, so we can talk?"

He asked as he looked at the chair across from him.

"Why do you have this chair if nobody sits on it?" I asked.

"Lots of people sit on it, you're sitting on it too, but I want to talk right now and having you over there and me over here isn't going to work."

"Why have it?" I asked.

"I like it. I sit on it when I am doing paperwork or working longer hours. It's a good chair to take a nap on."

I hobbled over to the other chair and sat down, noticing his yellow note pad with scribbles and handwriting all over the page.

"So what do you write about?" I asked.

"Lots of things. I write notes about what is discussed mainly. So, Rainy what day is it today?"

"Today is Wednesday."

"Yesterday was Monday. Today is Tuesday. Do you remember what I wanted you to think about from the last time we talked?"

"Yes, why is Emma's mom so mad at me, that's what you wanted me to journal but I didn't journal it though."

"That's OK, as long as you thought about it. What did you come up with?" He asked.

"I don't know, I think she is mad because Emma could have been really hurt."

"Let's talk about the accident. What is the last thing you remember?" He asked.

"Just driving, talking and listening to music. She won the state basketball game, I remember her screaming. Then I remember the paramedics coming, they took us to the hospital but Emma was able to go home."

"OK, and you said you were tired, how have you been sleeping?" He asked.

"Good I guess, I have bad dreams though."

"Do you remember any of your dreams?" He asked as he wrote on his notepad.

"No, not really. Except for this song that gets stuck in my head. It makes it hard to fall back to sleep." I said.

"Humm, what song?" He asked.

"Unbelievable by REM," I said.

As soon as I said it, I realized the song in my dream was the song Emma and I were singing to. This was the song playing when the car crashed and I remembered the instant it stopped. Recalling that moment put me in a trance which became obvious to anyone who tried to have conversations with me.

"Is that the same song you were listening to when you and Emma crashed?"

"Yea, actually it is." It took everything I had to look at him. Pulling myself out of a trance was like fighting for my life. I could stay completely zoned out, and let it take me out to sea or fight it and come back to shore.

"Well, that's good to remember. That might be why you're having bad dreams too. The fact that you can remember a little is a good thing." He reassured me.

"I guess so, but I really don't like that song anymore." My voice trailed off.

"Let's do something a little different today." He reached into a folder and took out some photos. "I want to show you some pictures and you tell me a little about each one." He added.

My mind wandered some while he was taking them from the envelope. I really disliked the way he pronounced pictures. Pictures…pronouncing the T in tures. I never said it like that, I've never heard anyone else say it like that either. Pic-sures…the T is replaced with an S.

He handed me a photo of my parents standing in front of our house, and I instantly recognized it. I didn't need to question why he had it, I figured he already talked to them about it, and they agreed to give him some photos.

"That's my mom and dad," I said.

"Right, but how do they make you feel when you see them?"

"Fine I guess, safe, loved. I said but also thinking it was such a stupid and stereotypical question.

"Take a look at this photo, tell me what you see here." He said.

"Emma, that's her last game! She actually won that game. State championship! She's so happy, and behind her are the other players. Hey look, that's me. That's a terrible photo of me. I look like a weirdo."

"What about this?" He flipped over another photo.

"That's my car. Holy cow! Is that what it looked like after the accident?" I asked.

"It is, you are very lucky Rainy." He said as he looked at the photo.

"By the looks of it, we both are lucky," I said proudly.

He flipped over a few more photos of the car. It was destroyed and completely crushed. It was difficult to look at and I was feeling uncomfortable.

"Looking at these make me feel uncomfortable. Are there more, because I don't want to see more." I said quietly.

"OK, we don't need to see more of the accident. But I want to show you a few other photos."

"Is that me? I'm in the hospital." I said as I took the photo from his hands.

"That's you after the accident. You were in the hospital for 14 days before coming here."

"I look so different, look at my face, it's black and blue," I said.

"Yes, as a parent myself, that would be difficult to see. Take a look at this photo." He handed the photo to me.

"Who is- oh my God! Is that Emma? That must be my blood on her because she looked so much better when she came to visit me." I handed it right back to him.

"This is Emma, this was taken in the hospital too." He said softly and followed by a long pause.

So the next thing I want to show you isn't a photo." He finally said.

He handed me a folded piece of paper with Emma's high school senior photo. I loved her photos, she is so photogenic. Mine were pretty too, that I will admit, but hers were more like the kind of photos you would see on a box of tampons. Free flowing hair, dancing in a wheat field and the sun highlighted her face just perfectly. Under her photo was her birth date and another date but I didn't really pay much attention to it.

"Do you know what this is?" He asked.

"Emma's Graduation announcement?" I questioned.

"Take a look again."

I opened the paper and a poem was on the inside cover and I read it out loud.

"Don't grieve for me, for now, I'm free. I'm following the path God has laid you see. I took his hand when I heard him call, I turned my back and left it all."

I looked up to Dr. Edwards and felt a little confused. I reread the first paragraph over in my head, but I was still confused.

"What a weird poem for a graduation announcement. I can't believe she would pick that." I said.

"This isn't her graduation announcement. Her mom picked the poem out. Why don't you read the whole poem?" He nodded.

"I could not stay another day, to laugh, to love, to work, to play. Tasks left undone must stay that way. I found that peace at the close of day. If my parting has left a void, then fill it with remembered joy. A friendship shared, a laugh, a kiss: oh yes these things I too will miss. Be not burdened with times of sorrow, I wish you the sunshine of tomorrow. My life's been full, I've savored much, good friends, good times, and a loved one's touch. Perhaps my time has been all to brief, don't lengthen it now with undue grief. Lift your hearts and peace to thee, God wanted me now: He set me free."

"What do you think of that?" He asked carefully after I read through the whole poem.

"I still think that's a weird poem to put on a graduation announcement, pretty though."

"What kind of poem is it?" He asked.

"It's more like a poem of someone who is leaving," I said trailing off into a whisper.

"Right, do you think it's a poem about someone that has left forever?" He asked.

"Yea, I guess so, it could be." I shrugged my shoulders.

"Look at the date on the front." He pointed to the front of the paper.

"Well, that's her birthday. And this is the date of…she won the championship game on that day." I said proudly.

"Yep, great. What else happened that day?" He asked.

"We were in a car accident," I answered.

"During the accident, you helped Emma out of the car. Is that right?"

"Yea, it's all kinda fuzzy but I remember pulling her away. She was telling me something… I can't remember it all, she wanted her mom, and she was really tired."

"Does that make you sad to think of the accident?"

Flashes of moments raced in my mind like little video clips and I started to feel sick to my stomach. The clips of memories flashing through my brain felt like electrical shocks and I didn't feel like talking anymore.

"I feel sick to my stomach," I said.

"That's normal." He said, "We can take a break and visit again tomorrow? How does that sound?"

"OK I guess, but do we need to talk about the accident again?" I asked through tears.

"Yes, we do. You will be OK though. Remembering, and knowing what happened will help you heal and move forward with your life."

That night was hell. Every time I fell asleep, I would jolt awake from remembering more of the accident. Sometimes, it wasn't the memory of the accident at all, I would just suddenly wake up from the pounding inside my chest. My heart felt like it could beat out of my rib cage, through my skin and out of my torso. Other times, I would wake up swearing that I could hear that song playing somewhere. I would be cold one minute and sweating the next; all the while bouncing back and forth between feeling fear, frustration, and sadness. Those moments in the dark, alone and in complete silence were the moments I missed Emma the most. I would close my eyes hoping that she would walk through the door, coming to see me when I needed her the most instead of random visits that were always interrupted.

Sometimes, I would have pain in my leg that would feel as if someone was stabbing me. I would wake up from shooting pains in my head and across my jaw that was so painful it made me want to bang my head on the wall. I felt alone and in some kind of torture chamber that my body and mind designed which was worse than if it were inflicted upon by some stranger. My mind and body were turning against me.

The next afternoon, my parents arrived and Dr. Edwards had us all join him in his office. One of my favorite nurses was also there, and she was sitting on the chaise lounge near the window. Two other chairs were brought in, and we all sat down in our self-delegated seats. The mood was light, my parents and Dr. Edwards talked about my dad's beehives and how impressive it was to Dr. Edwards that my dad is so knowledgeable on the topic. My dad offered him some honey for next time they visited, and he also offered it to Maryann who graciously accepted stating that she uses honey instead of sugar when baking.

"I wanted to have all of us here today to talk about the photos Rainy and I glanced through yesterday. Rainy, what day is it? He asked.

"Thursday, or wait. Wednesday? Yesterday was Thursday, or maybe it was Wednesday. I need a calendar."

"It's Wednesday. You're close, yesterday was Tuesday." He smiled.

"We were talking about a poem yesterday that you read out loud. We also looked at a date under Emma's picture and I asked what this date meant." He pointed to the folded paper with Emma's picture on the front.

"What does that date mean to you Rainy?" He added.

"It's Emma's birthday and the other date is the championship game as well as the accident." I yawned in between answering him.

"And the poem?" He asked.

"Weird that it's the poem her mom picked for her graduation announcements. Have you read it too?" I asked my parents.

"Yes, we sure have." My mom answered. "It is a beautiful poem."

"Rainy, you said that the poem was written to sound like someone was leaving forever. Do you remember saying that yesterday?"

"Yes, like going off to college maybe?"

"Yea, college…what other occasion do people leave forever?" He asked.

"When people die I guess."

"Yes, when people die. They don't come back, but we remember them don't we?"

I nodded my head and looked at my parents who wouldn't make eye contact with me, they kept looking at the floor or Dr. Edwards.

"Can you read the back of the paper for us?"

"Emma will be remembered for her love of basketball, her love for animals and her love for life. She will be missed by her parents, her friends, and the entire town. God Speed Emma."

I looked at my parents again who was crying and I shook my head no, still confused at what it all meant.

"What kind of occasion would someone write that about someone else?" He asked.

"Not really something on a graduation announcement. Is she getting married? That seems a little weird, I don't really know."

"What about when someone dies?" He looked at me to grab my attention and make eye contact with him.

"Oh, yea. That would make sense. The poem and all that." I said proudly.

Dr. Edwards didn't say anything and neither did nurse Maryann. My mom took hold of my hand and my dad pulled her over to his shoulder where she rested her head down. The room was completely silent and I couldn't tell what I was supposed to say or perhaps I missed a question. Dr. Edwards tilted his head to the side and continued to write on his yellow note pad while I looked at everyone, wondering what to say next.

"Did I miss a question?" I asked.

"No, you were asked why someone would write that, and we agreed that it would be appropriate words for someone who is having a funeral. You are holding Emma's funeral handout."

"No, that wouldn't make any sense because Emma isn't dead. Why would she have her photo on someone's announcement or whatever the hell this crap is?" I replied firmly.

"Because that isn't someone else's funeral announcement Rainy. That is Emma's, she died in the car accident."

I closed my eyes and a flood of emotions passed through every vein in my body. I felt like I ran into an electrical fence but unable to let go. A metallic taste washed through my mouth, and my ears were ringing. I could feel my face burning as my hands and feet turned ice-cold. I felt a cold, swift rush of air pass over my skin and raised the tiny hairs on end.

"Why would you say something like that? I feel guilty as it is. Am I supposed to feel more guilt?" I stuttered.

"Remember the promise I made to you a few weeks ago Rainy?" He asked.

"Yea," I whispered.

"What was the promise I made to you?"

"That you would never lie to me, and you will always tell me the truth," I said.

"So am I lying now?" He asked.

"Yes, I mean no, you're confused is all. Emma came to see me at the hospital, and she was fine." My voice was getting louder and higher the more I talked.

"You called her mom and wanted to speak with Emma, remember?"

I nodded.

"You asked to speak to Emma and her mom got really upset. Do you know why?" Dr. Edwards asked.

I didn't respond.

"Because she died in the car accident and you called her mom thinking she was alive and it upset her." He answered his own question.

"No." I snapped and glared directly into his eyes.

"Yes, I'm afraid it's the truth. Let's take a look at another picture." He said as he reached into the folder.

"No! And stop saying it that way! Its picture with an S not a T!" PIC-SURE! Not PIC-TURE!" I yelled.

"Neha, you need to calm down." My dad raised his voice.

"No dad, no! Emma is alive. I know. I was there!!!" I yelled as I pointed my finger repeatedly into my chest.

"Take a look at this photo. It's a copy of the news article, I know this is confusing Rainy, I know this is hard, but take a look and read it if you want." Dr. Edwards said calmly.

I refused to take the article from him, so he placed it on my lap. The headline read Fatal Accident Kills 1- Driver in Critical Condition. Below the headline was her name and the article described the accident. My name was not mentioned but the article repeated that she was the heart of the towns' people and when her service would be held. The more I read, the less I wanted to continue breathing.

I looked at my mom and dad, they know the truth, and I needed them to speak it to Dr. Edwards and Maryann.

"Neha, what doc is saying is true." My dad said choking back tears.

I wanted to run away but I couldn't with my cast. I wanted to scream but I couldn't find my voice. I was frozen and all I could do was repeat "no" over and over. I held my head in my hands and pulled at my hair, the pain was a distraction.

The nurse asked if I wanted help back to my room but at that point, all I wanted to do is call Emma.

"But, I just talked to her." I wept.

"You think you have, but you haven't kiddo." Dr. Edwards answered.

"I've seen her too!" I yelled.

"Same thing, you think you have but you haven't."

"So I'm lying?" I asked sarcastically.

"No, you're trying to cope. This is the only way your brain can process all trauma and pain along with all the other emotions pouring in at once. It's technically called disassociative disorder." He said.

"Please take me to my room. Please, I can't handle this. I can't do this. No, no, no, you're all wrong, please!" I begged.

"Maryann, why don't you bring her to her room and give her a little dose of Ambien. She really needs to sleep. We will talk more tomorrow." Dr. Edwards suggested.

As I stood up to grab my crutches, my mom squeezed my hand and I jerked it away. My dad told me he loved me, but I was so angry and hurt. I wanted to do was run away. Their voices trailed off behind me as I walked with my nurse through the doors of Dr. Edwards's office. I could hear my mom pleading to me, apologizing and telling me we would get through this and everything would be OK. *No, it will never be OK. I will never be OK again. No one will and it's my fault.*

I stayed at the Brain Integration Center for over a month and blended in with people who were diagnosed with OCD, bipolar disorder, depression, dementia, brain injuries, PTSD, and my favorite, paranoid schizophrenia. Not that there is anything funny about any of these people but it was amusing to watch them. During the day, after breakfast and before we were required to meet in a group, we wandered throughout the living area where there was a TV, a piano and several small tables to play cards on or any other board game a person can think of.

I grew fond of a girl named Rene. She was diagnosed with paranoid schizophrenia but most of the time, she was completely normal. We would talk about normal girl stuff and occasionally we would sit at a table and colored in coloring books. One day, she opened a coloring book where most of the pages had been colored in. She flipped through the pages quickly, almost frantically and became extremely agitated.

"Look, they are telling me something." She whispered.

"Who? Telling you what?" I asked.

"The others. Look, see this? This and this and this." She frantically flipped through page after page.

"Uhh, I don't see anything," I said.

"No, you can't. I am the only one who can. I am the negotiator between us and the others, they don't want to cause harm. I must remind everyone." She whispered again.

"Everyone? Hey, everyone!" She stood up, "I want to remind you all that the others do not want to cause any harm to us." Her voice increases.

"Oh my God, who moved the plant?" Another voice interjects.

That was Paul. He had OCD and was obsessed with a plant that sits on the table next to the couch. It needed it to be placed strategically and if it got moved, he fell apart. Every time he spoke, he had to tap his hand on his leg 3 times. He also pulled strands of hair out one at a time and laid them carefully on the table. He only did that when he was watching TV and I don't think he knew he was doing it.

"I'm thirteen weeks pregnant, do the others know I am pregnant?" A new voice said.

That was Brenda. When I was first admitted, she was preparing to give birth. It's no surprise that she thought she was thirteen weeks pregnant because days before that, she was seven months. She had been there the longest and the entire time, she thought she was pregnant. She reminded everyone, every minute of the day that she was expecting and would shout out random comments about the baby moving or the baby having hiccups.

"They mean no harm to us. They want to coexist in peace." Rene stated.

"Please stop dusting this area, the plant gets moved and it really needs to be left just like this." Paul would say to no one in particular as he would adjust the plant back to its rightful position.

Aaron was another patient in the center, but he didn't talk much. He was interesting to watch and most days I would watch him instead of watching TV. He was in the military and was sent there to deal with his PTSD. Aaron was much older than the rest of us and very protective. In his mind, he was protecting us from the enemy. He would crouch down holding an imaginary rifle keeping a lookout for potential intruders. He would run from one corner to another with stealth like maneuvers then stop and hold up his hand in a fist as if motioning the others to stop. He would put down his imaginary rifle and grab his imaginary binoculars then hold up 4 fingers as to warn the other soldiers of how many enemies were approaching. I was pretty sure he would throw an imaginary grenade now and then towards the nursing station but I can't be for certain. He would take cover behind one of the fake trees in the corner of the room covering his head in anticipation of the blast. At least that's what it seemed like to me. If a patient were called out of the common area by one of the nurses, he would stand guard until they came back. He would see them walking down the hall and motion to them to run as if he was rescuing them from the depths of hell. I particularly enjoyed watching him roll on the ground or crawl, all the while holding his rifle. Oddly enough, everyone ignored him and the longer I was there, the safer I felt knowing he was on the lookout.

Alice came in after me. She talked to people that none of us could see. I sat next to her one afternoon, but she freaked me out. She never talked directly to me except once when she mentioned that she knows I see people. In the process of her conversations with whoever she was talking to, she paused and looked directly at me as if she were as normal as a person can be. She stated that it's OK to see people, it means I can communicate with the other side. After she talked to me for a few minutes in a state of clarity, she went back to talking nonsense again and it reduced the value of her comment to me. I still couldn't shake it though. I actually went to the community library secretly looking for books on the topic, knowing full well that a mental hospital isn't going to let patients read books about seeing dead people.

Emma would come to me when I was sleeping and Dr. Edwards reminded me that this was OK, he said dreaming about someone who has passed away is just part of our mind processing information. I didn't tell him every encounter I had with Emma but I told him enough to be believed that I was getting better.

The other patients were the topic of the majority of my conversations with Dr. Edwards but I didn't tell him what Alice said to me about seeing dead people. I was well enough in my mental health to know that bringing this up might set me back in the eyes of Dr. Edwards. I found it fascinating that these people's minds were so broken. We talked a lot about my mind and how I was dealing with the realization of Emma being gone. I discovered that even though I wasn't seeing Emma as much, I needed to keep that to myself if I ever wanted to get discharged and go home. It was the last quarter of school and I missed the first 2 months. I knew I needed to get out of here, so I would graduate on time.

When we discussed the other people I saw; who I thought were my new friends, I learned that it was better to tell him that I recognized I was dreaming then too. If I disagreed and told him that I was really seeing them, even Emma, I don't think he would have understood. I didn't feel like I was seeing them as if they were alive, this I grew to understand a little more. I couldn't shake the feelings I got when I would see them though. The last time I saw Three was before I first got there. She or the others never came back. That gave me more questions, but I kept those to myself too. A person learns that talking about seeing dead people in a mental hospital won't get them anywhere fast.

I was getting better, I was accepting what happened to Emma as every day passed. When I would question certain things about the accident, Emma or my emotions, Dr. Edwards, would help me understand them. His words made sense to me, I trusted his words even though Emma seemed so real. I cried a lot, some days to myself and other days to Dr. Edwards. I missed Emma and the guilt I felt was almost too much to handle. I learned to cope using techniques that helped process the guilt and underwent other treatments that helped with my new reality. The last part of my healing would be how I reacted once I was out of my protective bubble of the mental hospital and back into the real world. My parents and Dr. Edwards had many conversations about me, but I wouldn't be there. The information my parents reported to him would be the guideline of that day's topic of conversation. We went through different scenarios that I might encounter after I left and how I could respond constructively. My parents felt that I would do better if I finished up high school from home and Dr. Edwards agreed and wrote a letter of recommendation to the board of education. Hearing the news that it was approved was a victory, knowing I didn't need to go back to school meant that I didn't have to face everyone.

After I was approved to be released from the Brain Center, I wanted to go home and stay home. I didn't want to see anyone or go into town for any reason what so ever. I was aware of their feelings towards me from what my parents would tell Dr. Edwards. He would talk to me about it and rehearse a plan not just for my reactions, but also what it meant. I knew I would be blamed for her death and didn't fault them for seeing that way because I too blamed myself.

The last week of my stay I went to get an x-ray of my leg to see how it was healing. I was able to come out of the cast and was given a boot to wear instead. I could put a little pressure on my foot but still needed crutches to keep from falling. It felt so freeing to have the cast off but I still had the weight of the world resting on my shoulders.

I had to undergo a series of tests and I met with Dr. Edwards every day for five days in a row. We concluded that I wasn't a suicide risk or at risk for other destructive actions. He would always tell me how proud he was of me, and I genuinely believed him but in the back of my head, I also knew I would never be the same. I would often respond to his praise in my mind thinking, *you're proud of me because I believe the fact Emma is dead and I killed her. If it wasn't for me, she would still be here.* That wasn't really the reason I would want someone to be proud of me over but I never said that out loud.

"Congratulations are in order young lady. You get to go home today." Dr. Edwards said.

I looked at my parents who were sitting on both sides of me, smiling. I felt like I should have been more excited, but I wasn't. In fact, I didn't really have any emotion at all and I wondered if that was normal. I questioned what kind of reaction would be appropriate and simply smiled in response.

"In three months, you will start to decrease your medication. You will do this very slowly and only under my supervision. You will still see me, but it will be at my office and not here."

"Oh, OK. That's a good idea, I would like to know how everyone else is doing." I said.

"Well, I might not be able to tell you much, but we can certainly talk about how you're doing and feeling. How do you feel about going home today?" He asked

"Good, I want to go home, but it's weird in a way."

"How is that weird?" He asked.

"I like the distraction of watching everyone here, besides they make me feel more normal."

"Rainy, that's not very nice." My mom interjected.

"No, that's OK." Dr. Edward raised his hand slightly, "She and I talk a lot about the others here and it's been healthy for her to realize that she isn't as broken as she once thought."

"Is there anything we need to keep an eye out for?" My dad asked.

"Well, we discussed a few things, but Rainy, I want you to be very aware of yourself at all times. I don't want you to distract yourself just to avoid feeling things."

This was a huge topic of conversation between Dr. Edwards and myself. We talked almost daily about staying inside the emotion and not outside of it. He warned me against creating a world of distraction to avoid feeling things I didn't want to feel. He always reminded me of how strong I was and I would get through anything as long as I let myself feel it. He saw that I was capable of checking out, and would use distractions to avoid what I was really feeling.

"I would like to go where they buried Emma," I said.

My parents didn't know what to say, and I was a little surprised at my forward statement.

"I feel like I need to say good-bye to her, I mean a real good-bye," I added.

"I think that is a great idea." Dr. Edwards said. "Mom, dad? I will be on stand-by if you need me. Rainy? I am the doc on call this week and through the weekend so if you feel emotions that you don't or can't process, I want a phone call." He looked at my parents.

"OK," I said. "But I think I will be OK, I have wanted to see her one last time. I mean, not see her, but you know… say good-bye."

I knew in order to go home, I had to be careful of the words I chose to use. Seeing Emma was a phrase I needed to avoid, it was considered a trigger for my parents to be on the lookout for. *I don't see Emma, I can see her in a dream, but I don't see her in my day to day life.* I would say these things to myself but I couldn't help but feel confused. I was taught that there was a difference in wanting or wishing to see Emma and actually seeing her. Dr. Edwards would remind me that wishing for her to be alive is normal and a part of grief, seeing her only meant that my brain was protecting me from emotions that I really needed to feel. I learned that I had to feel those emotions in order to stay sane which seemed so backward.

As we all walked towards the front of the building, I said good-bye to Maryann and gave her a hug. I thanked her for everything she did for me, and my parents thanked her too. I walked over to Rene where she was looking through coloring books and told her I was leaving.

"Just remember that the others are everywhere, but they are friendly." She said.

"OK, thanks for the reminder Rene, I will remember that."

Paul was watching TV and had an impressive collection of his hair neatly placed on a napkin. I wanted to say good-bye to him but it was exhausting to talk to him. It was such a production of tapping his leg and waiting for his words to come out in between counting and recounting. I just took notice of his plant sitting perfectly on the table next to him and smiled to myself.

Aaron was in position, he has been protecting me from the very beginning and I couldn't help to question that had I stayed there much longer, I would have eventually believed in what he was doing. I found relief that I noticed his behavior wasn't normal. I made eye contact with him and I said "thank you" but not with my voice, knowing that he was reading my lips. He took his two fingers to his eyes and then pointed the same two fingers back at me as if he were saying, "I see you, all clear."

On the day I left, Brenda was only 3 weeks pregnant. She had a miscarriage the week before and it was a difficult time for her. When

I discharged, she was back on top of the world, overjoyed with excitement from her little bundle of joy. I knew to say goodbye to her would result in a long conversation of how her pregnancy was going, and I just wanted to leave, but she was standing near the door so avoiding her wouldn't happen.

"Hello." She shook my parent's hands. "So nice to meet you both. I am 7 weeks pregnant, can you believe it?" She asked with excitement.

My parents didn't know what to say, and so I just stepped in between them and her and told her how happy I was for her. I took notice that just a few hours before that, she was only three weeks pregnant and I couldn't help but feel sorry for her. She took my hand and placed it on her stomach and told me to feel the baby.

"It's moving. Can you feel it?" She asked.

"You better not move my plant," Paul said in between counting and tapping. "Now look, my hair pile fell all over."

I hugged Brenda, I didn't want to feed into her fantasy or get caught talking with her because she would never stop. My dad held the door open as we shuffled out, but not before chaos erupted behind me. Paul was completely unhinged over his hair pile and Aaron launched a grenade at "the others" which angered Rene, their protector. On and on it went…

The rain was coming in a mist which then beaded on my window. I watched the drops as they raced each other to the bottom of the window and the focus it took to do that made me dizzy. I dozed off and on until we finally made the four-hour drive back to the dreaded town that knows me as the girl who killed Emma. The cemetery was covered with brown grass and bare trees yet to make spring and I could only imagine what it looked like in the summer.

Several people were scattered throughout the cemetery and staring in our direction and I couldn't help to notice how different they look compared to my mom and dad, and everyone else I knew. They seemed almost opaque or see-through but I couldn't focus on them or anything else for that matter. Since the accident, my focus and ability to concentrate had obviously changed.

"I'm glad to see that no one is here." My dad said.

I wanted to question what he meant by that but I decided the logical reason was that he was relieved Emma's mom wasn't there, I was too.

My dad pulled off the little paved drive that was not much bigger than a sidewalk. He parked off to the side far enough that another car could pass. My mom handed me my crutches and I hobbled next to my parents until I saw the mound of unsettled earth ahead of me. The dirt that covered Emma had not made its way flat and it took me off guard. Time seemed to stand still for so long and seeing the mound of dirt, knowing Emma was underneath it made it clear that time didn't stop; it just slowed down. I started to cry, something I did a lot of those days but I remembered Dr. Edwards telling me to stay with it and not avoid the emotions. There wasn't a headstone yet, my mom said they can take a few months to have made but fresh flowers lined the entire mound. Someone, probably Emma's family, were bringing flowers on a regular basis. It was beautiful, the color of all the flowers against the vast brown grass and bare trees brought a little life to such a dreary looking place. Sunflowers were her favorite and my mom made sure to stop, so I could bring something that didn't even come close to what I really wanted to bring. I wanted to bring her back to life and let me lay where she is instead. No one placed any sunflowers, it was all roses and lilies and other fancy flowers. Maybe I was the only one who knew her love for sunflowers.

"She told me one time that if two different men asked to marry her, and she loved them equally but one was holding red roses and the other had sunflowers, she would marry the man who had the sunflowers."

I felt remorse as I looked at all the flowers laying across her and not one was a sunflower. My mom held my crutches as I laid them over her, placing them as perfect as I could.

"I'm so sorry Emma. I am so sorry. I'm sorry. Why did this happen? I wish it was me. It should have been me. You deserve this life, not me."

"Neha, you can't think like that." My dad whispered.

"Dad, it really should have been me."

"If it were you, there would only be a different kind of pain and suffering, different people suffering and Emma would be standing here feeling the same way that you are right now. Would you want her to feel this way?"

He was right, I wouldn't wish that feeling on my worst enemy. My dad unfolded a piece of paper and walked between my mom and me, and said he wanted to offer a Native American poem that the elders of the tribe would tell to the survivors of the fallen.

"I give you one thought to keep, I am with you still- I do not sleep. I am a thousand winds that blow, I am the diamond glints on snow. I am the sunlight on ripened grain, I am the gentle autumn rain. When you awaken in the morning hush, I am the swift uplifting rush of quiet birds in circled flight. I am the soft stars that shine at night. Do not think of me as gone, I am with you still, in each new dawn."

As he handed me the paper, I looked up and saw Emma's mom walking toward us. She was moving quickly, and my dad quietly told us to stand still and let him do the talking. He walked toward her, but she went around him and directly over to me. My mom tried to speak through her broken voice.

"I am so sorry this had to happen," my mom whispered.

"Sorry? You're sorry? My Emma is dead and all you can say is you're sorry? No! I am the one that is sorry! You!" She pointed at me, "This should have been you! All mangled up and disfigured! I couldn't even tell it was her because of you! They had to bury my baby with her arms and legs broke, her face was disfigured! You're nothing! No! You're a murderer! Emma was all we had and you killed her!"

"Please," my dad said. "We are so sorry-"

"Go to hell!" She interrupted and pointed at me.

She started throwing all the sunflowers at me that I put down and yelled, screamed at me to leave. She threw flowers at me, but I just let her. I could hardly make out what she was saying half the time, but what I could understand were the harshest words I've ever heard spoken.

My dad tried to pull me away but I told him no. I knew it was what she needed to do and I could handle it. If I couldn't, I knew who would help me through it. I stood there while flowers and chunks of dirt were thrown at me, and to my face. If she missed, she picked it back up and threw it again. My mom was pleading with her to stop, and I was pleading with my mom to back away. Once there was nothing left to throw, she came toward me, and I took a hobble backward.

"Oh, I won't hurt you, because you're the killer." She snarled. "Maybe I should hurt you so you can kill me too. Do you hear me? You have killed my baby. I should go on a drive with you and you can kill me too. Do you hear me?" She continued, not making sense.

"I hate you, you should have never come here! You don't belong here! I don't ever want to see you here again! You're a piece of shit! I hope you go to hell." She continued.

"That's enough!" My dad yelled and stepped in between her and me, but repeated it again. "That's enough! Get her to the van."

"GO!" He yelled again.

"You have every right to feel hurt and pain, we are too, and we are so very sorry for what happened to Emma and to your family. We will never forget her or what this has done but you do not get to speak that way to my daughter or anyone else."

"You have a daughter, we have nothing! You get to take your daughter home, we will never see ours again!" She screamed hysterically.

"We don't doubt your pain, we feel it too. We are deeply sorry for what happened. There are so many other ways to handle this, attacking my daughter was unnecessary."

My dad got in the van, and we took off, leaving her mom standing there alone. I felt so bad, so guilty and I couldn't stop crying. My leg hurt, my head hurt and my heart was completely shattered. As I turned my head to take one last look, I saw Emma standing next to her mom.

"STOP!" I yelled.

"Dad, stop! Please!" I yelled again.

"What? God, Neha! You scared me!" My dad's voice was breathless.

He slammed on the breaks, and they both looked back at me. I watched Emma and her mom standing next to each other, and they looked so different from one another. Emma looked like all the other people that were standing around when we first drove up. Her mom was just like me, my parents but Emma looked like she did when I was in the hospital. It occurred to me that I was seeing Emma and all the other's standing throughout the cemetery but no one else could. I understood how unbelievable it was and how insane I would have sounded had I said anything. Thoughts of the movie The Sixth Sense with the classic one-liner, "I see dead people" along with Alice at the Center who told me she knew I could see people that no one else could, were racing around the reason section of my brain; the part of the brain that was told what was real and what was not. *People don't see dead people and if they say they can, most likely they are not right in their head.*

I couldn't say I knew for certain what happens when people cross to the other side and I never thought about it until then, but I was certain that nobody could actually see them. We all share ghost stories growing up, the rare and unusual events that can most likely be explained through other logic. We would ask each other if we believed in ghosts and someone would always give their personal encounter, but I was always the one explaining that it was most likely the wind or a loose hinge. I didn't believe in ghosts even though I believed that our spirit can transform or live past our physical bodies. It's the native belief but more than that, it's what I truly believed too.

At that moment, I couldn't tell what was real or if I might be mentally unstable.

My brain was processing information faster than it had in a long time, and I was aware that what I said next would be the deciding factor whether I went home or back to the Mental Hospital. My parents were both looking back at me waiting for me to reassure them that I was OK.

"I am never going to drive another person in my car for the rest of my life. This I promise."

Chapter 13

I can't get myself up fast enough. I run downstream and manage to cross back over the creek, stumbling my way through the water and frantically looking for the small path that leads me the hell out of here. All I want to do is get back to the house where I can control something, even if it's just the light switch.

Each step I take I can hear Dr. Edwards voice telling me that I was just dreaming. *Wake up…stay in the moment. Breathe…this isn't reality.*

I get to Ellie's house and run in through the broken screen door which completely tears it from the last hinge that was keeping it attached to the frame of the door. I flip the light on to the living area which blinds me for a moment. As my eyes adjust, my mind races back and forth from what I just saw and what to do next. *Think.* I look down and notice that my feet and legs are full of mud. *This is where Ellie goes every day.* I have so many questions, but I don't know whether to stay and ask them or run.

My back is facing away from the door when Ellie comes in and I don't want to turn around and look at her.

"I didn't know this would scare you so much," she said out of breath.

I spin around to find her standing in the door and I stare at her in disbelief. Her silky gray hair is falling across her face and her white nightgown hangs off her small bony frame, with one shoulder exposed. The bottom of her nightgown is weighed down by the heavy mud it picked up along the way. She looks so fragile and I can't feel any anger, I suppose I am just shocked. There are so many things out-of-place and I just need to get some answers.

Behind Ellie stands a young, handsome man and as she steps to the side, I can tell he isn't one of us. He is iridescent, like thin fabric in that you can almost see through him. He looks at me with a peaceful smile but the moment doesn't last. I feel a cold rush of air blow through my hair taking my breath away as he disappears. I have been smart for all these years not to discuss my occasional and random visions; if I can call it that. I like to think their hallucinations, a side effect from a head injury that still gets the best of me all these years later. This was different, what I just saw in the creek and what I saw standing behind Ellie were totally different because one was real, the other isn't.

The confidence in my ability to trust myself is slipping out from underneath me. Logic, reasoning, the unknown, the metaphysical realm of existence that sane people don't usually believe in, are all swirling together.

"Scare me? God Ellie. Please tell me what I just saw isn't real. Actually no, don't. Jesus Ellie! Did…who…what the actual hell? I can't even think straight!" I said raising my voice.

"Maybe I should have told you before I took you out there. I guess I thought Patrick may have told you yesterday."

If I hadn't been so wrapped up in his feelings for me maybe I would have pried further into his comments. I would have asked the questions my intuition was telling me to ask and furthermore, I should have made Ellie talk long before this. I knew something wasn't right. Now I am too invested in this to simply walk away.

"Ellie, if Patrick had told me yesterday what you have out there in the woods, I wouldn't have just let it go without saying something."

She doesn't respond, her gray eyes fill with tears as she sits down. I quickly grab the sheet from my bed and lay it across the couch, so I don't get mud all over it. I sit down knowing I'm not going back to sleep and Ellie is finally going to share her story.

"Ellie, talk to me. That is a human skeleton in the creek. Who is that?" I ask as I point toward the direction of the creek.

"My husband," she said as she wipes tears off her face.

"I married a good man that I loved more than life. We married when he was sixteen, and I was only fourteen. We were so young but back then, marriage at that age was normal. He was the only man I have ever kissed. And oh- he loved me. We were crazy for one another."

She stops for a moment and smiles to herself. She closes her eyes and I can tell she is going back in time, remembering everything about him.

"We loved to dance. Maxwell was a wonderful dancer. He was so strong and so full of life. He made me feel weightless when we would dance together. Life was perfect. Sometimes when I am almost asleep, I can feel him right next to me. It's a love so unlike anything I can explain. It's a love that, even though he is gone, I can still feel. I still smell him, in the rain. I feel him when the wind blows through my hair. That's him, touching me. And a butterfly that flies near me in the spring, that's him dancing with me. I know this with my heart. He is still taking care of me after all these years. He brought you to me. I believe that."

"I had no idea Ellie, I wish I knew this," I said softly.

She continues telling her story, she is ready to talk and I can tell that she just needs me to listen to her.

"We moved up here 40 years ago. Maxwell did some accounting in town, and he was a volunteer fire firefighter. Two very different jobs but he was good at both. That's how I know Patrick's dad. Max and his dad were very close and when he fell sick, he made Max a promise to always be around for me.

Thirteen years ago the doctors told him he had prostate cancer and unfortunately, it spread into his lymph system. They said with surgery and chemotherapy he might have a fighting chance but couldn't make any promises of his quality of life.

The day we discovered he had cancer, the drive home was the longest drive I have even been on. I drove him home that day which didn't happen too often. Not one word was spoken. He sat straight up in the seat and placed both hands in his lap, and stared out the window.

I was so sad for him but what does someone say to another when they have just been told that death was near?"

She pauses for a moment and I still feel like I need to stay quiet. She doesn't want her question answered and this is something I can understand more than most. I can tell the pauses she takes throughout her story are allowing the feelings from it to catch up to her. The action of giving is allowing yourself space and time to feel something between words is the exact action I need to see. After all this time, and processing my own pain and emotions, I could never understand what it meant to let myself feel it all. I didn't realize it could be as simple as remembering, pausing to experience it again and then moving on to the next memory. In the process of her doing this, she can remember the good times as well. She is able to recollect all the memories with grace and emotions because she is bringing it all together in one beautifully bound book. I can see where I didn't give myself this same right. When I was told Emma died, my mind broke and I created a world that left out the bad memories. The respected way to remember someone is to remember the good with the bad. Doing it any other way is an injustice to them and the memories shared together.

"After we got home, he didn't come inside with me, but instead, took a walk down to the creek. We usually did that walk together, but I knew he needed to be alone. After about an hour, he came in and informed me that he didn't want the chemo or surgery and I never questioned him or tried to convince him otherwise."

Ellie stands up in which was random considering the moment and tells me to go rinse off the mud and that she also wants to change into dry, clean clothing. I take the fastest shower of my life feeling frustrated at this brief intermission.

I curl myself up in a quilt on the couch briefly noticing the water dripping from my hair and down my back. Ellie sits down in her chair with her blanket and takes a moment to gather her thoughts. The sun is only a few hours away but the chill in the mountain air and the darkness of the morning sky still makes it feel like midnight.

"This is a photo of my Max. Those are my children. That on the right is Jacob and the little girl is Holly. This is the only photo I have of all of us together."

"Why? I mean, just this photo? Nothing else?" I ask as I take the photo from her.

"When the kids found out that Max had cancer, they were angry that I didn't fight his decision of not wanting chemo and surgery. They tried to be the voice of reason and it only made Max more frustrated."

She didn't answer my question but I figure it is an answer from another story. She also just keeps talking, so I can't ask more questions even if I want too.

"He spent the first 3 months after his diagnosis tiding up his life. I knew what he was doing but I never said one word about it. Our entire marriage, Max took care of all the financial business, so he was getting it all in order for me. He fixed things all around the house and worked quietly and diligently for months.

Every morning that he woke up was a relief to both of us. I couldn't possibly imagine what life would be like without him, in fact, we never spent one night away from each other since we were married.

His pain worsened over the months so the doctors gave him morphine which made him sleep all the time. The doctors put us in contact with an agency that cares for the dying, and they agreed to make home visits every other day as more of a palliative care program. Max was adamant that the kids not know how bad off he had become. In the beginning, when they were so angry with me for not insisting he fight it, he decided to tell them he was going to do the chemo and radiation. He even told them he had surgery. This was at the beginning of his diagnosis so when they came to visit, he appeared healthy and strong like he was beating it. They believed he was going to be OK, Max told them to not worry about coming up all the time. He insisted life was moving forward, and they came around less and less with his reassurance. Lying to your own children is a difficult thing to do. They didn't see or understand that it was his life and his body, they only saw him as their dad, and their need for him. We both thought it was for the best.

As the months carried on, he was getting weaker and cancer had taken over. The last time the kids came to visit, it was difficult for him to hide the fact that he wasn't as well as he led them to believe. But he got dressed and sat on the chair as the kids visited. He told them he started a healthy cancer diet where he has lost some weight and lied about how he was able to get around pretty well. He told them he was outside the day before and pointed to the pile of leaves outside the window. Evan, Patrick's dad had come to help around the place and Max asked him not to bag the leaves but to just leave them in the pile. After Max pointed out the piles to the kids, I understood why he told Evan to leave them. The kids told Max that he looked a little weak, and he explained that he was tired from working so hard the day before, and he was feeling fine. The kids left happy, knowing their dad was doing so well and Max felt better knowing he eased any worry they might have. Winter set in and the kids didn't come up this way when the weather was bad so this was the last time they saw their dad.

Three weeks went by and Max slept a lot. Some days, he didn't get up and others he would join me in watching the evening news. I ate with him for every meal even if he didn't feel like eating and when he did, many times I had to feed him because he would be so weak. He floated in between our world and his. Some days he felt distant and far away and others, he was more observant. I would lay next to him every moment I could, I just wanted to spend every second we had left together right next to his side. Sometimes I would just look at him and cry softly while he slept. I wanted to remember every line on his face, every crook in his hands and every expression he made. He talked less and less and his eyes would remain closed even if he was awake. Now and then, a tear would fall down the side of his face, and he winced in pain. Sometimes I would sit on the edge of the bed and catch the tears. It's silly I know, a little dramatic maybe but it meant something to me.

One night, as I was resting my head across his chest, his hand came up and touched my back. It was the first time he had reached out to me or touched me in a long time. I asked him if he was in pain even though I knew he was. He nodded to me that yes, he was. A tear rolled down his cheek and up to this point, he never complained of his pain, so I knew it had to be getting pretty bad. He could barely talk, but he didn't have to. I could see his words in his eyes. He looked at me in the purest form of helplessness and surrender. I will never forget that conversation.

"Eloise," he whispered to me.

"The pain?" I asked him, "Do you need more pain medication?"

As he nodded, his head fell heavily on the pillow. "Please, all of it, help me go, Ellie, it's time." His voice faded but I couldn't speak.

"I didn't," he paused, "do the treatments because I didn't want to suffer," he paused again, "I...don't want to suffer...now." He could barely get that last word out of his mouth.

Ellie continues.

"Talking was labored and I could tell he didn't want to say anymore. I knew what he wanted me to do even though we only talked about it once. He asked if I would be strong enough to help him when he felt ready. At the time, I didn't think it would be hard to do, but sitting next to him, knowing that moment had come, brought so much grief."

Ellie is crying, her eyes red around the edges as tears slid underneath her eyelids and down her cheeks. Her voice makes small sounds that can only be made when someone's heart is feeling the very person that they lived for, the kind of love they had for one another was simultaneous and all at once, all the time. They had the kind of love that never leaves when times get hard.

"How do you say good-bye to someone you know you will never see again? Not in this life anyway." Ellie said looking at me through eyes filled with tears.

I know I don't need to answer her, but my heart is breaking. Just as easily as she asked this question, I can easily ask how or what I am supposed to say or react. I just want to make her sadness go away but at the same time, through her story, she is able to feel him once more; or maybe he never left. She continues talking and I find comfort in her voice.

"At the time, I didn't feel like I said all I wanted to say to him. I was so concerned about how he was feeling that I never started to say good-bye. I had so many things to say but nothing could express how much I loved him or how much I was going to miss him. I wanted to talk about memories and feelings, the kids and our life together, but he was past that. That's what he was doing all that time and I knew my time had run out.

I told him I loved him. I touched his heart and expressed just how much I was going to miss him. I told him I would be OK, I didn't want him to feel bad for leaving me either. I told him we did a good job of raising our children and I loved every moment of it. I made sure he knew he was leaving a legacy behind and memories to last a lifetime.

I thanked him for loving me for as far back as I could remember, and he squeezed my hand. He could hear every word I said and at that moment, I was glad I didn't say it any sooner. As he listened to me, he would smile a little as I shared little moments that he and I only knew about.

My good-bye to him was interrupted when he let out a painful moan. I knew he needed me to give him the morphine. This was his plan all along. He never took a full dose and some days, he didn't take any morphine at all. I knew why even though it wasn't talked about. The nurses kept a close eye on the morphine so Max would transfer his doses from the bottle it came into another jar and hid it. They assumed he was taking it regularly and never questioned it. All along he was looking out for me, knowing that assisted suicide might get me in trouble.

I grabbed the bottle on his nightstand and reached for the jar he hid under the bed and poured it all together. I gave him dropper after dropper of morphine under his tongue letting him swallow a little after each drop. I was scared and my hands were shaking but I didn't stop until it was all gone. By the time I gave him the last of it, he was already having a hard time swallowing.

Max still managed to thank me, and I felt at ease watching the look of peace fall upon his face. I crawled into bed next to him and laid my head across his chest and listened to his breathing, I just wanted to hear his heart the same way I could feel it for all those years. He mumbled I love you, slowly and deliberately and I told him I loved him too. The last words he heard me say were, "it's been a beautiful life, Max."

Ellie stopped talking for a brief moment and repeated in a whisper, "It's been a beautiful life," to herself.

"I laid my head on his chest in silence, I was done talking and I didn't want him to try either. I could hear his heart beating and the sound was comforting and I knew at that moment the reason I didn't feel like talking anymore. I just wanted to listen to his heart. Time went so slowly and quietly. I laid with him like this for what seemed like hours, it was so quiet. The clock in the kitchen was the only sound I heard and even then, it seemed to stop from time to time.

Max's breathing shortened and become shallow. I could tell that he was no longer in my world. Even during the previous weeks when he seemed in between this world and the world we know nothing about, I always knew when he was there and not here. I could feel it physically as well as deep in my heart. In the last few hours of his life, that presence seemed to grow into a ball of light that had an energy source attached to it. It was almost a low vibration that was so comforting."

As soon as Ellie described what she felt and the way she articulated the words made me lose my breath. All these years of trying to understand the same feelings as she just effortlessly described, gave me hope in every sense of the word. In this very second, during the desperate inhale needed to catch the breath that leaped out of my chest just seconds ago is, is the same second I realized I wasn't alone. Ellie might be the one person in my life that can actually understand the complex questions I ask myself too often. What she described in the presence of Max as he was dying is the same thing feeling I have felt on and off for years. Sadly, I was stuck between believing in it and denying it because it felt so unstable.

"I kept my head on his chest, listening to the beating of his heart. Then, without warning, Max whispered something that I will never forget, "I'm going to miss her, my Ellie."

"He wasn't saying this to me Rainy." She said as she looked at me. "Even as he crossed over, I was the first thing he thought of and this gave me more comfort than anyone would ever imagine."

I nod my head as a few tears wander down my cheek as she continues.

"I kept my head down on his chest, listening passionately to the rhythm of his heart which was becoming weaker until eventually, I heard nothing. I sat up and smoothed the wrinkles on his nightshirt thinking that it was keeping me from hearing his heart. I listened again and nothing. I looked at his face and found all the years that rested in the lines of his skin were gone. He looked so peaceful but more than anything, I knew his pain was gone. He stopped breathing long before I noticed and it was then that Max, the love of my life and everything he was or ever will be had gone too."

Ellie stops talking but keeps her eyes closed. Hearing her talk about Max with so much love in her heart reminds me that love hurts but to know love; to really understand it, we must also feel the hurt that comes with it.

The longer Ellie sits in silence, the more certain I am that she is done talking. She still hasn't explained why Max's skeletal remains are still in the creek but if I am being honest with myself, I need a break.

I have so many emotions that are racing through every nerve pathway inside my head about my own experience with death. I ended Emma's life in the form of an accident. Ellie, on the other hand, ended life as an act of mercy. The only question I can think to ask is why I feel suddenly feel that someone understands me and what I have gone through but yet, the situation of Ellie's experiences are so much different from mine.

Not only do I find myself contemplating the differences between our experiences of death, I question morality and right versus wrong. One can argue that a person doesn't have that much control over another person's life because we live our life from a script that was already written, perhaps written by ourselves, so we can learn the lessons we missed from the life before.

Maybe we get one shot at life and when we die, we face a whole set of judgments and from those judgments is the reason heaven and hell were created. I can't find peace in any of that. For me, death never felt that far away. Since the accident, death, grieving, guilt, remorse, sorrow, and being on the edge of insanity has always been a shadow that follows me. Even though I am weighed down with questions that I can't even put into words, I have a feeling of weightlessness that has seemingly replaced those feelings in a matter of minutes. I stepped over the border of Kansas into the Land of Oz and now I can see that I have lived so many years inside a world without color.

My mind wanders back to a time when I first questioned all this and I can't help but notice the ironic nature of the whole thing. Had I just followed that path even just a little, maybe my life could have been different, maybe instead of running away from it, I could have lived it.

All I can do is make what life I have left mean something that is solid and stable. If this means letting go of my need to have a definition that dictates who I am; sane or insane or constantly wavering and denying aspects of myself, then I need to find that strength. If I don't, my life will continue down this meaningless road that leads too nowhere. I can't keep running away hoping that I will leave my past somewhere along the way.

PAST

I decided to go to a metaphysical fair one weekend, it was my first metaphysical fair but not new to the metaphysical world. After I spent time in the Mental Hospital and before meeting Zac I searched books on several topics regarding life after death and people who have died but came back to life. I was looking for anyone out there that might know why I saw Emma appear out of nowhere and offer an explanation for it other than a head injury, coma, delusional disorders, and PTSD. I was on different medications for the first six months after coming home, and I used this process to keep me company through the emotions I went through as I was getting off them. I didn't tell anyone or ask someone at the library for these books either. Even though I would go to a library in the next town over, I still didn't risk it. I knew if my parents found out that I was reading books about this topic, I would be sent back to Dr. Edwards.

There was a woman at the fair who was a self-proclaimed guru on the 6th sense. I was curious but couldn't get the nerve to speak directly to her. She was talking to someone who was standing at her section but their conversation fascinated me. I didn't want to eavesdrop but found myself gathering information, so I could hear what she was saying. Her brochure was laying on the table, so I took it upon myself to flip through it, half reading it and half listening to their conversation. The first comment on her brochure read, "You're not crazy."

As I continued skimming through the information, I decided I was interested enough to approach her. Maybe she would explain why I see what I do and reassure me that I wasn't delusional.

I approached the lady who was finishing up her conversation and smiled, holding up her brochure as to state my reasoning for being there. She directed me to sit at a table that was behind a set of room dividers. She had a pile of books sitting on a small bookcase randomly placed in no specific order. As we both sat down, I wanted to make sure she knew that I just had a few questions and not there to pay her for whatever it is she gets paid to do.

"I don't take money. I never have, it's a disgrace to the meaning of the work." She said.

"Oh, OK that's good then. I just have a few questions." I said. "I just don't know what those questions are. Does that make any sense?"

"Absolutely." She smiled, "why don't you tell me your story first, then the questions will follow."

"This is a little different I think," I said, embarrassed in what I haven't even shared yet.

"You're in the right place for different, whatever different means. If someone can define normal, then we might be able to define different. Anyway, it's all based on personal definition really."

I explained the accident, Emma and that I still see her in a unique kind of way. I explained that I often saw her in my sleep, sometimes I would see her while I was awake. I shared my time in the hospital and my brief encounter with Three and the other two that I only saw a handful of times. I admitted my breakdown, how I ended up in the Brain Integration Center and the denial about Emma dying. I described that the people I saw were not normal everyday people but more see-through or even specks of light that molded together to form a person.

The more I talked, the easier it was to format the questions I had. She was easy to talk to just like Dr. Edwards was, but she didn't write everything I said on a yellow note pad. Her facial expressions didn't contradict her vocal reactions which helped me get past the oddity of the whole thing. I might not be normal, she might not be normal but if there's a bunch of non-normal people all in the same room, we automatically morph into normalcy in which I subconsciously found comfort in.

"Why are they so random?" I asked her. "The people I see or hear are unexpected and I just sound so crazy. At the cemetery, I saw all kinds of people, just staring at me. I only see them for a brief second, sometimes they notice me, and sometimes they don't. Other times, I will see them for days." I finish.

"This must be the first time you have spoken about this." She stated as I nodded my head.

"I don't think you sound crazy." She said.

"I'm sure if I spoke to my parents about this, they might understand. They have a very deep respect and understanding of the Native culture and beliefs but I don't know if that culture went around seeing this kind of thing. Plus, my credibility has a shadow over it."

She picked up a book that has a photo of a Native American woman standing with a crow on her shoulders. The Healer, the Wise One, the Receiver- Tales from Tribal Elders.

"I almost didn't bring this book today. It happened to fall at my feet when I was gathering other books to bring and now I know why. I own a book store, a metaphysical book store. This is a good read for those who believe in the native way or simply want to learn the beliefs or spirituality but my favorite part of this book are the stories that have been told for many centuries, passed down and shared within tribal communities." She said as she handed me the book.

"This looks like a book I would love. Will it give me insight into the difference between sane and insane?" I asked.

"Probably not, most books you read on that topic are written from a physiological view and this is why you're questioning it in the first place. Long ago, psychology wasn't a thing. People didn't question the mental stability of a person, especially when they claim to see an event or a person. It was considered a vision, a gift and respected as such. It would be shared to the tribe or the people, perhaps it was a premonition or warning but either way, it was believed. This sort of topic has been written about dating back to the biblical era, Greek mythology, Vikings and so on. Take the story of Noah in the bible. God asked him to create an arc and bring two of every species into the arc because a great rain would destroy all the evil that spread. Noah was seen as a crazy person to so many people and very few believed him or understood what he was doing. It's not only a story of faith but also our mental capacity and what we choose to believe."

"So maybe I'm not delusional," I said, more as a statement than a question.

"The fact that you are even asking that question is a pretty good indication that you're not. Think of it this way, most crazy people don't go around asking if they are crazy. Right?" She smiled.

I smiled back but her comment stuck to me like an arrow. I repeated it back to myself because I didn't want to forget it. I also didn't want to lose track of what she was explaining after that, so I shuffled my attention to her words, wishing I had the ability to pause her.

"The scientific world has tried for many decades to explain a part of the human condition that can't always be explained. We can replace the heart, the kidneys, but we can't understand the soul or the spirit. Even though we have doctors who study the brain, they can't explain why we dream, what those dreams mean or even what we see in our awakened state. There's a lot of speculations but no science to prove a theory. When a group of people can't understand something, they will spin it into something they can because people need answers. Even those who believe in God will question why something happened and sometimes, an event or tragedy will weaken their faith completely. In reality, it's not up to us to question something that might or might not have happened. What we are meant to do is make something from it."

"But what about those people who are truly suffering from a mental illness, like multiple personality disorders or delusions? How does another person determine whether those people have a mental illness or if they are really seeing or believing in what they do?" I asked.

"I think it depends on their actions, who they are seeing or believing, how they manage life, what they accept and even the medications they take. There are so many dynamics to that. I'm almost certain you can tell the difference, the same way we know when someone is lying. The man I was talking to when you walked up was clearly being untruthful in what he claimed to be but you, I can tell. There's a difference and I can feel it."

She turned and looked for other books while I tried to let the whole conversation sink in, visualizing a pause button I wish I could have pressed. I think back to the patients at the mental hospital and understand the difference between myself and them. I think Dr. Edwards saw that too. I could also understand how a truly sane person would question their mental health while those who suffer might not. Reality versus perception are both real to anyone who experiences the event but the only difference is whether the person has the ability to question its validity.

"Sometimes, when we don't understand something we dig at it until we do. Then we try to fix it into something that is explainable or logical. It has become human nature, we discover a problem, over analyze it then put it back to together in a way we can understand it. It's a very shallow approach, and frankly an injustice to the complexity of who we are as human beings." She said while offering another book.

"What am I supposed to do when these people just randomly pop out of nowhere? I can't tell anyone because they would immediately put me on medication and send me back to the mental hospital." I said.

She continued, "Why do you need to tell someone? This is between you and those who choose you to see them. Have you ever talked to them? Perhaps ask them if they need help? Sometimes, people get stuck and can't cross over because of unfinished business, and they see people like you as a portal to those they need to communicate with. You are not the only one in the world who claims they can see or feel a presence that is bigger than they are. Like any new relationship, you will find out how to manage them as you go. The book I handed you will also explain what to do and maybe even why."

As the months went by, I read the books that she gave me, but in the privacy of my bedroom. Many theories seemed far-fetched and kooky but I decided to keep an open mind to the fact that the human condition is too complex to fully understand. I could comprehend the fact that there's a part of who we are as human beings that can't be discovered until death, and maybe even that theory was wishful thinking. I even wondered that perhaps the world between life and death is as simple as light or energy. I read about the different vibrations and gave thought to the idea that vibration was all we were. In conclusion to all the books I read, I felt that it could all be possible, but impossible to find the truth behind the complexity of life and death.

I dug deep into the world of all things metaphysical looking for answers, but nothing healed the pain and guilt. I became more knowledgeable in the idealism of enlightenment, but I was far from living it.

Enlightenment or even attaining the smallest amount of understanding as to the complexity of who we are in relation to space and time was very hard work. Especially after so many people told me that what I saw or felt was not real. It was real enough to have me admitted into a mental hospital and it was also real enough that I had to hide it. I didn't believe I had the capacity to do what it would've taken to fully understand, accept and work towards my higher self.

Instead, I discovered the more distracted I made myself to be, the less pain I was in. The more I disconnected from myself, the less pain and guilt I had to face. I went with logic in that somehow because of my brain injury, my optic nerves would go haywire causing me to see things that weren't real.

I became someone completely different but in order to do that, I needed to create chaos. Each distraction built another stepping stone which took me further away from who I was and what I did. I hoped those stepping stones would take me far away.

Chapter 14

The entire day following the conversation I had with Ellie is spent doing nothing. I manage to take a nap but doing much more than this feels impossible. I am lucky to have this time because the bird wakes me up every few hours to feed. Emotional exhaustion can be just as draining on the body as doing something that is actually physical. I feel comfort in allowing myself to do absolutely nothing and stay stuck inside my head.

This is the first time since the accident that I have been able to do this and oddly enough, I feel proud of it. This is what Dr. Edwards told me to do so long ago and I feel sorrow towards all the time I lost in creating chaos instead.

I admire Ellie in so many ways even though I still have so many questions. I decide it's easier to have questions that I don't ask than it is to have questions that won't be answered. I reflect on what it must have been like for Ellie and the magnitude of what she did. Her emotional strength inspires me, but not because she was strong enough to do what she did, it's the fact that she had the strength to feel the emotions that came with it.

Trust is earned but to trust in ourselves is when we master the art. I am not a trusting person and in order to protect myself, I've built a wall. Living inside the wall makes it impossible for anything to come through. I have a small little world that I can control and I never do anything that will produce consequences that aren't predictable and manageable. The unfortunate fact is the wall I built to protect myself is the same wall that keeps anything beautiful from coming in. Trusting myself means living in the open, unbound by walls because I will understand that whatever happens to me, I can handle. Trust is what builds strength. Life doesn't happen to us, it happens for us and it's time to let my walls down, it's time to trust myself.

The next day, I decide to sand the screen door that I tore off the hinges and Ellie is in the house doing whatever Ellie does. She takes a late morning nap after breakfast and I can tell her early morning walks are making her more fatigued than they used to.

Ellie makes me wear these ridiculous goggles to protect my eyes while sanding. I see her point but I still feel stupid. I enjoy working with my hands like this. I like the smell of wood and fixing things even if I don't know what I'm doing. It gives me time to think, and for some reason, I think about Jesus. After all, he was a simple man, a Jewish carpenter in fact. In doing this kind of work, I somehow feel closer to the man, not that I am particularly familiar with him. I only know a part of his story or the rumor of who he was but to say I have met him or felt his presence would be dishonest.

I take the same approach as my parents when it comes to religion. It goes back to the natives when they refer to God as, The Great Spirit. I love the stories my parents shared from when they lived on the reservation. A lot of stories were passed down, much like how I imagine the bible was created. The Christian God and the Native's Great Spirit are not as different as most people think. I believe it's the same God, but they are described differently.

I can sense someone staring at me, and when I look up I see Patrick standing in the door of the shed. Instead of removing the goggles from my face, I wipe circles on the lenses, so I can see clearly.

"Hi, how long have you been standing there?" I ask.

"Long enough." He answers. "Nice goggles."

"Oh yea, these. Ellie makes me wear them."

I take off the goggles and rest them on the top of my head. I am embarrassed to wear them and the fact that Patrick said something makes me blush. As he walks over to me, I quickly dust off my shirt and take off my gloves, another fashion statement Ellie makes me wear.

"Nice gloves too." He smiles. "Another one of Ellie's ideas?"

"Yup. She's looking out for me." I say playfully.

"Aren't those the kind of gloves you wear when you're doing the dishes?" He smiles.

"I suppose they are but I've never worn them to do dishes. So what brings you here?" I ask.

"You." He raises one eyebrow and I feel like my knees could give out.

"Oh, I feel honored," I respond as monotone as I can.

"So um, what are you working-?"

"Ellie told me everything," I interrupt.

"She did? Everything?"

"I saw him the other night. She took me to him." I said.

"To the creek?" He asks.

"Yes, she woke me up in the middle of the night. She told me to follow her and I have to admit, I knew something was going on but I never would have expected that." I said in disbelief.

"Well the whole thing is sad, isn't it? And then what happened to her afterward? It wasn't right, everything they did to her." His voice trails off.

"What who did?" I ask.

"Oh-she didn't tell you everything then." He said.

"No, I guess not," I said looking down.

"It was just the way people treated her, but she needs to tell you. She can tell you better than I ever could. It was bad Rainy. My dad and mom couldn't sit by and let it happen. Dad stepped in for Ellie, but it got ugly, so he was forced to back off."

I take a deep breath. I know Ellie will probably tell me all the details in her own time. Just like everything else, in her own time. I just don't want another surprise like the last one.

"So, you came up here for me huh?" I ask.

"It would be a lot easier if you had a phone. Why don't you have a phone?" He asks.

"I wanted to disconnect from the world, so I left it at home. Sometimes a girl just doesn't want to be reached."

"Oh, well that seems reasonable I guess." He sighs.

"We all have a story, don't we? One that we run from, or hide, or deny." I said feeling uncomfortable and surprised I would say such a thing.

"Uh, I'm an open book, so I don't really know. I mean, sure it's OK for others to have that kind of thing." He responds.

"An open book. OK. Well, I'm not so open." I said.

"I gather that. You never answered my question about going on a date with me." He smiles again.

"I don't date Patrick, I told you that. I can't." I said as I run my fingers over the screen door I'm sanding.

"Prearranged marriage I suppose?" He smiles.

I laugh, "No, you goof. I have been trying to fix my heart. As I said, I have my own story. My past isn't something I share all too often and when I do, I don't do it easily."

"I would love to listen sometime. I'm an open-minded kind of guy."

"Uh, sure. As soon as I feel like opening up, I will let you know." I said firmly.

"Hey, so why are you making this so hard?" He walks over to me, and nudges me with his elbow and runs his hands over the screen door. "You're making a fellow feel insecure."

"I seriously doubt you have any problems with insecurities Patrick. In fact, I almost guarantee you're not. Girls probably stand in line hoping to be your next trick."

"Ouch, and no. I don't date much either for your information. I don't really find the personalities of very many women attractive." He looks down. "They don't call me trick because of tricks I make with girls either." He adds.

"I'm sorry, I didn't mean to come across as judgmental or insensitive. It's just that I was married once, and I learned that I am not very good at relationships." I pause. "Not that I'm insinuating that you want a relationship with me."

"Maybe I do, but I won't know until you let me take you on a date." He winks.

"How about we just skip a date and make this screen door functional," I said.

"Well, that's a deal then."

"So, other than the obvious, why do people call you trick?" I ask as I sand the screen again.

"This." He taps on his lower leg.

"Your leg? What kind of tricks does it do?" I giggle.

"It disappears." We both laugh at our quick and witty sense of humor.

"Wow, a disappearing leg. Clever. Does it just walk off?" I ask as we both continue to laugh.

"It doesn't walk off, it comes off." He waits for my response.

"Oh, a removable leg, that's kinda handy in a sticky situation," I said without missing a beat.

"It gives the term, "kicking someone's ass" a whole new meaning." He said proudly.

I keep sanding as we both tease each other back and forth. It's so refreshing to have this kind of conversation. I can't remember the last time it was this easy and I like the fact that he feels comfortable enough with me to respond or add random and dorky facial expressions.

"Go with the grain, with the grain." He motions with his hands. "Nice and easy." He adds.

"Nice and easy huh? Like the time you told me to come back through on my way home and you'll give me a tune-up?" I tease.

He laughs at himself and said, "yea but hey, you remembered me didn't you?"

"I'm sure you used that line a time or two." I nudge his side with my hip.

"Nope, just you. It shocked my dad too. We still laugh about that. He gives me crap all the time now for my smooth pick-up line. He asked me the other day if it worked on you yet. I can't go back and tell him I didn't get a date with you again. My ego is already black and blue."

"Well, it was cute." I smile. "Now you have something to report back."

"I think the moment I knew you were different was the second I saw a glob of jelly on your cheek. God, that was perfect." He laughs.

"It was embarrassing!!!!" My voice cracks from laughing.

Patrick and I continue working on sanding and repainting the screen door, but before long the clouds roll in. The thunder and lightning begin to rumble, sometimes cracking so loud that it startles both of us. Rain starts gushing from the sky, and we debate on sticking it out or making a mad dash to the house as we simultaneously decide to make a run for it.

"There's a problem with the reactor!!! We're all gonna die!!!" I yell as we're running through the pouring rain back to the house.

When we reach the porch, Patrick is laughing hysterically. We are both soaking wet and our shoes are muddy and wet. I can't help but laugh because he is laughing so hard.

"What the heck is so funny? I don't even know why I'm laughing. I'm laughing at you laugh! What the hell?" I could barely get the words out.

"Oh, man. You are one funny girl. We're all gonna die?" He leans over to catch his breath. "Seriously, it was completely random I guess."

"It just felt like an appropriate moment to shout out a Homer Simpson quote."

"Oh, yea!" He pointed at me. "There's a problem with the reactor!!! We're all going to die!!! The Simpson's, I always knew the girl of my dreams would be able to quote Homer Simpson."

As we walk into the house, Ellie is waiting for us with towels, so we can dry off. She is smiling and excited for us to come in and tells us to take off our wet shoes and have some warm tea.

I slip my shoes off quickly and follow her to the kitchen as Patrick stays behind to unlace his boots. The kettle is already going and I grab the tea from the drawer as Ellie places the honey on the table. She reaches into the refrigerator and hands me some flavored creamer.

"Patrick likes creamer in his tea." She whispers.

"Oh, good to know," I whisper back, wondering why we are whispering in the first place.

Patrick stands in the entrance of the door shirtless with his pants rolled up to his knees. I am absolutely mesmerized at his body but his tattoo almost makes me gasp for air. It is on his chest and upper arm of a black raven in flight with what looks like paint splatter dripping down his chest. It is a stunning tattoo, beautifully done and it looks good on him. His muscles are stretched out past his arms and his chest looks like something you would see on a Greek God statue. His hair is messy and wet and I take notice of how long it is, not too long but just long enough that it carves out his jawline with precision. He is a gorgeous specimen of a human being and the fact that he sees me as his dream girl stirs something in me that I have never felt before.

He tells Ellie that he put his shirt and socks in the dryer and it warms my heart hearing him say that. The fact that he feels so comfortable with Ellie and knowing they have a past together brings a sense of belonging.

As I glance down, I can see where Patrick was not kidding around when he told me about his magic leg. It didn't surprise me, but a part of me questioned whether he was being serious about it until now. He is so handsome standing there that the fact that he's missing the bottom part of his leg doesn't matter one bit. He has a prosthetic device but the foot part looks like what a runner would have. It looks robotic and oddly, I find it extremely sexy.

"I guess you were serious, you do have a magic leg." I smile.

"Yep, it's real all right. All the way down to the bank account."

"Well, it suits you. It really does." I said.

He looks surprised that I said that but happy. It must be something he is a little insecure about or at least one would think. He said he was an open book, so I'm sure he will tell me how it happened but until then, I need to get out of my wet clothes. I pass by him as he continues to stand in the entrance to the kitchen and I brush up against his bare skin. He doesn't move much as I pass by and when I glance up, he is looking down at me with an expression so intense that it makes me flush. I can tell he feels it too and now I understand what people mean when they try to describe chemistry.

I change as fast as I can, feeling bored with the lack of clothes I have to choose from. I can hear what they were talking about even when their voices lower as if they are telling secrets. I stop and listen to them feeling guilty that I am doing this and also fully aware of the embarrassment I would feel if I get caught.

"Patrick, looks like you are having fun with Rainy," Ellie said.

"Jeez Ellie, she has me all kinds of messed up. In a good way. She is just so unique and quirky, she's funny and my God, she is beautiful." He whispers.

"Well, yes she is, and she is very kind. Why for a girl to help out an old woman like me is pretty significant." She states.

"Did you know she was married?" He asks.

"I did, does that bother you?" She asks?

"No, no… not at all but… I have a feeling there's a lot more to her." He whispers even more.

"There is," Ellie said. "She will tell you I'm sure." She patted his hand.

"I don't want her to leave Ellie. I've never felt this way." He said.

I immediately walk back in the kitchen pretending not to hear a word they spoke. I need to stop their conversation from going any further. I don't want to know how he feels about me because I don't want him feeling anything. It will only complicate my life and right now, I'm discovering a part of me that needs to be discovered on my own.

We decide to stay inside enjoying Ellie's company instead of going back out to work on the screen. She asks Patrick to stay for dinner that she already started making when we were outside. He accepts her invite and makes sure we understand that he is doing the dishes. He teases me about this being our first date because I refuse to go on a real first date.

After Patrick does the dishes, we migrate to the living room. Ellie doesn't have a T.V, not that I want to watch T.V but it feels like a good time for a movie. Patrick sits next to me, his pants dry and his shirt on and grabs my hand in his.

Ellie begins talking as she pulls her blanket over her lap. Her gentle voice begins to wander into the air where space and time seem to stop.

Chapter 15

Ellie begins.

"When the kids graduated from college, they didn't want to come back up here where there are no real jobs. They wanted the big jobs in the corporate world, but they always kept in touch, and we went to visit them. Of course, they still came home around holidays or birthdays and Holly would bring a friend, or boyfriend and Jacob would bring over different girls every time. Max and I understood that kids grow up and start lives of their own. Jacob was not short on confidence and when he got the position at The Firm, his ego grew even bigger. He always wanted to be a lawyer, and he is so extremely intelligent. Holly was bound and determined to become a police officer but decided on criminal psychology, forensics, and crime analyst. She completed more training in Virginia for another 3 years before getting her first assignment but to her disappointment, was not in Colorado. About a week after Max died, she was given a team that worked with human trafficking which is something she wanted to do after working in Florida with a task force that stopped shipments from Cuba of women and children being sold.

You can imagine their surprise when Max died. I didn't give them much detail because I didn't know what to say, I was pretty overwhelmed by the whole thing. The last they knew about their dad was he was healthy after going through chemo and surgery. It took a few days for Holly to come home and I asked that Jacob wait for her and come up together. This gave me time to get my mind about me, I needed a little time to figure out what to do next.

The night Max died, I called Evan, and he told me not to call anyone but it was too late. I already called Tully, he was the funeral director in town, and he was heading up to take his body.

I have always known that Max wanted to be buried up here near the creek. There's an Aspen grove on the other side of the creek where Max and I would sometimes have lunch or watch the stars in the summer. It would be really dark at night back in the trees but the clearing near the patch of aspens was wide open to the sky. He made me promise once that I would bury him right where we were sitting. That's an easy promise to make when you're young and don't have other situations to juggle.

I told Evan and Beth that I wanted to get Max's body back and that I made a mistake in letting Tully take him. I knew I couldn't go to the mortuary and just bring him back, and I was also aware of the laws of burying people on private property so the idea of getting Max back felt pretty hopeless. Beth and Evan told me to just be patient a few days, and they will try to come up with something.

The service was scheduled ten days after he died which allowed me to make arrangements carefully and slowly. It also allowed your dad to come up with a plan." Ellie looked at Patrick as he nodded his head.

"I just don't know what I would have done without your parent's young man," Ellie said straight to Patrick.

"They loved Max, he was like a brother to my dad, an uncle to me. They will also do anything for you to Ellie." Patrick said.

I didn't realize just how close their families are until this moment. I see where Patrick is right at home here but the interaction at the diner tells a different story, one of disconnect or distance. So hearing how close they are, comes as a surprise. Ellie continues.

"Evan came over four days before Max's service and proposed his plan. That afternoon I called Tully and asked that I meet with him to go over Max's final wishes but first we needed to make sure Tully was finished preparing Max's body. Tully reassured us that he completed the preparation of his body and placed Max in his final resting position, awaiting the service. We agreed to meet the following evening.

Evan and Beth drove me into Silverthorne and Tully was waiting for us in the reception area. As we sat to discuss how the service was going to be arranged, Evan took it upon himself to use the restroom but in reality, went to see how hard it would be to get Max out of there. My purpose was to explain to Tully of Max's last wishes of me being the last person to see him. I couldn't believe how smooth the lies were coming out of my mouth, and not just to Tully, but my own children.

He was very generous with his understanding and figured I would want to say my last farewell. I had to explain how we decided on a closed casket after all. I explained that Max didn't want the kids to see him that way and that he asked to leave the last memory of him being that of strength and life which really isn't far from the truth. Max would have never wanted an open casket.

Tully took me down a flight of stairs to the holding area where they keep the prepared caskets for transportation to the service. Through a separate hallway were a set of doors where bodies were brought in and this is where Evan would be while Beth kept Tully engaged in his favorite topic of conversation, HAM radio.

Tully opened Max's casket and I quickly asked him if there was anything else he needed to do before closing it permanently. He reassured me that he was completely finished and once I closed it, he had no reason to reopen it. He gave me his word and added that this is a common request by a lot of loved ones which was also a relief because I didn't want to raise any suspicion.

I could hear Tully and Beth upstairs talking, so I hurried down the hallway to the doors that opened to a large concrete driveway with tall concrete retaining walls surrounding the entrance. Evan slid through the doors and didn't waste any time unfolding a sheet and placing it over the top of two appliance casters that he hinged together.

It took all of Evans strength to lift Max from the casket, and we were both surprised at how little Max was able to bend. I held on to his feet as we gently but not gracefully placed his body across the rolling casters. He quickly wrapped him up, and he pulled as I pushed Max back down the hall and through the doors. He told me to close the casket and make sure the area was clear.

When I came back, Evan had lifted Max's body into the back of his truck and rolled the hard truck bed cover back over the top, out of sight. He quickly drove back to the parking area and I went back to the area where Max's casket still remained. I doubled checked the outside of the casket to make sure there wasn't any fabric sticking out and glanced over the whole area one last time before calling for Tully that I was done. I was so scared and nervous that he would know instantly of what we had just done, but he was more interested in finishing his conversation about how HAM radio signals get transmitted.

The three of us were completely speechless on the drive home. I'm sure we all had the same single thought going through our heads.

I couldn't sleep that night. Every time I closed my eyes, a panic would engulf me. I was not only worried about getting caught but more importantly, I didn't want Evan and Beth to get into any trouble.

Every little detail that was executed successfully was one more breath I could exhale. Getting him back up here felt impossible, yet we managed to pull it off. I knew that it wouldn't be over until Tully had the casket in the ground and buried. As morbid as it sounds, it was critical.

Evan and Beth came over the next morning with Max still in the bed of Evan's truck. It hadn't reached daylight yet as the three of us pulled Max along the path and to the area he wanted to be. As Evan unfolded Max from the sheet, he asked me again if I still wanted him placed in the water."

"Wait," I said. "Why did you want him in the water and not in the opening of the aspen trees?" I ask.

"Because when I die, I want to be placed with him together in the tree clearing. This was our spot and this is where I want my body to lay with his." She states firmly and continues.

"It was a cold and wet winter and the creek had a layer of ice formed across and I will admit, because of that, I felt a little defeated." She pauses, "But your dad Patrick," she looks directly at Patrick and nodded, "your dad took some large rocks and broke the ice off and laid him down in the cold water. He told me not to go back until he said it was OK and I trusted that he had his reasons."

Patrick squeezes my hand as Ellie continues.

"In truth, that little place in the creek was the perfect place for him to be. It is deep in that section and the banks that surround it keeps him from moving. The steady rush of water from the waterfall above keeps the water constantly flowing and makes it almost impossible to see through.

The day of the funeral was a complete disaster, to say the least. I was so worried about the empty casket that I didn't think about much more than that. Dr. Roberts was Max's oncologist, and he came to the service to pay his respects to our family. I never thought about the fact that he might come when the public obituary was posted. I was standing next to the kids when he introduced himself as Max's physician. Holly mentioned what a surprise it was to have him pass away when just a few months prior, he looked so healthy and felt well. Jacob asked Dr. Roberts if it was common for cancer to come back so quickly after being in remission." Ellie recalled.

"That's when Dr. Roberts shared that Max certainly would have lived longer had he gone through surgery and chemo. I knew Holly and Jacob picked up on the discrepancies between what we told them the instant they shot each other the same look. They were angry."

Ellie begins to recall the moments after Max's service and their conversation. My only thought is how hard it must have been for Ellie to know she had to face her own children with the truth about their dad. *How does a mother and a grown woman who just lost the love of her life try to reason with her children?*

"I felt an overwhelming sense of doom knowing I would need to tell the truth about his wishes and his death." She continues. "Holly and Jacob looked at each other as I thanked Dr. Roberts for his time and consideration in paying his respects. I tried to keep myself together for the rest of the service as I spoke to everyone who came. The kids made it home before I did, and they were waiting on the front porch for me." Ellie explains.

"As soon as I stepped onto the porch, Jacob demands the three of us talk. They didn't really talk to me though, they yelled at me. They were not interested in anything I had to say either. They would ask me questions, but wouldn't let me answer. Holly asked me why I would lie to them but when I tried to explain it, I would get bombarded with other questions or judgments. She told me that I didn't own him, and that's when I raised my voice to them and yelled that I simply did what their dad asked me to do." Ellie pauses.

I can tell Ellie wants to cry, she is on the verge of tears, but they have yet to roll out of her eyes. Tears collect and once she blinks a few times, they will eventually spill over and down her cheeks.

"That's when they finally stopped yelling but I knew things went from bad to worse. Holly looked at me suspiciously and asked in a very slow, monotone voice what I did exactly. So I told them. I never told them that Max was up here in the creek. I knew that would not go over well based on their reactions up to that point. I was certain after I explained the whole thing, they would understand or at least understand over time.

I will never forget the way they looked at me. It broke my heart knowing I caused so much pain, hurt and anger but I held firm to the fact that I did what was best for Max. Jacob couldn't look at me, and Holly was speechless. Imagine my surprise when she finally asked me if I understood what I did was considered murder."

"Oh my God," I whispered. "I am so sorry. You know that isn't true, right?" I said as I lean toward Ellie.

"To this day, I might not remember every word said but I can still remember their disgusted looks. I know I didn't murder Max." Ellie explains. "But remember who they are. Jacob is a criminal lawyer for the DA's office, he prosecutes murderers and holly works for the FBI. My children believed I murdered their father, they will never see it any other way. Jacob finally spoke but it wasn't my son talking, it was more like a man who was presenting a case in front of a jury. He said, "let me get this straight, mom, you killed a man who was distraught and probably not thinking clearly. He was dying of cancer that could have been treated and you let this man make decisions that he had no business making? Then you take his life? This is what the court of law will see. Nothing more. Do you understand what you've done?" Ellie stops talking.

I don't know what to say to her and I feel so much sadness for her. Ellie is crying as she remembers the day when her children became strangers. I take the stillness of the moment and ask myself how I would respond if this were my own parents. Certainly not like they did.

Ellie continues, "I waited for three weeks before they eventually called me, they were both on the phone when they called. Holly said they decided not to say anything to the authorities but will be taking my punishment into their own hands. Holly reminded me of their careers and that this would destroy it if the truth ever surfaced. I was to keep my mouth shut and Jacob said he would come up here to discuss the details of the next steps.

They just cut me off from the rest of the world. I had no way of making any calls, I couldn't watch TV or drive. They even took my eyeglasses. Jacob took control over all my money and told me that someone would come up weekly to bring me to the little convenience store attached to the diner, so I could get groceries. I was also told that when I get sick, I would not be able to see a doctor.

I was hoping Jacob would come to see my side of this, his own father's wishes, but he made it clear once he came up to discuss it, that I was to keep quiet and never speak of it to anyone. He couldn't even look at me when he was talking to me, he just followed his list of things to be done and left. He didn't say good-bye, but he did leave me an envelope on the kitchen table. After he left, I read what was inside there was a copy of an article of a similar situation. A woman who helped her husband commit suicide and convicted of second-degree murder and would live the rest of her life in prison. At the bottom of the article was a handwritten note from Holly that advised me to take this as a warning to what will happen to me if I ever tell anyone or step one foot away from the rules they set. I signed all the papers he told me to sign and I felt like my whole life was over.

Jacob wrote one last thing that absolutely broke my heart. In a separate letter, he explained that he told everyone he possibly could, everyone who knew me, that I had abused the kids when they were younger, starved them and neglected their needs. Evan and Beth told me this later as well. Apparently, Jacob went to the local bar where everyone knows everyone up here. He got really drunk the night he found out the truth about his dad, and what I had done. He warned everyone and anyone who tried to help me or give me aid, even check in on me, that he would make their lives a living hell. He threatened them that he had the power to ruin them. But no one would go against him anyway because by the time the night was over, he had them convinced that I was a monster, and they all felt my punishment was fair and just. From there forward, I never wanted to be seen again.

New generations have come forward but the story has remained for all these years. I get picked up every week to get food. Some weeks, nobody comes, so I was forced to live on what little I could. Evan and Beth would come over, but they too were afraid of what would happen. Jacob and Holly threatened them once that they had the power to take down their shop in town and put them in prison for drug trafficking. A surveillance camera was placed at the entrance to the driveway and this deterred anyone from stepping over the line. Because they lived up the road from me, they could walk through the woods and not get noticed but I'm sure the fear of getting caught was immense.

Since you have come, Evan, Beth, and Patrick have come over more often and you and I have come and gone yet, nothing has been done; at least not yet anyway.

Years later, I received a surprise letter from my son's wife that she was handling all the money from there forward. I never knew my son got married and it depressed me more than you can imagine. Their lives continued without me, and my son carries on with his lies to this day.

Money was given to the store every month, and she made sure it was just enough to get food and necessities. About a year ago, she left a letter for me at the store informing me that she and Jacob have divorced, but she was given custody over my money and estate. They weren't married long, this was her second marriage, and they didn't have kids together. She never wrote much in her letters, most of the time it was just money but sometimes, she wrote little notes that consisted of a sentence or two. When she told me she was divorcing Jacob, she wrote, 'through the death of one also kills the heart of another.' I'm not sure what she meant by that but I came up with more than a few ideas. Apparently, Jacob transferred everything to her, and she would continue her duties of sending me money. I suppose you could say that I am surprised she still sends money. For all I know of this woman, she could have taken every last dime and left me up here to wither away. I still don't know how much money I have but now and then, I will get an envelope with extra money wrapped in a folded piece of paper. I can tell it's from her by the way the paper smells. From the first time I ever got her letter, it has always smelled the same, like perfume. It was a welcome scent that I looked forward too, more so than the money she left inside."

I looked at Patrick who was trying to get my attention anyway. He smiled down at me, but I couldn't smile back. I found myself leaning on him but quickly moved once my thoughts caught up to me.

"Were you aware of this? All of this?" I ask Patrick.

"Yea, but I never believed Ellie abused her children." He tells me.

"But you let this happen anyway?" I ask in shock.

"What choice did they leave us Rainy? Holly had the ability to frame us and Jacob had the law on his side. They were very specific as to what they could do to us, and we had no proof to claim our innocence. It's not like we could save a letter or record conversations. They would come up out of the blue and warn us in person. It was random and it was very scary. The details of how they could destroy us were shocking. They had scenarios planned out that scared people, especially my parents, half to death. Rumor has it, they even have strands of hair and DNA on certain people. So even if someone wanted to go against them, they quickly learned not to. No one knew what they were capable of but planting some kind of evidence on a murder scene seemed probable." Patrick explains.

I suppose I can understand it. I want to believe that every part of me would fight against this but in reality, I know better. It is such a tragedy and injustice to Ellie who was simply doing what Max wanted. But for me, well… I know I have nothing to lose. These people will eventually find out who I am, but I have nothing they can take from me. *Let them try* I said to myself.

"Well, they can't scare me." I finally said. "Let them try."

"They should scare you. They will take down anyone who loves you, they will expose you, they will frame you and there's nothing you can do to stop it." Patrick said shaking his head in disbelief.

"So why now, why come around openly? Why risk it all now?" I ask Patrick as Ellie listens.

"Because we have something we can fight back with." He said.

Chapter 16

"It was a car accident. I was with my best friend when we were hit on his side by a drunk driver. The driver was going over 70 miles an hour through a stop sign. We didn't even see him coming. My buddy and I were coming home from a music festival outside Estes Park. We decided to take a different way home because of the traffic but when we started to go through our stop sign, the guy came out of nowhere and completely creamed us. He killed my buddy and left me with this." Patrick says as he taps his prosthetic leg.

"Wow, that is a lot to take in all at once," I said.

"Well, it is what it is. Ryan was killed instantly." His voice trailed off. "I don't remember much after that, but I do remember the impact and seeing Ryan lay lifeless next to me." He adds.

"I'm sorry Patrick. I had a friend die in an accident too." I said quietly.

"Really? So you know what I'm talking about."

"Umm, I do. Except I was the one driving." I whisper.

"Oh Crap, that must have been- how did you- I can't-" he stutters.

"It's a story of its own," I interrupt." "It was sad, more than sad and it broke me," I admit.

I can't remember a single moment in my life where I didn't feel the need to clutter empty voids in conversations with meaningless topics. Patrick holds my hand while we weave in and out of the trees but when he talks, he lets go and uses both hands to gesture, an adorable trait passed down from his dad.

"The accident," I ask. "What happened to the drunk driver?"

"Not a scratch. That's typical, isn't it? He was driving without his lights on. That's why we never saw him coming." He said.

"Did he get prosecuted?" I ask.

"Yep, vehicular homicide." He said. "And you? Did you get prosecuted?"

"No, I never did. I wasn't drinking though. Plus... I went kinda crazy." I was embarrassed to admit.

"Hum, like you went skydiving kind of crazy or like literally crazy." He smiles.

"No, I went into a mental hospital because I believed she was still alive," I said knowing that it might be hard for him to understand.

"Oh." He said quietly.

He doesn't say anything for a while, and we walk quietly. The probability that he will feel differently about me after knowing my mind is capable of breaking as it has in the past is very high. His accident was caused by a drunk driver but that is the only difference between me, and the driver that hit them. I wasn't driving carelessly, but I wasn't paying close enough attention to the road. I killed my best friend just like that driver killed Patrick's and left him with half a leg. He talks about his accident so freely and I question if he really understands what I went through as the person who caused the death of someone else. I can't decide if I should offer more details or give it time. If the tables were turned, I would want to know if someone I am interested in went nuts and spent time in a mental hospital for an accident that killed someone. I would want all the details but it doesn't seem to matter to him.

In saying that, I don't know if I am willing to be open to the idea of a relationship. I have a job waiting for me back home. I have a life to return to even though I don't want that life. It's not a life I am running from anymore, it's a life that simply doesn't fit me any longer. Being up here has taught me more about myself than I could have hoped for and I don't want to go backward. I need to start planning my next steps moving forward but the thought of going home makes me feel sorrow to the person I have become in such a short time.

Walking next to Patrick, I visualize a circle that represents my life. Death, love, loss, and victories all move within this circle and it's never ending but it's also part of my life. It is what makes me whole regardless of the fact that it fractured and broke me during its creation. I find myself envisioning a completely different life that doesn't include hidden emotions, checked out behavior and missing parts of my life's chapters. I see where I have grown to enjoy the silence. I have grown to enjoy being with myself, and what it means to love and accept who I am and what I have done. Forgiving myself hasn't happened and I question whether it will.

These two lives are so different but my past is so much more established and familiar. The walls I created are shifting more every day, I'm trusting myself that I have what it takes to cope with what might happen next. I have no idea if I am mentally unstable, the voices or the unseen still sneak in when I least expect it. I wish someone would see them with me, or even hear them. I crave the relief I would feel if someone saw them for just a split-second. What I feel today is new and scary but it also promises hope.

I can't stomach the thought of leaving Ellie up here alone. I also can't forget the potential of our lives being flipped upside down for simply associating with her.

"Has anyone been affected by Ellie's kids?" I ask.

"My mom was, at least we think she was. She had a small cupcake store down in Silverthorne and one day, someone from the health department came in to do a walk through. My mom's little store was always in perfect order, so there wasn't anything to report but after they walked through, they brought out dead mice in a bag along with a bunch of dead bugs. They said the health department was flagging the bakery and a public notice would be filed. They told my mom she would need over thirty thousand dollars to bring the bakery up to industry standards. Up to that point, my mom passed every inspection but after that, she decided she would eliminate the risk, and we took it as a warning. That's what it was, a warning because in no way was the bakery in the condition they said it was."

"Do you really think it was Jacob and Holly?" I ask.

"Pretty sure. We knew that if we kept helping Ellie that would only be the beginning. My dad had the shop in town, and we could only imagine what they might do to it. As soon as my parents stopped being a public advocate for Ellie, their life wasn't disrupted again."

"So how do you plan to stop this then?" I ask.

"Well, Jacobs's ex-wife has asked to meet with Ellie sometime soon. She said she can end it all but wants to meet somewhere to talk about it, she knows about the surveillance cameras and is not comfortable coming to the house. My dad and I are planning a way around them, so she can come up and talk freely. She told Ellie that her car has a tracking device as well. My dad said he would meet her in town when she was ready. He will remove it for her, so she can come up here. We don't need any lose lipped locals running off to Holly or Jacob with this news. She also told my dad about a secret recording she has of Jacob and Holly discussing certain things that could end the whole thing as well as both their careers, maybe even send them to prison."

Patrick leads me off into the trees away from the trail in a direction I have not walked before. It is the middle of the afternoon and the rain clouds are building up like clockwork, they form every day around this time, some dropping huge buckets of rain and some just make noise. We reach a section of trees where every direction I turn is more trees. If I were here alone, I would be completely lost. I wouldn't know what area I just walked from or which direction to go. Everything looks the same, every tree looks like the next and the ground offers little guidance. It is both beautiful and intimidating at the same time. I can understand why people get lost in places like this. One slight turn and a person can lose all sense of direction.

"Rainy!" He calls from behind me.

I look back when I realize he has stopped walking and is no longer next to me. He is standing between two huge pine trees and staring at me with his blue eyes and my breath slips away from me. *How can I ever get tired of seeing this beautiful man?* He doesn't walk toward me, and I stand where I am waiting for him to say something.

"You are beautiful." He said while having to raise his voice a little.

"You are beautiful in so many ways." He adds. "I don't want you to ever leave. I don't care if you're brokenhearted. Let me in there, let me in your heart. I won't hurt you. I'm a man of honor and since the first time I saw you, I feel what I think a person feels when they say it was love at first sight." He said.

"You make me smile Patrick." I holler back to him.

"Is that all you can say?" He smiles at me and shrugs his shoulders.

"I have a whole life that I lived before this one. Heartache. Pain. Hate. I went crazy once! I'm complicated Patrick." I raise my voice even more.

"I don't care if you're crazy. You can have conversations with a kiwi for all I care. I just want to start this new chapter with you." He said as he starts walking toward me.

"What makes you think my chapter is over?" I ask.

He reaches out with his strong hand and tucks my hair behind my ear and grabs the back of my neck and pulls me close. Our lips are only an inch from touching and I know he is about to kiss me.

"Your last chapter is over." He whispers.

Patrick sucks the air out of my mouth as he kisses me. He is slow for a moment, then intense with passion. He will bite my lip gently and with his hands tangled in my hair, he pulls my head back and kisses my neck. He stops only long enough to look at me then kisses me again. I've never been kissed this way. I never felt this way physically either. I feel like I am on fire, every last nerve is heightened and his touch is more than I can process. He is unbelievably strong and forceful but the kind of force that shows confidence, not anger.

He slides his hand up my skirt and takes my panties off as he kisses my navel in one single movement. He pulls my shirt down and now both of the most intimate parts of myself are exposed. His breathing changes with mine, both knowing what we want. We glare into one another as I unbutton his pants, and he takes me again, kissing my neck and pulling me back exposing my chest to his lips.

He lifts me up like a rag doll with one hand as I cross my legs around his waist, gripping on to him with both legs. He puts himself inside me, and I have never been so captivated by the action of making love. His strength, his force, and passion are for his gratification but that only makes me want him to be more selfish. It's so cliché for a man to try to please a woman but as soon as he takes it for his own, it instantly becomes exactly what a woman craves and I crave him more than I ever have with any other person.

His facial expressions, his touch, his fierce strength surge through him and into me as if we need each other to power our individual selves.

He leans his back on the tree and effortlessly brings us to the ground as I am still straddling his waist. He kisses me slowly, his movements slow with mine and the numb feeling I am left with makes its way to him. He holds me, and never touch the ground as he stays inside me. Once again, he tucks my hair behind my ear.

"Your last chapter is over." He orders.

Chapter 17

Patrick and I have become even closer as the weeks have gone by. He stays up here most nights but was sleeping on the couch out of respect for Ellie. We were speechless when she told him that while she was born at night, she wasn't born last night, and she was open-minded enough to know that we should be sleeping in the same bed.

Patrick and I will lay in bed and talk into all hours of the morning but sometimes, we will talk with Ellie in the living room. She enjoys the chatter between us, and we love her stories just as much. She will ask me after Patrick leaves what my plans are for the future. She reminds me all the time about how crazy he is for me and suggests I stay. *I wish it could be that simple.*

Ellie and I decided to name the bird Raven. Simple yet, meaningful especially to me. He is starting to eat more solid scraps of meat and his feathers are filling in. He looks less like a sick chicken and more like a raven. His beak is strong already, and he's almost ready to start perching on branches. He isn't waking me up as much through the night, but he likes attention during the day. He likes to be held and practices perching on my arm while Patrick has shown me the "step up" command. I am surprised at how intelligent he is already, and I am growing more and more aware of the fact that sometime soon, he will fly away and be a raven, doing what ravens do.

Patrick and I work on Ellie's house just about every day, fixing as many things we can see to fix. She is so grateful and talks about how Max would have loved watching us. She maintains her routine throughout the day but I notice her growing increasingly more tired as time goes by. She goes to the creek every morning and sometimes I meet her out there, and we sit together. She rests in her chair near the window and stares out into the world as she knows it to be. Ellie joins me from time to time on the porch and loves the rocking chairs that Patrick and I fixed. We talk about Emma and Max and I take notice every day in how far I have come from the beginning of this journey. She always ends our conversations by asking me if I have decided to stay up here.

Until meeting Patrick and Ellie, my parents are the only other people in this world that offered a sense of belonging. To belong in a particular place or tribe, we must also have something to offer and I know I offer something to Ellie that is valuable, even if it's just my time. To give her an answer is difficult because I simply don't know but I always remind her that I will be right here tomorrow and the thought of leaving now makes me feel incredibly sad.

A few days ago, I made an eye appointment for Ellie to get new glasses. She doesn't know that she will get them today but I want to keep that a surprise. When the topic first came up, she said that getting the exam and having to wait for the glasses is as bad as taking candy from a child but I finally convinced her.

Patrick has spent the past few days messing around with the car in the garage. When we leave for her appointment, Ellie is completely surprised as she opens the door and finds the old car waiting for her in perfect condition. Patrick holds her door open like a perfect gentleman and I sit in the back seat. Watching Ellie through the side mirror brings so much happiness to my heart. Her window is down and the summer mountain air blows her gray hair wildly around her thin face. Her eyes catch a ray of sunshine and once she can see again, she will find the world more beautiful than she could have ever remembered.

As Patrick and I wait for Ellie in the waiting room, his dad calls to make sure we made it into town with the car. Those two talked for hours the night before about what might be wrong with the car and why it wouldn't start. Of course, it was the simplest solution and the last to try. It has been sitting for so long that in order to get it to start, Patrick had to do something with the gas but I don't understand enough to know whether it was intentional on their part or a last-minute mistake that provided the victorious result.

"Would you mind if I use your phone to call my parents? Last time I spoke with them was 2 weeks ago. I'm sure they want to hear from me." I ask Patrick.

"Sure, as long as you tell them you're staying up here for good and you found a man that fell in love with you." He said.

"Wait just a second, is that your way of telling me you love me?" I tease.

"I suppose it is. I love you and that scares the hell out of me because you're so damn close to slipping out of my grip." He whispers.

Patrick proclaims his love for me inside the eye doctor's office where a waiting room full of people listening. Some pretend to not hear while others smile at me or to themselves. I want to say it back but I don't. I haven't thought about falling in love with him because I am too busy figuring out my life and what to do next. Falling in love with him will change everything and take away the choices I have. Patrick knows this, or he wouldn't fear losing me. I admire how he can feel emotions even though those emotions might bring a broken heart. I wish I had more courage to love freely but I'm getting so close.

"Hey mom," I said as I walk outside. "How are you guys? I want to check in."

"Hi sweetie, I'm really glad you called. I was starting to worry. Dad was about to take me up there." She said.

"Well hey there Neha." My dad said on the other line.

"Hi! Are you both on the phone?"

"We sure are. Your mom was about to foot it up there to check on you." He said.

"So where are you?" My mom asked.

"What number are you calling from?" My dad asked.

"Are you doing OK?" She asked.

"Guys! One at a time here." I can't help but smile. "I am at the eye doctor for Ellie. It's a long story and even longer time coming. I'm using Patrick's phone."

"Patrick? Oh, well OK. I didn't realize how often you two see each other." My dad questions.

"Well, she is a grown woman. She is also a very beautiful grown woman with a great head on her shoulders." My mom tells him through the phone.

"So, hey guys. I'm right here? Maybe you can talk about me after I get off the phone?" I smile.

I find it rather adorable that the two of them are on the phone together rather than just talking one at a time. One phone is next to my parent's bed and the other phone is in my dad's office. They are cordless phones but if they get to close to one another, the feedback will make a god awful sound forcing them to stay separate. I know after all these years that even though they are across the house, they still look at each other when talking. It's comical to watch and I know without a shadow of a doubt, they are doing it now.

"So any thought about when you might be coming back?" My dad asks.

"Well, I don't know. My boss told me my position won't be available for another 3 months." I said.

"So you're staying up there that long? Oh Rainy, you don't need to wear out your welcome." My mom said sounding concerned.

"I don't think I am going to run into that issue. I'm seeing more and more every day about how much help Ellie needs." I respond. "Oh and Raven, he still needs help. I think he will start perching any day now. His feathers are coming in, his flight feathers…oh, the thought-"

My dad interrupts, "You might be surprised how attached you

and Raven might get. You have always had a connection to those birds. Neha, he is a wild bird, he will someday leave the nest."

"What about her family?" My mom asks.

"It's such a long story you guys. Way too long for a quick phone conversation- and dad, I know. Raven is so smart and I don't know... I love the little fella." I said.

"Maybe we can come up there? I wouldn't mind meeting Ellie and seeing Raven too." She said.

"And Patrick." My dad adds.

"Sure, that would be nice. I just... I have so much to talk about and not much time. I will call again when I'm not waiting for Ellie... I miss you guys. I really do."

"We miss you too." They said together.

"I'm going to be in touch. This is Patrick's number so you can call him if you need me." I add at the last minute.

"We love you. Be happy!" My mom adds.

"I love you guys," I said.

I give the phone back to Patrick and let him know that my parents have his number if for whatever reason they need to contact me. A part of me feels overwhelmed after talking to them. They asked questions I can't answer or don't want to answer and thinking through my future plans isn't something I want to do. I want to continue in the moment and live my future as if it's happening now.

While we wait for Ellie's glasses to get ready, we grab lunch which is one of her favorite things to do. At some point, I need to discuss with both of them about the possibility of me leaving.

"Ellie, you would tell me if I wore out my welcome wouldn't you?" I ask her.

"Oh for heaven's sake. You must have talked to your parents again." She said in a huff.

"Yea, I did. Just for a few minutes. They always remind me of not over-staying." I said.

"Well, I have half a notion to call them and tell them that you are never going to overstay with me, and to stop feeding silly thoughts about it into your head," Ellie said.

Patrick barely talks at lunch, but he never misses an opportunity to hold my hand or kiss my forehead. It's endearing and kind and I return it by looking at him in the eyes and smiling. I hold his hand and at times, when I least expect it, I feel a surge of sexual energy pass between us and I know he feels it too.

The second Ellie puts her glasses on and looks at me is a moment I will never forget. I laugh at her facial expressions and Patrick teases her about being disappointed in his looks. It has become my favorite memory with her so far. She is completely taken back at what she can see in focus and what she has been missing. She doesn't want the optometrist to take them off for fitting because she doesn't want to miss something.

"Would you take a look at that?" She asked. "Just look at- oh, and that tree. It has a lot of branches. Oh my, look at me- and can you believe this is little Patrick?" She said as she turns and looks at him. "Look at you, a young man." She gasps.

"Ellie, look in the mirror, how do you like them?" I ask.

"Oh, good lord. Is that me? I look old…what am I saying? I am old." She said looking in the mirror.

On our way home, Patrick pulls over at the entrance to the campground where I spent a night in hell. I almost share that experience but decide after Patrick pulls over, it isn't the time. The fact that I want to tell them about that night shows just how much I have accepted my past as a chapter once written, once very real and still is for all of us, just in different ways.

Patrick tells Ellie to get behind the wheel, and I feel a little nervous knowing that she probably hasn't driven in over a decade. To add fuel to the mix, as of… now or, less than an hour ago at best, she is able to see further than 6 inches away. I wonder if Patrick has lost his mind but, one glance from him is all it takes for me to realize that he has this under control. Ellie sits behind the wheel, but she is too short to see over the steering wheel, so Patrick takes his hoodie off and lets her sit on it, so she can see out. Not only is he shirtless, but I am also speechless. Before Patrick could close his door, Ellie already put the car into drive. She slowly rolls forward and giggles, commenting that she doesn't even have a driver's license.

"Just for clarification purposes, you don't have a driver's license now or are you telling us you never had one. I'm asking for a friend." I ask from the back seat.

"She had one, I remember her driving us to the store for ice cream as a kid," Patrick answers for her.

It only takes a few minutes to realize that Ellie can, in fact, see where she is going, and she can drive just fine. I don't know why I was in doubt in the first place but, I am able to relax a little, and enjoy the late afternoon breeze blowing in. With Patrick sitting where Ellie was, I have full access to look at every part of his face without risking the likelihood of getting caught, making it awkward for both of us. His face is powerful and serious with a jawline that defines his facial features. His hair is being tossed around from the wind through the windows and now and then, he rests his head back and takes it all in with a deep sigh. I can tell he is deep in thought and every time he clenches his jaw, the muscle tightens up reminding me of the first time he ever did that, I was wrapped around his waist. He is a good man, this I can tell and Ellie is right in saying he is crazy about me. It still doesn't change the fact that this life and my other life do not go together.

While we were in town, I bought Ellie a few magazines and a coloring book full of mandalas. I bought her fancy colored pencils to use knowing that she will enjoy seeing the detail and colors for the first time in a long time. I can't wait to get home, so she can see what I got for her.

She doesn't go see Max that night but instead, goes to bed early. It saddens me that she is as tired as she is but I remind myself that she has done more in the past few months than she has in years.

Patrick and I sit on the porch in the dark, swinging on the newly installed porch swing. I am curled up next to him while he controls the movement of the swing. His shoes are off and I can see his prosthetic leg that up to this point, I never paid much attention too. Not because it bothers me, quite the opposite; I simply don't care. I let my hand feel the smooth finish and ask him if it ever hurts. He is honest and raw with his emotions explaining that he was actually in a lot of pain when it happened but as soon as they discovered they couldn't save it, it went from physical pain to emotional.

"Once I healed and got my prosthetic leg, I took a little road trip, like what you're doing. At least I assume that's what you're doing." His voice trails off.

"Yea, something like that. Did you come back feeling different?" I ask.

"I went on a backpacking trip to Grand Teton. I suppose I needed to prove to myself that I could still do and be the same person I was before the accident." He responds.

"Are you?"

"I discovered that I'm better than before. This thing changed me. It humbled me, it took me down from the invincible platform I was on and placed both feet on the ground." He said.

"No pun intended?" I giggle.

"Yea, no pun intended. I was thinking I would have to quit my volunteer work in search and rescue and everything else I was born to do, but it just made me better, stronger and I take nothing for granted." He said firmly.

"I love you." I blurt out.

I can't believe what I just said but it is the truth. I have fallen in love with him and I can't go a single second longer without telling him. I don't care about what might or might not happen, he makes me a stronger person. This whole experience has made me so much stronger than I ever thought I was.

"You don't know what that means to hear you say this to me." He sighs. "With all I am, I love you too." He adds.

I sit up straight and place both feet on the deck to stop the porch swing from moving. I feel sadness for the relationship, not for myself or for Patrick, but genuine sorrow for the feelings between us.

"I don't really know how to use the right words, I'm used to living in my own head that talking about my feelings doesn't come naturally to me," I explain.

"Patrick," I add, "I have a whole other life waiting for me. I have a job lined up, I have parents, and I have a past..." I said as my voice fades.

"We all have a past." He said.

"I see that now, I really do. My past doesn't give more pain than yours does, or Ellie's. I understand that pain is pain and it isn't mine to own. We all have it and no one is immune from it. I get that now, I understand that we all process pain differently and I'm OK. I'm not as broken as I thought I was." I said, almost in a panic.

"I told you a few weeks ago that it doesn't matter what your past is. I want you every morning, every night, I want to give myself to you. I want to live adventures with you, I want to be bored with you. You have become the best part of who I am." He said.

"Do you ever think about what happens when we die?" I ask, completely changing the subject.

"What the hell kind of question is that?" He asks sounding irritated.

"I need to know Patrick. I want to share my feeling too but I also need to get this off my chest." I explain.

"It was not the response I was expecting but I don't want you to think that just because I say something about my feelings that I expect you to do the same. I'm not saying these things just to get responses. I hope you know that. It was just surprising, you surprise me a lot. You're different, quirky and I love that about you." He said as he twists his fingers through the ends of my hair.

I smile at him but I don't want to ask again. I know I need to share a few more "quirky" things about me that in reality, if the tables were turned, and he shared with me what I am about to share with him, I would think he was nuts.

"OK," he sighs again. "I'm not a religious guy. I believe in a lot of things when it comes to issues that are bigger than I am. I consider the topic of all things that require faith to be bigger than myself. If it wasn't, then it would be a fact, and we don't have factual evidence when it comes to life, death, purpose or meaning. I know we as human beings are functioning at a small percentage of who we are as a soul, light source, energy…all that stuff. I believe that after this life, we transform into our higher self or what we originated from." His voice fades.

"Wow, I don't know about that…you sound like a real weirdo." I laugh. "I'm kidding! Seriously, that is actually beautifully said."

"It wasn't until I went to the Grand Teton's that I really felt connected to something that was more alive, bigger and…I don't know…better than myself. It was just me out there but something else was with me. Maybe God, maybe a great spirit, I don't know but it was showing me strength in myself that I didn't know I had. Especially after losing my leg." He said as he looked down at his leg.

"Here is my strange little story. No laughing." I smile and pause for a few minutes in order to find a good place to start. "I was hurt, really hurt after the accident. I stayed in a coma for a week and remember very little about that time. When I woke up, I found out my leg was broken, a few of my ribs shattered but the head injury was the most serious. The only thing I can remember is seeing Emma. She visited me frequently and so did a few other people. I didn't know them, but we became friends, it's not really the definition of a friend but you get the idea right?"

"I thought your friend died?" He asks looking confused.

"She did, but I didn't believe it and no one believed me. Of course, they didn't believe me, she really died that night. But in no way was I going to believe it because I was seeing her all the time. That's when my parents placed me in a mental health hospital. Not necessarily because I was delusional, but they thought it would help with my brain injury and rewire all the areas that needed rewiring. I don't need to go into all the details but to this day, I still see, sense or even hear Emma. Here's the other part of that, I can also see other people that are not really there. I mean, they're there, but I am the only one who sees them." I wait for his response but I don't get one.

"Ugh!" I moan, "I sound so stupid, it's so unbelievable and I get that. I'm not saying I'm psychic. I never want to be considered as that because that's not me. I don't know why I see them, and they don't look like us. They are different. It's like their iridescent and made of light or energy or...vibrations..." My voice turns to a whisper as I remember the way Ellie described Max.

"I used to deny it, think that I was hallucinating or just ignore them. Emma, I can't ignore her. I can't ignore any of it anymore. The other night, after I saw Max in the water, he came in. Not him as who he was when he died, nothing gross like that. In fact, I wasn't scared. He was young though, he only stayed a second and it was like he left through me. I felt his...whatever it was, it seemed to just kind of go through me. I didn't tell Ellie. I had too many other questions to ask. But, Emma...sometimes she scares me. The night before I met Ellie, she was with me. I didn't see her, but she kept calling my name. I was terrified."

"What's the reason these people come to you?" Patrick asks.

I am shocked at his response and especially his question. It's not at all what I am expecting and not prepared to answer it, so instead, I just look at him. It is like I'm in a trance because I can't say anything and my brain was not computing.

"Hello?" Patrick said as he waves his hand in front of my face.

"Sorry, I umm... no one has asked me that before. I don't... I really don't know why."

"Well, number one," Patrick starts, "I believe you. We don't know what our brains are capable of right? So even if it was the accident or some other phenomenon, I believe that you are seeing someone that others can't." He stops.

"And two?" I ask.

"This is your thing. We all have a thing we master right? So master this, find out more. Or better yet, you might need to just accept it for what it is." He questions more than he makes a statement.

"Yea..." I pause. "Maybe. I can see what you mean. But that's not easy, I have literally fought for years against this. I constantly worried about being insane. I mean like really delusional."

"Crazy people don't quest-" He starts.

"I know... I've heard that before." I interrupt. "Crazy people don't usually question if they're crazy."

"Right." He smiles.

"Look," I sigh. "I love you. That is the easy part. I just don't know how to put it together. My other life and this life are not one of the same Patrick. I don't know how or if I even want to blend it together. I would need to find a job up here, I need to find a place to live and essentially start all over. There isn't a prison up here either."

"Whoa, back up." He interrupts. "Prison?"

"I didn't mention? I am a fugitive. Guilty." I smile.

"Seriously, how in the world does a prison fall into the mix?" He asks.

"I work in surgery. I assist and organize surgeries for the federal and state prison systems. I have my privileges with several hospitals in the state for criminals who are being sent to prison or already in the system." I explain.

"Why am I just now finding that out? That's pretty fascinating." He raises an eyebrow that has become something he does that I find irresistible and extremely sexy.

"Well, you never asked, I suppose I never really talked about it either." I climb into his lap, wrap my legs around his waist and on and on it goes.

Chapter 18

I wake up to the sound of people talking but I can't make out the words. I lay still for a moment, trying to find familiarity in their voices but all I can hear is Patrick laughing. I slip on my hoodie and sweats and wander into the living room where my parents, as well as Patrick's parents, are laughing as if they all go way back.

"Mom? Dad? How in the world- when did you get up here?" I said as I rubbed my face.

"Patrick called us, he wanted to meet us. We drove up early this morning." My mom smiles.

"And my mom brought some muffins and fruit for breakfast," Patrick said.

"Oh, well good morning then. This is a nice surprise." I smile.

Patrick stands next to me, and I thank his mom for bringing muffins and fruit. I assume Patrick has properly introduced himself already and I hug my mom and dad, it feels good to see them.

"Well..." My mom looks at me. "I'm very happy that Patrick called and asked us to all meet. I...we had no idea what was happening up here and how... Rainy never mentioned... well... it's a lot to take in."

"I adore your daughter." Patrick smiles and kisses my forehead. "She sure took me by surprise, I wasn't expecting to fall in love like I have. I wanted all of us to formally meet."

"Patrick, you're a good man." My dad stands up. "I appreciate you putting this all together, and meeting your parents."

"How about you boys go take a look at old Chevy or something while we girls get to talking." Patrick's mom said as she heads into the kitchen.

I give my dad a hug as he tells me he loves me. My nickname is something I'm sure I will need to explain Patrick and I make a mental note as he looks at me with a little confusion. As the boys head out to the shed, I look to Ellie for assurance that this is all OK. I can tell she wants to tell me something but in private, so I nod my head to let her know I understand. As Patrick's mom and my mom head into the kitchen, Ellie whispers how thrilled she is to have everyone here, but she also tells me that Jacob's ex-wife is coming soon. She feels more comfortable having us here.

"Does everyone know she's coming?" I whisper back.

"Yes, although you need to talk to your parents because they don't know everything that has happened and why she is coming." She said.

"OK, I will talk with them, don't worry though. You couldn't have asked for a more open-minded duo." I explain.

"Mom, I thought we could go for a walk?" I ask my mom who is chatting with Patrick's mom. "I will get dressed, we can go before the afternoon storms roll through."

My mom and I find the guys looking under the hood of Ellie's old car and I make eye contact with Patrick. He gives me a charming smile and I want to give him a huge rodeo type of hug but wonder if my parents really understand how I feel about this man. My dad joins us, and we begin walking along the tree line until we reach the entrance to the path that leads to Max.

"I am taking you on a little path, so we can talk but all I ask is that you stay opened minded."

"We are so happy you have found these people. Ellie is so kind, and Patrick, oh my…he is just so taken by you. He's very handsome Rainy." My mom smiles.

"He means so much to me, so does Ellie and being up here has made me feel wanted, I have a purpose. I just don't know if staying up here is my next step or if I need to come home and continue on with my life." I said.

"I just wanted to say something real quick to my ladies. Patrick asked his parents and me if he could marry you." He blurts out.

"What?" I gasp. "Hell no. No way. What did you tell him, dad?" I beg.

"I like that kid. I really do, from the second I spoke to him on the phone. We have talked a few times for long lengths. He is fully aware of your past, and I said yes and so did his dad. His parents love you as well." My dad said proudly.

"Dad, you don't even know Patrick. Hell- I am just starting to know him too. Plus, I didn't come up here to get married, or even get a boyfriend." I said in frustration.

"I know, so I told him to wait." He said.

"You did?" I stop walking. "I mean, that's good but how did he take it?" I ask.

"He will wait his whole life if he needs too." He said. "Plus, he knows you have decisions to make and thinks it's best for you to make them without giving you any contributing situations to consider."

"I don't know what to say, dad. I mean it seems a little fast. Maybe a few years from now?" I question. "Mom? Did you know about this?" I ask.

"No, I am just as surprised as you are, but I can tell you are both crazy for each other." She answers.

"We are. It just happened and things make sense but it's not because of Patrick. It's also not about me anymore, that's why I wanted to go for a walk." I said as I start walking.

We get to the creek and I cross over as my parents follow, removing their shoes first. I tell them about Max and how Ellie followed through with his last request and what she went through to bring him up to the creek. I show them the water where Max is and I tell the whole story as they listen carefully. I'm surprised at their reaction because I reacted so differently when I first saw Max. Then again, presentation is everything when it comes to this kind of thing.

"Why would Ellie's kids do that?" My dad asks.

"I don't understand it either dad, but she has all of us now. Ellie also told me that Jacob's ex-wife is coming up today to talk to Ellie."

"We're really proud of you Neha. Standing Bull would be too. He always said you would bring happiness." He said.

"No dad, he said I would bring rain. Nice try though." I smirk playfully.

"Rain is what makes things grow, and growth brings happiness so..." He said back with the same smirk.

"You're stretching it dear." My mom laughs.

"Oh, and by the way- Patrick has a magic leg. He lost his leg in a car accident. His friend was driving and someone hit them. He lost his leg, but they gave him a new one." I said.

"Well then, you two have more in common than we thought. That's too bad that he went through that. No one should have to go through that, the pain is spread over so many people." My mom rambles.

"A magic leg huh?" My dad interrupts. "Now who's stretching it?"

Another car is parked in front of the house by the time we get back. It doesn't look familiar and I assume it is Jacob's ex-wife's car. I quickly hurry back inside hoping I didn't miss anything but also wanting to be there for Ellie.

I open the front door and a woman has her back to me and sitting down in Ellie's chair. She has long, thick brown hair that is turning gray and I can instantly smell her perfume. This is the smell Ellie was talking about on the letters she received from her. It smells oddly familiar but I can't really figure it out. Ellie motions for me to join them and introduces the woman as she turns around.

Oh no, oh my God no.

Chapter 19

I take a step back and trip over her bag, losing complete balance and fall into Patrick. I feel a sharp pain in my lower back as I scream. My breath leaves my body and I can barely get enough air in my lungs. Every single move I make or gasp of air I take only makes it worse.

My parents jump up and rush over to me as Gwen leaps from her seat and gets as far away from me as possible without actually leaving the room. Everyone starts shouting and voices start to blend together, and I can't keep up with that has happened. *Gwen? Why is Emma's mom here?*

"Rainy, Rainy!" Patrick is shouting over me. "Do not move, do you hear me? Do not move. You are OK."

I nod my head that I understand what he was telling me. I look at my mom who was looking at me, then back at Gwen.

"What did you do to her Gwen?" My mom sobbed. "Why are you here? How could you?"

"NO!" Patrick shouts and the room instantly gets quiet. "Everyone needs to calm down. Dad, go to the truck and grab my medical bag. Rainy, I know it hurts but I need you to listen to me very carefully. Everyone needs to listen and stop what you're doing." Patrick ordered.

"Now, I don't know who you are, or what you're doing here but those questions need to be addressed later. Does everyone understand? OK. I do not want anyone to move. Is that clear? No one. Rainy, you have fallen back on the metal plate to my prosthetic leg. I don't know how far it has gone through but from what I can tell, it's in pretty far. I can't move and neither can you." He said slowly.

"Can't you pull it out?" My mom's voice is shaking.

"No, I am going to detach the metal plate from my leg, then we are going to leave it there until we can get the medics up here to get her to the hospital. I don't want to remove it; it might be what keeps her lungs from collapsing."

"Dispatch, I need immediate support to C.R 14 over." His dad calls into the radio.

"Dispatch to 17-Copy that. What is the address?"

"9856-I've got a potential pneumothorax." He said calmly.

"We have EMS in response. Stand-by 17."

"OK, dad I need you to get the tension release tool from my bag. Then I need the biggest syringe you can find in there. Rainy, I have help on the way. I need you to hold still. I am going to detach the metal plate from my leg. It is going to stay inside you until we get you to the hospital. OK?" Patrick said calmly.

I can't respond, I am too short of breath to say anything so I nod my head. The pain has taken over the whole left side of my torso and catching my breath is impossible to do. I cough a little but I feel like I am drowning. I can hear several voices coming from different directions, but the only person I can actually see was Patrick.

"This isn't going to feel good, I need to make some space for the air to come through," Patrick said looking straight into my eyes.

The pain is extreme, but I can't vocalize any of it. I want to find a comfortable position or try to take the metal piece out of my side but the pressure keeps me from moving. I can hear Patrick's dad talking into the radio and static voices answering in between high-pitched beeping sounds and static.

"Rainy! You have got to stay still. Someone needs to hold her hands down." Patrick yells at me.

I can feel the pressure on my chest easing up but the pain is incredible. Patrick stands up as other people who I don't recognize file in around me. They move me to a board keeping me on my right side and strap me down and before I know it, I am in the ambulance. I start shaking but force myself to stay with the pain. I just keep telling myself this over and over. I don't want to pass out or fall asleep even though I am absolutely terrified.

I lost a lot of blood while in transport and feel lightheaded once we arrive at the hospital but I still keep myself somewhat aware of my surroundings. I can't get an x-ray because the piece that is sticking out of me is metal. Patrick doesn't leave my side but once he sees my parents, he goes to them. A nurse comes in and tells me that I am going asleep for a little while but reassures me the metal will be gone when I wake up.

I don't want to go to sleep and yell for Patrick. He runs in with my parents behind him and I can see Ellie in the hall standing next to Emma's mom and I suddenly feel betrayed.

"Don't let them put me to sleep," I whisper.

"Well, they can't take my foot out of your lung with you awake." Patrick smiled as he looked down at me.

"Last time, please. Mom. Dad. Remember last time. I didn't remember when I woke up."

"Honey, it's not like that this time." My mom said.

"You are going to be OK Neha. I promise." My dad smiles and let's go of my hand.

Patrick and my parents walk down the hallway while I am transferred into a cold, white room with huge lights hanging from the ceiling. Someone tells me to count down from one hundred.

"Ninety-nine, ninety-eight, ninety-seh…vaann…"

"Hey sleepy girl, how do you feel?" Patrick's voice is soft and smooth.

I am relaxed and groggy but as I wake up a little more, I can't fight the urge to laugh. Once I start laughing, I can't stop which makes Patrick laugh too. The only thing that seems to stop me is the pain that follows. Once the pain eases up, I laugh again.

"The sedation is making her a little goofy." He informs my parents who just came back into my room.

"Well, laughter is the best medicine." My mom said as she brushes the hair from my face.

"Can you guys believe this happened? Did you get your foot back?" I said with a groggy voice and can barely ask without laughing.

"I did," Patrick said. "You sure know where to land."

"Hey, what the hell was Emma's mom doing up at Ellie's? Whose bright idea was that?" I ask.

"Gwen? Rainy that is Jacob's ex-wife. Your mom and dad also told me that she is Emma's mom too." He said.

"That's actually way too hard to believe. It's impossible; Jacobs's ex-wife? When did Emma's parents' divorce?" I ask.

"We divorced a few years after Emma passed away." Emma's mom is standing in the door.

"Um, let's give them time to talk. Neha, we will be right outside, the little waiting room. OK?" My dad said.

Everyone left, and I am at the mercy of Emma's mom. She sat down next to me, and tears roll down her cheeks as she looks at me.

"I'm sorry about what happened to Emma. I'm so sorry." I whisper.

"Shhh…listen kiddo, I owe you an apology as to how I handled myself all those years ago. I know it was a difficult time for everyone." She spoke softly.

"I miss her every day. The pain is still inside me as if it just happened yesterday."

"You need to forgive yourself for what happened Rainy. It was an accident, a terrible accident. I miss her too, I miss her to the point where some days I want to leave this life just to be with her again." She said.

"I know it's all I seem to say but I really am so sorry," I said again.

"It was a huge surprise to see you, looks like it was an even bigger surprise to you." She smiled.

"I was shocked." I wince. "I actually thought you stabbed me at first," I add.

"I think everyone did."

"How did you, why… I mean Jacob. Ellie's son and you? Married?" I ask.

"Emma's dad and I divorced a few years after the accident. We just fell apart. We had problems before that and the relationship wasn't strong enough to handle her death." She sighed. "I was still a mess when I met Jacob and I had no business marrying him but I did. He is not a good person."

"I've heard his sister isn't either," I said.

"I don't know her all that well, but I wouldn't want to be on their bad side." She said. "But, it doesn't matter anymore. I have a plan to keep them from doing anything stupid or make more threats." She added.

Having her mom here brought back emotions I thought I lost all those years ago and I realize that having her here in this way is what I have needed for so long. To hear her tell me that I need to forgive myself is difficult, but I can understand it now. Before when people said that, I had no clue how to forgive myself but now, I can see where I never have and it's time.

"After the accident, I went through some things that put me in a hospital where they could help fix my brain injury, I am so sorry I called you back then. I really thought she was alive, I could see her so clearly and… I got confused… I'm so sorry." I whisper.

"I had no idea, I heard you went to a recovery center, but because I was so unreasonable, I was never given information about you. I feel Emma like she is right next to me, but I have never seen her. I can dream about her, but even then I don't see her. I suppose that's not how it works… you know… with the afterlife." She said as if she is embarrassed.

"I understand, I don't know much-" My thought process is interrupted as I shift my focus to a very faint light with an iridescent figure that became clearer the longer I looked. I know what is about to happen but I don't know who it is until I hear a gasp come from Emma's mom. It is Emma and to say I am shocked that her mom can see this is an understatement. This is the first time I have seen her in a while but I know the voices I heard at the campground were hers. This time, I don't feel scared and rather than looking at her, I can't take my eyes off Gwen. Her face has a glow cast over it as she looks directly at Emma.

"Oh, Emma." Her hand covers her mouth, and tears build up in her eyes. "My sweet Emma, I miss you so much." She tells her.

Emma is outlined in the most beautiful and angelic light one can imagine. Her smile was kind, warm, and loving as she reaches out to touch her mom softly on her cheek. Her mom brings her hand out to reach for her, but the light fades, leaving completely.

Cold air flows through me and blows my hair back slightly as she disappears into thin air just like it did when I saw Max. Emma and Max are the only two who came through light and I wonder if the others who came before Max had a light but I just didn't believe it enough to really see it. A feeling of pure content and happiness falls over every part of my soul I can tell her mom feels it too. For the first time in years of breathing and surviving, I was able to feel love for myself and what forgiveness, true forgiveness really feels like.

"She is beautiful, tell me you saw her." Her mom quickly turns to look at me.

I saw her, but the best part is the fact that you saw her too. Emma heard me…she gave me my answer…but what do I do with it?

"I saw her, I've seen her before too, and now I know why," I whisper.

Chapter 20

The doctor said I can go home after spending two nights. I am relieved that I only need stitches, but he warns me that my lung is still jeopardized. While the risk is low, my lung can still cause complications. Patrick is given orders to take care of me which he seems a little too excited about. Admittedly, I am looking forward to lounging around with him.

I am quiet on the way back to Ellie's and I know Patrick senses that something is wrong, but he doesn't ask. I wouldn't know what to say anyway because I can't really figure out what is wrong in the first place. Something feels off balance and I can't put my finger on it.

My parents are waiting on the porch holding Raven in their lap as we drive up. I can't help but smile, and I am comforted to see them. Then I realize why I feel so disconnected.

"Hi! Are you glad to be back?" My mom asks.

"Yea, I feel much better. Where is Ellie?" I ask as I pick up Raven who is now able to perch on my hand.

"She is in the house taking a nap." She answers.

Ellie has been sleeping a lot lately, she seems more tired and less engaged as to what everyone is saying and doing. She will quietly listen to the conversations but won't say much, and sometimes I wonder if she is able to follow along. She doesn't complain of pain, she doesn't seem depressed either, she is simply tired.

When I get to her room, she is laying on her side curled up with her knees to her chest. This isn't the first time I've seen her this way but it was the first time I see something in her that I fear. My heart goes to my stomach and I have a sick feeling deep down inside where emotions are raw and fragile. She has herself covered with a thin blanket and it outlines her bones and sharp curves that send chills down my spine.

"Ellie?" I whisper. "I'm back. Do you need anything?"

The length of time it takes to focus her hollow eyes on me makes me want to cry. It is such a huge shift from the quick-footed little lady I met just a few months ago. As she begins to focus more, I ask her again if she wants anything. She slowly unfolds her weary body and I sit a few pillows for her to lean up against.

"No, honey. I'm OK."

Her voice is weak as she coughs, barely able to catch her breath. I can hear a deep rattle in her lungs and I instantly know why she has been so tired and lifeless.

"You seem a little sad. Are you OK?" She finally wheezes the question.

"No, I'm OK. Yea... I mean Ellie?" I sigh as I look out her door. "The doctor said I can go home. Go home. Home has always been where my parents are. Now, I just don't know." I said as I wring my hands together.

"Home is anywhere..." Ellie coughs and finally catches her breath. "Love lives."

I can't let Ellie struggle another second. I call out to Patrick and explain that I think Ellie is sick and needs to see a doctor. He brings his medical bag over and checks her temperature, listens to her chest, takes her blood pressure and checks her oxygen level.

"Ellie, you have a fever and your lungs are rattling. You also have low oxygen. I think this is a good time to take you to town. We need to get you on some antibiotics and maybe give you a nebulizer treatment." Patrick said as he holds her hand.

Patrick and his parents make arrangements to get Ellie to the doctor while I stay behind with my parents.

The house is empty, my mom and dad are on a walk as I lay back in bed. The last few days are catching up to me and filling my heart with uncertainty. There seems to be so much happening all at once and normally, this is the life I craved. I needed this kind of chaos in order to function and now, it feels so overwhelming. I have grown to enjoy the solitude the past few months has given me.

I worry about Ellie, a woman that not only do I love like a family member but also admire. Her strength is untouchable. What she has faced over the years is unthinkable and heartbreaking. It can't be possible that just when her freedom is within reach, she falls sick. It's unfair, unfair to her. I am determined to understand the plan Gwen has proposed yet, I still can't wrap my head around the fact that she also plays a huge role in my past.

I have cautiously fallen in love with Patrick knowing that it might be just another thing I will need to let go of. He loves me more than I ever could ask for, especially from a guy like him. I love him too and until I can see how my life unfolds, I can't fully surrender my heart.

Any day now Raven will take flight. He will fly away and find a home and the thought brings more sadness than anything else. Having a pet raven isn't logical but I want it to be. I want him to stay with me, but I also know I have to do what is best for him. I am not his home and it's almost certain, he will forget me.

I don't know where home is, I can't tell where I belong and at least before coming up here, I knew those things. It's so cliché to think of my life as a fork in the road but essentially, I have two very different paths to take and I'm not sure which one makes sense.

One path leads me home to all things familiar and steady. It holds my career, my parents and my financial security. I created a stable future that looks good on even the most torn up piece of paper.

The other path leads me to where I am today, here with Patrick and caring for Ellie who has forever left her mark on my heart. It is so unsteady, so unpredictable and it's everything I needed to get away from; everything I created, so I could forget what I created.

I think of different scenarios, like taking Ellie back with me which quickly dissolves when I realize this is her home, this is where she belongs. I can date Patrick and see him on weekends or days off but the idea pulls on a section of my heart that brings a sense of loss.

Somehow, I can see where sometime soon, I will need to make a decision and I hope the decision can be made for me, in the same way I was led up here; the part of life that is more of our destiny rather than our plan.

Chapter 21

"What do you mean she refused treatment? She can't do that can she?" I whisper to Patrick.

"Yes, she can, and she did."

"That's the silliest thing I have heard." I shake my head. "She isn't thinking clearly."

"Do you know who you sound like right now? Jacob and Holly." Patrick said quietly.

"What? No, I'm not. I'm nothing like them. I would never do what her kids did to Ellie after Max died. Why on earth would you say that?"

"That's not what I meant. I know you wouldn't do that, but you're saying the same things they did."

Our voices are starting to rise and I don't want Ellie to hear the conversation. I am done talking about the subject, so I go outside. Patrick follows me and precedes to try to explain himself but I can't talk about the subject. However, I stop in my tracks when he apologizes to me. I have never known a man other than my dad to say sorry to me. Zac never did, even when he told me he cheated on me.

"Please, Rainy. Just understand? I'm sorry I insinuated that you were like them. I know you're not." He pleads.

"Thank you." I turn around to see him standing in front of me just as genuine as I hoped.

Patrick sighs once I turn around to face him. He is relieved that I stopped to acknowledge his apology, and I am comforted by his authentic response. His shoulders relax and I can tell there isn't anything more he would rather do than see me happy.

"Maybe you can start over? What did the doctor say?" I ask hoping we can simply move past it.

"She has phenomena, they did a chest x-ray and all four quadrants are full of fluid. She is also in possible renal failure, her test results will give us more information in a few days. They wanted to admit her in the hospital but as I said, she refused all treatments. The doctor gave us an inhaler and antibiotics which will help clear the phenomena but even then, she needs oxygen and fluids to fully recover."

"Why? She doesn't have cancer, I mean all this is curable right?" I ask.

"Maybe, elderly people die of phenomena all the time, even infants. Her kidney issues are more serious. We also discovered that she hasn't been to a doctor since before Max died. She isn't the healthiest person right now, and she doesn't have insurance. We are asking Gwen to drive up and give us the details of Ellie's financial situation, and get her on insurance. Until then, we don't really have much we can do until the results come in."

"I thought Ellie talked to her already," I ask.

"They did talk but Gwen left shortly after visiting with you and we never talked to her. She agreed to come up in a few days when we know more. She also told us that there is some information she can't disclose. Ellie asked her not too."

"I have a feeling I know what it is." I sigh.

Ellie sleeps most of the day now and has not walked the path to Max since getting sick. The antibiotics are doing very little and her test results came back with full renal failure along with other disheartening medical concerns.

My parents have gone home and Patrick comes up in the evening after work to help out, not that there is much any of us can do at this point. When Patrick arrives, I go for a walk. I always go see Max for Ellie and report back to her which she appreciates. She loves listening to me, just like the first night we met. She finds comfort in this but will stop me if I am not being descriptive enough or if I'm not going into enough detail.

When I go see Max, she asks about the wind, or how the earth feels under my feet. Fall is settling in the forest, so I will bring her leaves that are changing and with her new glasses, she can see every detail of the colors. She likes the smooth texture of the leaves and will hold it between her fingers. She explains that she always get the blues this time of year. Even though the pine trees stay green throughout the year, the maple or aspen trees lose their leaves in preparation for winter. I share a story from the native's about a tree that my parents used to share with me.

"Our lives are like the life of a tree. In the spring, a tree blooms with color and enthusiasm for life. A tree in the spring offers hope, it shows us that even the deepest and coldest parts of winter can't keep it from coming back to life. None of us are immune from heartache, tragedy, or loss but what we make from it is proof that we also have a spring season to bloom.

In the summer, a tree shows us a slightly different shade of green from the pine trees that surround it. These are the trees that leave us in the fall and winter but return, always showing us those differences. We also learn that not one kind of tree is better than the other. A pine tree stays through the harshest conditions and thrives while the other trees go to sleep but both have important reasons. In the summer months, a tree offers shade, protection, contrast, life, and stability.

In the fall, the tree changes into more colors we ever thought possible. The rich green leaves turn yellow, orange and red preparing us for what lies ahead, reminding us of the legacy it will leave behind but reassuring us through the beauty of it all. Some trees reward its receivers with sweet fruit to gather in preparation for the coming winter. We all have the ability to give away what no longer serves us, and we do this with such grace.

In the winter, a tree is bare, leafless and venerable and like a tree, we all have a winter stage in life where all the wisdom, life, and offerings we had from the other seasons become a memory. We contemplate life, what was, and all the memories we store in our hearts. We don't look as beautiful as we might have been in the other seasons, but we carry wisdom. Maybe we take this wisdom with us, but we definitely pass it down and that becomes our legacy.

The roots of our tree represent things in our life that keep us grounded and centered. Those are the same things in life that we can't live without. We are rooted deeply into the ground, stable and accepting to the life mother earth offers. Without a root system, a tree wouldn't be a tree in the same way we wouldn't survive. Before all else, before seasons or leaves, the roots must be nurtured.

The trunk of the tree is the same as our personality. How flexible we are plays a role in how we react to life's storms. Will we have the mental stamina to flex enough through the dangerous winds that threaten us? Or do we snap? Flexibility allows us to survive giant storms much like the storms throughout a person's life. What we do to maintain this flexibility depends on how we think, how we grow and nurture our well-being.

The branches of our tree represent our interests. It's what we love to do when all the other aspects of the tree are being cared for. This is the reward, each branch holds a tiny part of who we are. These interests are what our branches are made out of.

So you see Ellie, a tree is just like us. Sometimes, our seasons don't go in a particular order, but we celebrate each season knowing it serves a purpose."

I finish my story knowing Ellie has slept through most of it, but not caring. It feels good to repeat it and in doing so, understanding it more than I ever had before.

Conversations with Ellie are deep and meaningful, we have very little small talk these days and her time is the most precious gift she has. Her eyes, gray and light are changing in color, almost turning light blue creating an eerie effect against her gray, relatively white hair. We laugh together, cry together, and while she naps during the day, I sleep with her.

Raven loves to run across the bed and I make sure Ellie gets to see him when she is awake. He is making typical raven sounds and sometimes, it's loud enough to wake her up. He hops around the house usually and will follow me from room to room, sometimes flying to me. Raven is a happy little guy and expressive. His excitement to see me is contagious, especially when he simply wants me to hold him. I take him outside several times a day to let him fly, but he is always tethered. Soon, he will be ready to fly away.

The wind that once blew through her white sheer curtains has now ceased. The chill is too much for Ellie. I have closed the windows, and every time a breeze comes up, her house protests with creaking sounds.

She has a bible sitting on her nightstand and I pick it up, seeing it bookmarked in several places. I have not opened a bible and read it since the accident but today, with the stillness in the air and the sun warning us of winter, I open it to the first marked page and realize the bible is written in a storybook format which I like even more. She opens her gray-blue eyes as soon as she realizes what I am reading. She loves the story of Noah and I remember my connection to it as well.

Ellie has lost most of her appetite but enjoys sipping on chocolate milk. Patrick suggested not to let her drink milk, it tends to make her cough more; somehow causing her saliva to thicken making it difficult to control. When she asks, I don't have the heart to tell her no when this is about the only thing she likes. She also appreciates the way I make soup, particularly chicken and stars. I don't add as much water when I cook it, making the flavor more intense. She is starting to lose her sense of taste and the robust flavor of chicken and stars soup tends to liven up her appetite.

Her breathing has become short and weak and in my moments of fear, I become obsessed with the rhythm. I hold onto the sound of her inhales and exhales, timing them with the tick of the clock coming from the kitchen. Tick-inhale-tick-exhale-tick-inhale...

Chapter 22

"You can take me to Max now," Ellie whispers to Patrick. Ellie is getting frailer as the days drag out. I can see where she has lost almost all muscle and any fat she had vanished a long time ago.

He leans over Ellie and wraps his arms around her tiny frame, supporting her as he covers her up in a blanket. He carries her as if she weighs nothing at all which at this point, she can't weigh much. I open the doors and walk ahead of them until we reach the opening of the forest. He walks down the path carrying Ellie like my dad used to carry me to bed.

I am concerned about crossing the creek but quickly realized it was no match for Patrick.

"Where do you want to lay Ellie, under the tree?" He asks.

"No." She said in a whisper, "Lay me next to Max, on the bank."

The ground is coated with fallen aspen tree leaves, making it yellow and shades of green. I lay extra blankets down creating a soft place for her to rest.

"Are you comfortable?" He asks.

She nods, so I place a blanket under her with several small pillows for her head. She looks to the sky, the trees that tower over her and the golden colored ground that surrounds her and eventually she turns towards Max. Her face softens as she places her thin hand over the water as it flows between her fingers.

Fall is almost at an end but today is warm, the sun peeking through the tips of the trees. My heart aches for what is coming next and staying in the moment is almost impossible. I have no words to speak and even if I had them, I'm not sure they would come out.

Patrick heads back to the house, we're waiting for Gwen to arrive. At this point, she has not been detected up here and if she has, no one has heard from Holly or Jacob. Patrick and his dad disconnected the surveillance camera more than a month ago which makes us all believe Jacob and Holly are not actively watching.

"Did you bring everything?" She asks in a cracked and weak whisper.

All I can do is nod my head. What I have done to get to this point is beyond my own comprehension. We have been in close supervision with a doctor from the same agency that cared for Max and now, I find myself in the same footprints Ellie was.

What I am about to do absolutely crushes my soul. It goes against everything I have ever known. I can't do this without the support of Patrick, his parents or mine. Gwen can't know, all she knows is Ellie is dying and needs to speak with her one last time.

I caused an accident that killed my best friend which destroyed many lives, as well as mine. I functioned but at the lowest level a person can. Gwen's marriage broke up and my parents had to emotionally support me since the night it happened. At this moment, I question whether I have what it takes to survive this after it is all said and done. I am helping Ellie, my friend and personal hero, end her life. I am doing this as her last wish knowing, my actions are taking another life.

I can't say for certain if this was Ellie's plan all along. Perhaps this is where her desperation came from in wanting me to take her home so many months ago. Even if it was, I don't mind. I suppose it can only mean that she saw something in me that I didn't.

I still don't know if I acquire the traits that she sees in me. I don't feel courageous or strong and I don't know if I want the life that follows this. I will live the rest of my life in this shadow, much like the shadow of Emma and I lost myself in it.

As Gwen and Patrick weave the path to where I sit with Ellie, I can understand how bizarre this looks to anyone from the outside. Patrick and I faced Ellie towards the waterfall where Max's body has been for so many years, only his structure remains, pinned down with heavy stones. We can't allow Gwen to see him and realize the risk we all face if she does. When she talks to Ellie, her back will be away from the waterfall, assuring us that she won't notice. The runoff is steady from the recent rains making the waterfall flow faster than it did months ago when I first saw Max. The area where Max rests is deeper than before and the crashing of the water makes it difficult to see through. As the creek is met with gravity and force, it creates an abundance of oxygenated water flow creating a white barrier making it impossible to see through. This is our only protection, Mother Nature at her finest.

We leave Ellie to speak with Gwen and give them privacy but I can't help to wonder what they are discussing. Gwen smiles occasionally and nods her head but I question how well she can hear Ellie considering the sound of the waterfall and Ellie's voice being so weak. She doesn't stay long, it doesn't even seem like she was here for ten minutes at the most. She glances over to us as our cue that Ellie has said all she needed to say.

Even from a distance, I can smell Gwen's perfume, such a familiar scent reaching back to when Emma was alive. She never wore her mom's perfume, but she always had a vague scent that lingered on her, possibly because she gave her mom a hug. It's the same scent that Ellie looked forward too. She kneels down to give Ellie a hug and as we get closer, Gwen smiles sweetly and tells us that she can see herself back.

Both Patrick and I sit next to Ellie, not talking much and when we did, it was conversations between Patrick and myself. Ellie listens and would dangle her hand over the top of the water. Leaves from the surrounding aspen trees slowly fall onto our blankets or in the water which is a pleasant distraction. Ellie isn't interested in eating, and she hasn't been for a few days.

As the day turned into evening and before the dark set in, Patrick collects firewood. It is only when Patrick is gone that Ellie talks to me.

"If you could do anything in the world, what would you do?" She asks, barely able to get the words out.

"Well, I suppose I don't really know. As far as a career, I never thought much about it… I don't know if I would keep doing what I do now…maybe something more meaningful I guess." I respond.

I look to Ellie as I speak, and she has her eyes closed listening to me, but when I ask why she wants to know or what she would have done in her life, she doesn't respond. She will cough and at times, I wonder if she will catch her breath again. Her lungs are rattling worse than even the day before and I can see for the first time how much she's struggling to breathe and how scared this makes her.

"Any…time Rainy." Ellie coughs. "I can go now."

Tears flood my eyes and all I can do is tell her how much I love her. I want her to know that in the end, she is loved and admired. I need her to know she has friends she is leaving behind. I explain that family isn't always from blood. I remind her that she is family. I want to say everything I can, knowing that after today I won't see Ellie on this side of life.

Patrick starts the fire and the smell of pine burning along with the freshness in the air makes my heart ache. Oddly, it smells like what I imagine an ending to smell like and the sorrow that comes with it.

Patrick helps me give Ellie drops of morphine quickly, so she can get enough in her system before she falls asleep and can't swallow. My hands are shaking and I can't see clearly because of the tears welling up in my eyes. There are other medications that needed to be taken but I don't know what they are, all I know is that she needs to take them. She coughs with every dropper of morphine and it scares me. Patrick can tell that I am reaching my own threshold of capabilities and steps in to comfort me, eventually taking over. Once he gave her the last of the medicine, he holds my hand, and we both hold Ellie's.

"Thank…youuu…boooth…aaand I looove youuu too-." Ellie whispers.

"You're my person Ellie," I said through tears. "You're my person…"

I take Ellie's head and lift her on my lap like I did Emma all those years earlier. Ellie is dying in my arms like Max did years ago with Ellie and the sadness I feel is unbelievable. Being responsible for death whether in mercy or from an accident is the same. It feels exactly the same.

Patrick makes eye contact with me several times and I need this more than I realize. I don't feel alone and that in of itself is more than I could ask for. He keeps hold of her hand as I smooth her hair. The shadows from the campfire dance around through the reflection of the water or across our faces completely dependent on the random movement of the flames. He uses his stethoscope to listen to her heart while looking at me. Her breathing becomes shallow and fewer in between until eventually, she takes her final breath.

Patrick listens to her heart once more and shakes his head, letting me know her heart has stopped but before I could react we are suddenly distracted from a sound coming from deep within the trees.

The snapping of broken timber gets louder as we hold our breath in anticipation of what or who might be coming. Suddenly, a massive bull elk walks into the light of the fire and stands tall. He holds his head high with his majestic full rack of perfectly shaped antlers looking directly at us.

"Whoa," Patrick whispers.

"Shhh…it's OK. Max is taking Ellie home."

Patrick is startled and confused at what he is seeing as we sit in complete silence. I feel a sense of pride in the fact that I am the brave one, the calm and reassuring one. For the first time, I feel normal, human and honored to witness something that up until

Gwen and now Patrick, only I was capable of witnessing. I realize again that Gwen was meant to see Emma and Patrick was meant to see Max. I am the connection, confirming that I am not unstable.

Ellie walks toward Max and when she turns around, it's clear that she isn't the same person laying in my lap, she is young, like Max and so beautiful. They are outlined in a soft light that I have grown used to seeing and I can feel the love and peace between them. I want to give Patrick the same eye contact he offered me just moments earlier but when we looked at each other, his reaction of shock and uncertainty reminds me that Patrick doesn't understand what he is seeing.

Ellie raises her hand to me, and I raise mine back, the whole time Patrick is in disbelief. I can feel her words as if they are spoken from her mouth even though nothing is said. She is thanking me, and I feel her gratitude. This is something I need but didn't realize until now. I instantly feel OK, I don't fear the fallout of emotions that I worried about experiencing going into this. I know at this moment, what I've done is the best gift I could have given her. Both Emma and now Ellie are giving me the gift of solace and peace. Feelings that seem to transfer from them to me that takes away the pain of death.

Just as gracefully as they appear, they fade away. In the silence of the moment, somewhere between our shallow breaths and from deep within the trees, the elk announces his final call; echoing through the forest. *Bye, Ellie…be free.*

Chapter 23

We decide to wait until the sun comes up before heading back to the house. We wrap ourselves in blankets while we sit together, leaving Ellie covered a few feet away.

"I suppose this whole thing, the Elk and seeing Ellie… Max, is this the crazy you talk about?" Patrick asks. "Because I have never seen anything like that in all my life. This is what you see? People like that? How do you sleep? Does it scare you? It would scare me. I can understand why people don't believe you, I don't believe what I saw-"

"Hey, slow down." I interrupt. "It's taken many years to understand it myself. I still don't fully grasp it, but I don't feel like a nut case every time I have this kind of interaction. I should probably explain it more but I can't. I really didn't believe it myself until Emma came through while her mom was with me. This just happened the other day, Gwen saw her too and for the first time, I felt like what I see is real. The fact that you saw Ellie go to Max is so surreal to me. For all these years, I have created huge distractions and chaos trying to run from crazy/not crazy emotions. I needed others to see it."

"Why you? I mean, why do you see them, how do you get others to see them? I've never seen anything like this before."

"I don't know, I really don't understand it," I answer.

"Maybe that's what you're supposed to do, show others." He adds.

"Could be, and the longer I am on this journey, I can see the meaning of it all. I'm starting to understand myself, my direction but there are still things I don't understand."

"Isn't there TV shows or something, I know people go on TV and do these shows, maybe it's real after all?" He asks.

"I think some people have the capability to see, hear, and even feel the presence of those who passed on. Others lie about it but the bottom line is who believes it and who doesn't." I answer.

"But it's more complicated than that," I add. "I had a massive head injury, I was in a medically induced coma for weeks. When I was growing up, I had an active imagination but never saw people others couldn't. After the accident, that's when my life changed."

"I'm sorry, I didn't have a lot of understanding before this. You told me you… not that I didn't believe you… I just couldn't picture how it… now I can… I'm speechless…" He said but not making sense.

"I still struggle, now I do it with support from those who I never thought would support me. Emma's mom, she never would have seen Emma in the way she did if it weren't for me. You wouldn't have been able to see Ellie go to Max without me either. There's a connection, I know that I am meant to do more with this but up until this point in my life, I decided to run from it." I said with my voice trailing off.

"There is something pretty special about you Rainy. It scares me in some ways, Max… it was like he was talking to me, and he told me things without actually talking to me. It… I will never for it." He said shaking his head.

"I know, it's really unbelievable. Patrick, I'm exhausted. I need to shut down, sleep or disconnect for a while. There's so much that I need to do, and we still have Ellie at the creek, your dad needs to head over so you guys can take care of what Ellie wanted to be done with the burial. I need to call Gwen I guess."

When I walk into the house, the smell of lavender fills the air just like it did the first time I walked through her door. Raven, who is perched on twisted branches that Patrick and I built for him, holds his foot out as I walk by, so I pick him up. He loves going outside but I can't seem to find the motivation to take him.

I am relieved to be inside and alone so instead, I decide to let Raven hang out on my shoulder. Patrick left to get his dad, and I just need time to think, to breathe. I am emotionally drained as well as physically weak. So much has happened and I need to let all the emotions catch up to me.

As I start to cry, I grab hold of Ellie's old quilt and wrap it over me as I head into the kitchen. She is gone now, the first time I have been in her home without her and I feel lonely. I close my eyes and remember her face as she turned to me one last time, she was happy, content and free. Death is a beautiful ending or beginning to those who believe in eternity, heaven, or even simply returning to their highest self; the self that is enlightened. Death can be a selfish emotion felt by those who are left behind but it doesn't need to be. If we take away our personal sadness and grief we are left with a feeling of pure content knowing they have been set free.

Its morning but not ten in the morning as the clock suggests. I hold my breath a moment to completely silence my existence long enough to not hear what I have heard for so many months; something I depended on to remind me that time keeps ticking away regardless. The clock on the wall has stopped at ten and even though I can't say for certain, ten last night is about the time Ellie died; the same time Max died. I believe this, I have learned to surrender to a feeling like this as if it's already been written, and for me, coincidences just don't seem possible.

Sitting on the table, several piles of papers and envelopes we scattered with my name written on them. As I pick up the first one, the familiar smell of Gwen's perfume gave away any sort of mystery as to who they were from even though they regarded Ellie. Some were in Ellie's shaken and unsteady handwriting and other envelopes had my name meticulously written in perfect handwriting.

Dear Rainy,

If you are reading this, it means I have gone to be with Max.

For so many years, I wanted to walk next to him again, but after you wandered into my life, I found myself wanting to live just a little longer. You have shown me a life that I only thought would happen after my death.

I have so many reasons to thank you. You gave me hope in two realms of existence and I don't have the words to express my gratitude.

Gwen has tied up some loose ends regarding what I leave behind. I have given careful thought and consideration to the following decisions.

My son and daughter will not be notified by either of us for reasons you can understand. It will be your choice whether you decide to inform them. Regardless of what you decide to do, everything you are about to read has been legally bound and can in no way be altered.

Everything I have, all of my money and the estate are now yours. You will discover shortly just how much you are inheriting and like me, you will be shocked. I asked you what you wanted to do in life if you could do anything and in writing this, I don't know what your answer will be and at this point, you are the only one who will know. Think about what you told me, then I will ask you to consider one last idea.

This money is yours to do as you wish, the estate is yours as well and you have brought it back to life. Whatever you decide, I ask that you make it count. Use yourself and this money as a way to bring life to others, understanding that life isn't always what we think it is. You will never need to work again, you will have the freedom to make a difference in others like you have done for me.

I have separated all the papers and documents with phone numbers and names.

To Patrick, Evan, Beth, and Gwen, what would I have done without you? You made so many things possible for Max and I. Gwen has agreed to take a small amount of money after I convinced her to do so for her time and dedication to handling this. Patrick, I want you to drive Max's car, you have always loved it. To Evan and Beth, I have given you enough money to start your bakery again. I know my children took that away from you and it was something I couldn't forgive myself for.

Patrick and Rainy, the love you have for one another doesn't happen every day and so many people will never know a love like this. Don't let it go, don't get in its way and let it happen. Trust me, in the end, it will be what you live for.

Because life lives on…

Love, Ellie

Chapter 24

We all managed to come together, and place Ellie and Max together under their tree. No marker is set and it isn't needed or even wanted. The tree's roots are firmly planted deep below and the branches reach high above into the sky marking their existence. My dad performs the native offering ceremony and I read the same poem to them as I did to Emma.

Many moons have passed and the harshness of winter has come and gone. I live in the shadow of Ellie, and the smell of her lavender. The trail created years ago leads me to her every morning before I start my day. I keep the clock on the wall in the kitchen, never fixing it so it remains at ten o'clock. It won't work again because I removed the long brown cord that went into the power outlet.

A few weeks after Ellie died, I decided to let Raven take his final flight. As majestic as I wanted it to be, it was awkward and clumsy. I wanted to do this alone, a moment between Raven and I that I needed to keep between us. That morning I held him until we got to the clearing of trees at the front of the house. I talked to him, told him it was OK to fly away even though I was sobbing through it. I scratched his forehead as he held his head down. This was his favorite place to be scratched. He stretched a wing, a clue he wants me to scratch under it. I said my final goodbye and on the count of three, I dropped my arms from under him, forcing his flight. He flew in a circle and straight back to me. A part of me wanted to walk back inside and never let him go. This went on for another four attempts until he finally flew to a tree. He perched there for a few minutes and crackled his voice loudly but flew back as if he scared himself with his own voice. The last time I let him fly, I ran back to the house, stayed inside and cried.

As I peeked out the window, I could see Raven on the ground standing in the same place where I let him go. He would hop a little and stop. He would make a screeching sound and hop a little more, I knew he was looking for me in the last place he saw me. It was breaking my heart, but I was sure he would eventually fly away.

That evening, before it got dark, I heard a tap at the door. I opened it to find Raven standing on the ground tapping his beak against the screen door and the porch. I knew then that Mr. Raven didn't want to go home because I was his home. He was my home too and I felt content letting him come back inside knowing that I tried.

To this day, I take Raven outside so he can fly around. Sometimes I won't see him for hours, but he always comes back. Every time he does, I know he is flying home.

I removed all of Ellie's old furniture, keeping a few things that my heart wanted, including her chair. I purchased a new bed for the spare room that is now mine. Ellie's room is my masterpiece in so many ways.

I am still a secret up here for the most part. Gossip mainly suggests that Ellie left me all her money and I just make art all day long. I love the rumor and play along easily. The only people who know the truth are Patrick, his parents, and mine.

Ellie also left a handwritten letter but this came in two parts, unlike the other letters she left. The first was a clue as to where I would find the second letter. It simply read, 'answers on how to survive the apocalypse.'

The second letter was located under the front porch in between a small crack in the boards. I was fixing the porch one afternoon, and I was frustrated by a gap between the boards. She told me to leave the crack and said it made for a great little hiding place in the event of some sort of end-of-the-world apocalypse.

Rainy,

I am asking you to meet with a friend, Dr. Kelly. She knows you will contact her, and she will share our many discussions but I ask you to stay open-minded. This will surely come as a surprise. Just know that I am always with you.

Ellie

To say I was surprised was an understatement. I was shocked. I left Dr. Kelly's office before the conversation was over for the simple reasoning of my own mental well-being. Even though I didn't stay to get all the details, I heard enough and I spent many weeks feeling anger toward Ellie.

Ellie met Dr. Kelly through an agency that cares for the dying and even though she didn't have cancer, Dr. Kelly was able to use that as a viable excuse to see her. I never sat in on the appointments she had with Dr. Kelly, I assumed it was all a part of Ellie's plan. To this day, I still do not know how the subject came up or whose idea it was but it's clear that Ellie told her about her wishes and how she wanted to die at home… and, who would help her. She asked me to do the same for others who fall under Ellie's sort of circumstances.

Months of unannounced visits from Dr. Kelly forced me to evaluate death and how I feel about it. Dr. Kelly would leave every visit with a thought to ponder. Usually, it was a question about how I personally would want to die. I finally came to the conclusion that if we could all choose our own death, it would be pretty similar in that we would have control over when and how it would happen. No one in his or her right mind wants a slow and painful death.

One thing I can say for certain, why we die is not the question to ask. To ask why we die, or why someone had to die, is pointless. It's better to ask what we are willing to make from it. With this question, we not only get answers, but we can also understand the dying process altogether.

We live for reasons that are logical. We live for love, memories, and happiness, for our family and friends. If we can view death the same as we view life, then we can live and die without battles. Living a life with dignity is a human right, dying with dignity is also a human right but religion, government, fear, and ultimately selfishness have shadowed the simplicity of this. What we do in this life is only a small part of who we are meant to become. Death is a phase, just as life.

The people sent to me share their story of fighting the good fight but in the end, they tell me how they lost. This is a great place to start because I am able to show them that life and death don't need to be at war in the first place. Death isn't an ending, just as life isn't the beginning. Life isn't a battle that was lost to death. There doesn't need to be a battle between life and death at all. Life has a place, so should death.

In having these discussions, we are able to gracefully move forward accepting that the next phase, the dying phase, is coming. Fear of dying is always a topic of conversation but I try my best to explain in my own way, through my own experiences, the beauty I see as I watch someone find their way. Some people fear going to hell, others worry about not going anywhere and a few people fear the unknown. Fear is one of the first feelings to leave and usually gets replaced with grief. It's not very often that I hear someone say that they didn't have any regrets. They grieve for what could have been and what they wish they would have done differently. Sorrow always finds its way in and out of the many multitudes of emotions and I try to show them that every emotion in this journey is fair, reasonable and normal. Anger sneaks in with some people, not everyone and humor can make a hard day seem a little less overwhelming. Forgiveness is the most difficult need to attain. So many times, they wish they could be forgiven for something they have done or said. Other times, they want to forgive someone who might have left a scar in their memories. Forgiveness and the ability to do so is one of the most freeing emotions a person can feel. Forgiveness doesn't excuse the wrongs, but it does set them free. Being forgiven isn't always possible, so I try to show them how to forgive themselves.

When I can, I find ways to make the little things they wish they would have done become a reality. Such simple things, like watching someone eat a slice of cake from the middle, applying a fake tattoo or coloring someone's hair purple, I make it happen. I help them live the life they needed to live in a short amount of time we have, so they can find peace in leaving.

I am not the gatekeeper of death and Dr. Kelly doesn't send me people to simply die. She sends me those who want to make death part of their life. Most of the time, an end of life group or agency will take care of them, but now and then, someone comes along with a certain set of circumstances. Some have been alone and lonely for so long that the only thing they really want is to not die alone.

Terminal cancer is usually the diagnosis but once someone arrives, they are not yet dying and this is the first thing I remind them of. Death is when we take our last breath but before that, there is still a beautiful journey yet to unfold. Death is so personal, everyone is different but there's still a little life left to live when they come up here to the trees.

I can't do this without the help of Patrick and our parents. Without them, I wouldn't do this work because I don't have the emotional strength all on my own. They make it possible, they make what we do up here just a little more beautiful, natural and simple.

In the end, after their last breath, perhaps their last exhale, their final departure is done deep in the forest with a ceremony my dad offers that was passed down from the elders on the reservation. Their ashes rise to the trees where they are kept, continuing to live in the embrace of every leaf or branch. Their souls shift to a new vibration but the forest keeps them, it keeps the part of them that holds proof of the fact that they were once here and their lives mattered.

I have become aware of one last unsettling emotion in my heart that I know is being occupied by the anger I feel towards Jacob and Holly. I decided to write them a letter but held off mailing it in hopes that the simple act of writing it would release that anger… but it didn't.

Today, as I walk down the long path from the mailbox, I see a warrior dressed in full ceremonial attire, standing at the edge of the trees. When I make eye contact with him, he simply nods his head in approval. I knew instantly that he is here to tell me I found my way. I finally found my place, where I belong. Raven finds me too, he swoops down like the many times before, finds my arm and together we walk through the forest that keeps them.

Holly and Jacob,

We don't know each other, and this is a good thing. I met your mom many moons ago by what seemed to be a total accident at the time. Now, today as I write this, I know it was more than that.

The purpose of this letter is not to inform you of her death because I know you don't care. However, I wanted to let you know that your mom was an incredible human being.

Through all the alienation and disgraceful acts placed upon Ellie, she thrived. She did so because of the love she carried in her heart, even towards you both, her children who cast her into what you both assumed would be a lonely and isolated life. She forgave you both a long time ago, not because she thought you needed forgiving, but because she had so much life to live.

Ellie quickly became my best friend and I will miss her deeply. I have learned so much from her, especially about love and what it means to be a human being. I'm sure this is a difficult topic for you to understand but maybe someday, you will. If you ever find the definition of compassion and love, you too will seek forgiveness. Until then, you will know it was given. Forgiving yourselves will be something you'll need to discover on your own but it won't happen if you can't love.

I never would have known Ellie had you both not walked out of her life in the name of justice, so I owe you my gratitude. She was loved by so many people, a love that wasn't bound by fear, intimidation or resentment.

Her story reminds me of the many battles white man had with the Natives. Lives were lost, many tribes wiped from existence as the white man took land, traditions, and cultures that didn't belong to anyone but Mother Earth.

Through the battles, the injustices and complete destruction, the natives surrendered to conditions that were completely unjust, unfair and morally wrong. They did this for many reasons, but mainly because of their wisdom. They were wise enough to understand that their love, their history, their legend, and heritage would live on well past their existence.

Your mom had that wisdom. She continued to love, free from all the restrains you forced upon her. The one thing you couldn't take from her was her ability to love, her memories and legacy. In fact, the last words she spoke were, 'I love you too.'

Like many battles and wars, someone needs to lose. While the white man assumed victory over the land and the native population, they didn't really win. You see, the white man lost everything that defines the meaning of humanity. However, the white man's greatest loss was the fact that they believed in what they did.

You both went to battle just like the white man but you lost. This whole time, you assumed victory and justice but the reality is, through forgiveness, love wins.

Neha

THE RAVEN

A Tale from the Cheyenne

Long ago, the land was dark. Nothing had light and all people had darkness. This is what they know.

A woman near water take a drink and soon she was full with baby. This make grandfather happy.

Baby was unhappy and cry for 2 moons pass. A boy cry a long time…

Grandfather gave a boy a small sack and the boy cry no longer. A boy opened it and light went to the sky, light spread all over the sky. The lights became stars at night.

The boy cried again…long cry, many stars passed through the sky. Many stars.

Grandfather gave a boy another sack. Larger sack than before. The boy open and light went to the sky, a circle. Circle became the moon. The moon came at night…it bring light.

Boy cried many moons, many stars passed through the sky.

Grandfather gave a boy a sack and boy turns into raven, dark bird, night bird. Raven boy bring sack to sky…raven goes to the sky… sack is open and fire goes up. Fire in sky take night away, take moon and stars. Fire is the sun.

Sun will rise and moon, stars sleep. Always light from a raven boy…a boy who cries.

Raven, a boy bring many moons, stars, sun. Raven, dark bird, night bird rise to sky with light for dark, brings light back for day.

See a dark bird, a raven and know he make the light.

Her Name

"She bring Neha to this ground below us…The sky has not bring water for five moons…today sky water has fallen, and today, girl is given her call… Neha…she who make rain.

From Neha, make many great things grow… Neha also take away... every thirteen moons, she will listen from your voice until she can listen from her own…guides of Neha, teacher of girl who makes rain…when sky water fall and take away, teach the girl…she is for good, Neha from the sky, water falling, rain maker.

Neha falls…"
– Chief Standing Bull